ADVANCE PRAISE FOR
DON'T LOOK BACK

"A crisply written page-turner, *Don't Look Back* is a story of tragedy, tenacity, and the continued importance of a free press. From the terror of the final moments inside the World Trade Center towers, to the incompetence that doomed hundreds of city firefighters, to the principled mutiny inside a major newspaper to get that story out, the story never lets up. Calderone writes with moving affection and respect for the blue-collar men and women who do the hard work in our democracy, who fight to preserve it, and who sometimes pay for that struggle with their lives."

— MARK BOWDEN, author,
Black Hawk Down

"Joe Calderone, one of the city's great reporters, uses those skills in a brilliantly suspenseful novel about 9/11, the city's worst tragedy, and the first responders who lost their lives that day and their families' search for the truth."

— NICK PILEGGI, author of *Wiseguy*
and its screenplay, *Goodfellas*

D0111818

"Joe Calderone is a former *NY Daily News* investigative reporter who knows his stuff when it comes to the FDNY and he has crafted a novel that helps shine a light on the incredible challenges and sacrifices firefighters made on 9/11, including the 343 members of the FDNY we lost that day under the most tragic of circumstances. There were communication failures on 9/11 that no doubt contributed to the loss of life and this novel will help remind us to not repeat those mistakes ever again. Calderone has done the FDNY a service."

> — MICHAEL REGAN, former First
> Deputy Commissioner, FDNY

"This is a novel about the most painful day in New York City history and its aftermath, as reporters and investigators struggled to uncover the official blunders of Rudy Giuliani's City Hall that made a tragic day worse. Joe Calderone uses all his tools as one of New York's best investigative reporters, as well as a panoramic knowledge of the city, to offer a vivid tale of people in search of a difficult truth."

> — TOM ROBBINS, Pulitzer Prize finalist and
> Investigative Journalist in Residence
> at the Craig Newmark Graduate
> School of Journalism at CUNY

DON'T LOOK BACK

A NOVEL - BASED ON REAL EVENTS

THE 343 FDNY FIREFIGHTERS KILLED ON 9-11 AND THE FIGHT FOR THE TRUTH

JOE CALDERONE

Post Hill
PRESS

A POST HILL PRESS BOOK
ISBN: 978-1-63758-400-2
ISBN (eBook): 978-1-63758-401-9

Don't Look Back:
The 343 FDNY Firefighters Killed on 9-11 and the Fight
for the Truth
© 2022 by Joe Calderone
All Rights Reserved

Post Hill Press
New York • Nashville
posthillpress.com

Published in the United States of America
1 2 3 4 5 6 7 8 9 10

To the 343 FDNY Firefighters Who Perished on 9/11

This is a work of fiction woven into a historical setting. With the exception of Rudolph Giuliani, all of the characters (as well as any companies or other entities named) and their words and deeds are products of the author's imagination. Though some job descriptions or titles within city government or within fictitious companies are referenced, the characters who occupy those roles in this book are just that—created characters; they never existed and are not intended to reflect any actual persons who may have held those or similar positions before, during, or after September 11, 2001, or to convey actual facts about any such persons. Any resemblance to actual persons, living or dead, or actual events involving such persons is purely coincidental. As for Mr. Giuliani, any conduct attributed to him in this book is also fictional and is expressly not intended to convey any actual facts about him.

CHAPTER ONE

SEPTEMBER 11, 2001
9:05 A.M.

A s they headed west over the Brooklyn Bridge, Peter Murphy double-checked his gear, making sure he had all his equipment. It might have seemed silly, but the precaution was something they taught in the FDNY Fire Academy, where only weeks ago he had been training. Guys had been known to leave the firehouse without a helmet or a radio or a fully charged "can"—as the silver hand-held fire extinguishers were known. And that could be troublesome and embarrassing, especially for a "probie" like himself. As the junior man on Ladder 389, it was his job to be the "can man," meaning he would carry the small fire extinguisher during a forced entry, positioned behind the "irons" man, who carried the tools to break through a locked door or window at a fire scene. Peter's job was to suppress any fire during the entry and help search for victims while waiting for the engine company to arrive with hoses and more men to put water on a fire.

At the arc of the roadway on the bridge, speeding along toward Lower Manhattan, Peter and the rest of his unit could see clearly the fully engulfed upper floors of the North and South Towers of the World Trade Center. It was a surreal sight. More than once during the short ride from Brooklyn Heights—the truck's sirens screaming the entire way—Peter thought how ineffective the little handheld fire extinguisher would be in this situation. The other men also glanced at each other in the cab of the truck but said little. They knew this would be the biggest fire of their lives, and the senior men also knew if things didn't go right, it might be their last. Their adrenaline was pumping.

"Listen up, probie," said Lieutenant Kevin Callahan, the senior man on the rig. "No matter what, you stay right next to me. I want you so close I can smell your awful breath. You got me? And do exactly what I tell you, when I tell you. No thinking. Just follow my orders, okay?"

"Copy that, Lieutenant," Peter shouted back.

A six-foot-two former marine with a shaggy crop of brown curly hair and a six-pack of abs that he worked on daily at the gym, Peter Murphy had learned how to follow orders without question, even when they seemed asinine.

Peter tried not to let his thoughts run away from him as the truck and his comrades drew closer to the blazing Twin Towers. But this was easier said than done. This would be his first actual fire while with the FDNY, which he had joined at his mother's urging, following a year off bumming around the beaches of Southern California. He was eager to prove himself to his fellow firefighters. They were a tough and seasoned bunch. Mike the Termite (known for his carpentry skills); Patrick (aka the Irish), who never missed a Notre Dame football game and who, yes, could drink them all under the table; Sal (the Eggplant), who brought his Italian mother's recipes to the firehouse, perfecting them over the years, and who had the most experience on the job; and the Lieutenant, who the other men simply called "Lou," in deference to his rank.

Peter Murphy knew his mother, Sarah, and father, a recently retired NYPD detective, must be watching the drama unfold on the TV in their Pelham Bay apartment in the Bronx, a few miles north. He thought about calling her. But most cell phones were down, and he didn't want to seem like a wuss in front of the other men. He tried to concentrate on the task ahead. And he recalled the lessons learned at the fire academy. Above all else, the instructors taught safety. Over and over, they stressed how to size up a fire scene, conduct a safe search and rescue, and then know when it was time to get out—without getting yourself or your fellow firefighters killed. The ultimate goal of every FDNY member was to live to fight a fire another day.

As their rig barreled over the bridge, Peter replayed his instructor's safety messages in his head. But none of it seemed applicable to what he and the men were facing today. No one had foreseen this ultimate Manhattan high-rise fire, caused by hijacked airliners being piloted into two of the tallest buildings in the world. It was not a scenario that they had ever drilled for in the academy.

Peter had no idea what to expect. He knew he would have to trust his lieutenant and the more senior men from his firehouse. He knew part of their job was to protect the probie—him—from danger. That was the unspoken, unwritten rule of any firehouse: The senior men could harass the probie as much as they wanted at the house, but—on the fireground—the other men instinctively tried to keep any probie out of harm's way while giving him enough room to learn the job. They had all once themselves been probies, rookie firefighters who generally lacked the experience to avoid getting killed, the kind of experience that could only be gained by years of responding to calls big and small. From the stovetop pot burners to car accidents on the FDR to fully engulfed apartment fires where a roof could cave in with little notice, the men of Ladder 389—based in Brooklyn Heights, near the foot of the Brooklyn Bridge—had seen it all, at least until this morning.

Lieutenant Callahan had his own misgivings coming over the bridge. The radio traffic on the FDNY communications channels already was jammed beyond anything he had experienced, making it difficult to get any useful information about the situation he and his men were about to face. It seemed as if every member of the FDNY was responding to the WTC, which was not necessarily a good thing. Callahan knew that too many firefighters—all eager to help and arriving at the same time—could lead to chaos at the fire scene if the bosses didn't control the situation. And the attack had occurred at the time of an FDNY shift change, so many firefighters who were just coming off their tours joined those reporting for the next shift, jumping on rigs together across the city—all heading to the WTC. Some firefighters whose rigs had already left the firehouse commandeered MTA buses, ordering the bus drivers to take them downtown to the Trade Center so they could be part of the action. This was the biggest, baddest fire in a generation, and no one on the FDNY wanted to miss it.

Lieutenant Callahan concentrated on how to protect his men, especially Peter. The largely Irish and Italian-American workforce at the FDNY took care of their own. They often passed the job itself down from one generation to the next, from father to son and from uncle to nephew. This made the FDNY an insular place, one that remained an overwhelmingly white and male world. Whatever the FDNY lacked in diversity, it made up for in family ties and brotherly bonds—on and off the fireground.

Lieutenant Callahan felt the burden of that tradition as the men roared over the Brooklyn Bridge, especially when he got his first good look at the Twin Towers in the distance, wrapped in flames and smoke beneath a perfect blue September morning sky, knowing that anything could happen.

"This doesn't look good," Sal said to the Lieutenant, out of earshot of the probie. "What's your plan?"

"We'll have to size it up when we get there, but make sure the other guys stay close," Lou said. "It's going to be a crazy scene. I'll check in with command—if there is a command. You get everyone else ready. Make sure they have their masks and their Scotts are fully charged. But don't load them up with any extra stuff. It could be a long climb up those stairs. No way are we going to be able to put water on that fire. It's too intense and too high up. I assume this is a search and rescue operation at this point."

"Roger that, Lou," Sal responded.

Today, though, all their skills would be put to the test—just to make it out alive. Lou glanced at Peter and the other men.

Peter caught Callahan's look and wondered if he would ever get to see his mom again. It was a fleeting thought, one he pushed to the back of his mind. He had dreamed of the life he wanted to build for himself with his girlfriend Anna, his high school sweetheart. They had recently started to talk about marriage and about saving up enough money for a down payment to buy a starter house out in Suffolk County in Islip or Commack or Ronkonkoma, more than an hour's drive from Manhattan but where a young couple who scrimped could still afford a modest home. They both wanted to move out of the Bronx.

Like generations of firefighters before him, Peter had begun taking jobs in the home renovation and construction trades to supplement his FDNY salary. He did mostly unskilled tasks, like helping to rip out an old bathroom or laying down lumber for a new deck, working as a helper on jobs secured by the Termite and the other more senior and more skilled firefighters from his firehouse. Eventually, Peter would learn one of the skilled trades—laying tile or basic carpentry—from the other guys in his house and strike out on his own. Working two jobs was how the guys afforded the two-car, one-house-in-the-suburbs, middle-class lifestyle they and their wives and children had come to expect, even on an FDNY salary. The flexible schedules at the firehouse, where you could work a twenty-four-hour shift and then be off for three days, allowed them to juggle it all. And juggle they did.

As the Lieutenant predicted, it was chaos when Peter's company arrived at the base of the North Tower. A few senior officers manned a makeshift command post in the lobby. They appeared to have only the slightest sense of what was going on in the 110 floors above them. They had no TV to help them see what was unfolding. It occurred to Peter that anyone watching the drama unfold live on television probably had a better view of what was happening than the FDNY officers at that command post.

Peter's FDNY unit was among the first to arrive.

Peter saw some units from other companies racing up the nearest stairs, not bothering to check in with the chiefs at the command center, who were trying unsuccessfully to keep track of which firefighters were going where. "Let's go," one FDNY captain yelled to his men. "We can't wait for orders."

Peter and his unit began their ascent on foot—all ninety-nine elevators in the North Tower were inoperable. As Peter, Mike, Patrick, Sal, and the Lieutenant worked their way up the stairs, each carrying up to seventy-five pounds of protective gear and equipment, they squeezed passed hundreds of civilians making their way down, mostly on their own.

The cinder block-lined stairway with its concrete steps and steel railings was mostly clear of smoke; those coming down were calm. As Peter's unit checked in on each floor they passed, making sure no one else had been left behind, the offices they encountered looked as if it was a weekend and everyone had simply gone home. Desks, chairs, phones, and cubicles were all in their proper order. But for the chaos in the lobby and on the street below, it looked like a regular workday inside on the lower floors, except for an occasional jarring noise outside the windows—the sudden, unnerving, and regular thuds from street level.

It was a strange sound, not one Peter had ever heard before. It took Peter and the other guys a while to figure it out. On the tenth floor, they stopped, rested for a moment, and peered out the narrow, ceiling-to-floor-length windows. As they watched from inside, they noticed objects whizzing past.

"Is that what I think it is?" the Lieutenant asked the other guys.

"Jumpers," Sal said solemnly. "It's got to be a beast up there if they are jumping."

Peter at first didn't get it. He had heard the term "jumpers" before, but he thought it referred to people committing suicide and choosing to do so by jumping off one of the city's bridges. Why would people be jumping from the upper floors, especially if the FDNY was on the way?

He asked his lieutenant. "What's going on? Why are they jumping?"

"The heat must be so intense up there that they are choosing to jump rather than be burned to death. It happens," the Lieutenant said. "Let's keep moving,"

The senior officers in the lobby had confirmed that their objective at this point was a rescue mission, not to fight the fire, which was too huge and too high up. They were to check each floor that hadn't already been cleared, making sure no civilians were left behind, and report back via radio to the command post in the lobby—if they could reach their superiors, which often they could not. They would ascend as close to the fire floors as possible. With the elevators out of service, they knew this could take hours.

The Lieutenant's "handy-talkie" radio suddenly crackled to life. "Ladder 389. Report position."

It was Pete Ganci, the chief of the department, the highest-ranking uniformed officer in the FDNY and one of the first to arrive at the scene. The Lieutenant was surprised to hear him, but not surprised that Ganci was in the thick of it, directing his troops.

"We're on ten heading to eleven," the Lieutenant answered. "All present."

"Ten-four," the chief replied. "Stay in touch. Use this channel."

The Lieutenant turned to Sal. "You know the radios in here didn't work during the '93 bombing. I hope they fixed them."

"I hope so too, Lou," Sal replied. "The higher up we go, the more interference we likely will get ."

Ladder 389 moved up through the fifteenth floor with little to report. These floors of the North Tower were deserted.

"Hey, Lou, there's nobody up here. Seems like everybody has gotten out already," Peter yelled to the Lieutenant.

Peter was starting to get a bad feeling in his gut. His mind was racing. *What are we really doing here? He kept his thoughts to himself. He didn't want the other men to think he was weak in the knee, not on his first real fire.*

Peter's unease about the mission only grew as he saw police officers race down the stairs as he and the guys from his unit continued their ascent. Some of the cops didn't even bother to stop to share information.

Peter blocked the path of one cop on his way down. "Hey, what's your hurry? Where are you guys going? Isn't the fire up that way?"

The descending cop tried to push past Peter and gave him a look as if to say, "Buddy, if you want to die in here, that's fine. Not me." Other cops were jumping down the stairs two at a time. Their NYPD captain stopped briefly. "We made it up to twenty-five. A Mayday to evacuate all first responders came over about five minutes ago. Didn't you guys hear it? I'd get your guys out of here if I was you. They said the building might come down."

Peter thought the cops were acting like wusses. No way was he heading *away* from the fire. Can you imagine trying to live that one down? The biggest fire in the tallest building in the city and he was going to leave before he even opened up a nozzle or saw a flame or, at the very least, make a rescue? No way. Just because the cops were leaving didn't mean that the FDNY should be doing the same. The cops weren't trained for this. The FDNY was.

"Thanks for the intel," the Lieutenant said. "We'll hang around a bit longer."

Still, Peter thought, if a Mayday had been called, why didn't they hear it on their FDNY radio? An order like that would be across the board—for every first responder to get out as quickly as possible.

The Lieutenant turned to Peter and the other guys. "Let's keep going," he said, trying now to reach the chief again on his radio. If there was a Mayday, he was certain the chief would have tried to reach him.

"This is Ladder 389 to Command Post. Ladder 389 reporting. Please acknowledge. K." The "K" meant Lou had ended his transmission. He waited patiently for a response but heard only static.

CHAPTER TWO

A s they reached the twentieth floor, Peter spotted something out of the corner of his eye, far back in the office space, that didn't look right. He made his way to the spot.

"Hey, Lieutenant, over here."

A guy in a wheelchair, about fifty years old, dressed in a dark business suit and tie, was sitting at his desk, calm as day, as if he was waiting for a bus.

"Wondering when you guys were going to show up. I could use some help getting out of here," the man said.

"Didn't anyone get to you before now?" Peter asked.

"Some other guys saw me and told me to stay put. They said they would be right back. That was about thirty minutes ago. I've been dialing 911, and they told me to stay low to the ground and hang in there, that help was on the way. It's hard for me to stay low, as you can see," hitting the arm of his wheelchair. "I'm sure glad to see you guys."

"What about the other people on this floor? Didn't anyone stay with you?"

"No, I told them to get going. We've been through this drill before."

"Man, this is no drill," Peter said. "This is the real thing. The building's been hit."

The other guys in Peter's company glanced at each other. They instinctively knew two seemingly conflicting facts: It would be a bear to get this guy down twenty floors without working elevators, but at the same time, he was their ticket out of this mess. It would take all four of them to get him down the stairs, each taking turns bearing his weight, which Peter estimated at two hundred pounds.

"We're going to get you out of here," the Lieutenant told the guy. "Don't worry. But the elevators aren't working. We are going to have to take you down the stairs."

Peter knew there was no time to waste. If the cop they had passed was right and a Mayday had been issued, they were in immediate danger. It seemed impossible that the Twin Towers, built to withstand the impact of a plane and barely shaken by a 1993 truck bombing in its basement, could be in danger. Yet the cop they passed seemed pretty sure about what *he* had heard on *his* radio. And he sure was in a hurry.

"Lieutenant," Peter asked, "do you want me to try again and get the command on the radio to see if they called a Mayday?"

The lieutenant nodded. "Go ahead."

Peter pushed the transmit button on his handy-talkie radio. "This is Ladder 389 to Command Post. Please update status. Repeat. This is 389 to Command Post, looking to confirm orders. K."

Peter got nothing but static in response.

"Keep trying," the lieutenant ordered.

Meanwhile, they couldn't wait around for an answer. Right now, they had an obvious and more immediate task ahead. Peter and the others gathered around the man in the wheelchair. "We're heading down. When we reach the stairs, we'll have to take turns lifting. Drop all your Scotts. We're not going to need them."

The other guys looked at the Lieutenant for a moment but didn't move.

"Lieutenant, you sure you want us to ditch them?" said Sal.

Telling firefighters to leave their Scott paks was like telling a lifeguard to dive into the ocean for a rescue with no life preserver, no rope, no surfboard, no boat. It just wasn't done. The Scott Air-Paks the firefighters wore on their backs provided a self-contained breathing system and could mean the difference between living and dying if they encountered a bad smoke condition. The guys would feel naked, exposed without them. What if the fire from above spread down to them? Then they'd be defenseless.

"We have no choice. Our job now is to get this guy out of there. We can come back up later for the paks. Stash them in a corner over there."

The guys knew the Lieutenant was right. They jettisoned their Scotts, covering them with some boxes in case some other crews came by and were tempted to help themselves. They kept their tools, which were relatively light in weight and could be invaluable in the event they had to pry open a door or dig themselves out of a collapse. Then, they started moving the wheelchair toward the stairs.

It was slow going. Some workers from the upper floors were still making their way down the stairs, making it harder to get the space and time they needed to lift the wheelchair down. Peter and his unit had to wait at each landing to let the others go ahead before they could begin again to hoist the wheelchair down another half a flight. One guy on each front wheel and two on the back. It was tedious, hard labor, even for four physically fit firefighters. Peter took his turn on the wheels, where most of the weight shifted during the descent.

More cops streamed down the stairs, passing them quickly. None offered to help. They seemed to know something Peter and the other firefighters didn't. Finally, one of the cops yelled to them as he fled down the stairs.

"The South Tower came down. Hit the street like a pancake. Collapsed on top of itself. We're next. Haven't you been listening to the radio? You've got to get out now and get as far away from the building as you can."

"And what exactly are we supposed to do with him?" the Lieutenant asked to no one in particular, motioning toward the man in the wheelchair.

"That's your call," the cop responded over his shoulder, already a half a flight of stairs ahead.

The Lieutenant tried his radio again. "This is 389 to base. Anyone there? Please advise on evacuation order. How much time do we have?"

Static answered him back.

The guy in the wheelchair knew what was going on. "You guys should go. I've had a good run. I appreciate what you're doing, but it's not worth five of you getting crushed for one of me. Just leave me by the elevator. Maybe it will come back on."

"Listen, pal," said the Lieutenant. "I said we're going to get you out of here, and that's what we're going to do."

He turned to his men, gathered now a few feet up the stairs from the landing.

"You guys are free to go," the Lieutenant told them. "There's a Mayday to evacuate. The South Tower is down already. I don't know how much time we have left before this one comes down too. I can't hold you. Make a break for it, and when you hit the street, don't stop running until you are far enough away or have some serious cover. You might be best going into the subway. If this thing comes down, it's going to be like Hiroshima."

Peter and the other guys looked at the Lieutenant and the wheelchair guy and didn't say a word. They knew they couldn't just leave them behind. This was what they signed up for. For a moment, Peter imagined reaching the street, saving himself, eventually being reunited with his colleagues and family and having to explain that he left the Lieutenant behind with a man in a wheelchair. It was an unthinkable choice.

"Cut the shit, Lieutenant," said Sal in a take-no-prisoners tone that only he could get away with. "Let's keep going."

Peter grabbed a wheel again as they started down, this time with more purpose, more speed, sometimes going two steps at a time, hitting the second step pretty hard. The wheelchair guy didn't object. He was just as anxious as Peter and the other guys to get to the street. Peter thought that this was going to be one hell of a rescue if they made it out alive. Probably would make the *Daily News*. And it would be one heck of a story to retell back at the firehouse. It was the kind of reputation-maker that a probie like himself could live off for a long time, maybe his entire career, considering that this was the biggest fire and disaster the city had ever seen. But he gave their chances of making it out fifty-fifty. They had made it to the fifteenth floor. There was a long way to go, and they had no way of knowing how long the North Tower would stay upright.

Peter silently repeated the Lord's Prayer, the one prayer he remembered from his days in Catholic grammar school in the Bronx.

Before he could silently mouth the "Amen," his thoughts were interrupted by a crackling sound that resonated through the staircase, floors, and stairway handrails. Peter could tell from the reaction of the others that it wasn't a good sign.

None of the men had actually been inside a building during a full collapse. But they all had survived partial collapses—a roof caving in, a stairway giving way, a section of a wall or a floor going out from under you. Sometimes, there were no warning signs. It just happened in a flash, and you suddenly found yourself under a bunch of debris or a full floor lower. Hopefully, you didn't break a leg or get crushed by a flaming piece of floor joist. But the World Trade Center wasn't built anything like a five-story tenement: It was made of steel, concrete, and glass.

The men listened for the telltale sounds of a building collapse.

"Did you hear that?" Sal asked.

Another faint, slow rumble followed by a low-decibel screech could be heard in the distance, coming from the floors above. At first, no one reacted. A few minutes passed before they heard another similar series of sounds—this time a little closer to their location. This time, they all started moving as fast as they could. There was little doubt what it foretold.

"Pick it up. Let's go. We still have twelve floors to go. We've got to move it."

The men who had been reluctant to leave their Scott paks behind now started shedding their remaining fire gear. Turnout coats—the most basic and critical protection against fire and water—were quickly peeled off and left behind in the stairway. Bunker gear, the heavy pants designed to protect legs and the body's core against flames, also were stripped off. Peter and his unit were down to T-shirts and shorts, almost running down the stairs now, juggling the wheelchair from one landing to the next, desperate to reach the street. If they ran out of time, there would be no escaping this one, not with ninety-five stories of steel, glass, and furnishings above. The top floors would come down first and pick up speed as they crashed into the floor below.

"I'm telling you guys, leave me here. You aren't going to make it," the man in the wheelchair said again.

"Just shut up, will ya," the Lieutenant shouted. "Just hang on tight."

"Lieutenant, maybe he's right," said Sal. "The sounds are getting closer and closer. I don't think we have much time."

Peter was surprised to hear Sal speak up, but he was secretly glad he did. This seemed now like a suicide mission.

"I told you, you guys can go anytime. There's an order to evacuate, a Mayday, so there will be no repercussions. You have a right to save yourselves. I'm staying with him."

Peter and the other men said nothing and got back to hoisting the wheelchair down the next flight. They were on the tenth floor now. Soon, they would be on the street. Another fifteen minutes was all they needed. If only they had that much time.

The Lieutenant pushed the transmit button on his radio one more time. "This is Ladder 389 to Command Post. We have one man in a wheelchair coming down. Any unit nearby, we could use assistance. Does anyone read me?"

All he heard back was static. If anyone with the FDNY was still left in command at the WTC scene, they either couldn't hear him or were running for their own lives. Either way, it left the men of Ladder 389 completely on their own.

The Lieutenant yelled now to Peter and the other men. "Pick him up and carry him down. We've got to get down to the lobby now."

Peter—the youngest and strongest of the unit—moved first, picking the man out of his wheelchair and slinging him over his shoulder. They ditched the wheelchair in the stairwell and started almost jumping down the stairs two steps at a time now with Sal in front and Patrick behind in case Peter stumbled.

The Lieutenant stayed by Peter's side. They made it a two-man carry with the Lieutenant helping to shoulder some of the man's weight by locking hands with Peter under the man's buttocks. The man hung on to their shoulders, one arm around each of their necks. They could move faster this way, but it was still a slow go.

"Save yourselves," the wheelchair man cried out, one last time. "Put me down. I'll be okay."

Peter and the other men ignored the wheelchair man's advice. They kept carrying him down, one flight at a time. Peter's arms were getting weary. His legs started to cramp up. *This guy is awfully heavy*, he thought. For a moment he felt like putting him down, abandoning him in the stairwell. Then his thoughts turned to his mom and dad. He knew what they would expect. And he recalled his marine training and the motto of the U.S. armed forces:... "Leave No Man Behind." On the battlefield, no marine left a fallen brother behind. Peter thought the marine creed applied just as well to this situation. *We are, after all, under attack.*

They kept descending as quickly as they could and reached the fifth floor, but then, suddenly, the walls and most of the floor in the stairwell gave way beneath them. Peter instinctively tried to protect the wheelchair man, covering him with his own body to protect him from the falling debris. He saw the Lieutenant and his FDNY brothers fall away into the void where the stairway floor had been moments ago. He tried to grasp on to something—anything—to stop his own fall, but there was nothing left to grab. It all came crashing down.

All that was later found of Peter Murphy was his crushed probie helmet.

CHAPTER THREE

11:00 A.M.

Sarah started calling Peter's firehouse—in the Brooklyn Heights section of Brooklyn—late that morning. Like almost everyone else in NYC and millions throughout the world, she watched live as first the South Tower collapsed at 9:59 a.m. and then the North Tower went down at 10:28 a.m. Her husband told her not to call, but she couldn't help herself. The phone at the firehouse rang and rang. No answer. She got no response on Peter's cell phone either. Not even his voice mail. The cell phone calls weren't going through.

Peter had graduated from the FDNY Fire Academy only six weeks earlier. That had been a very happy day. Sarah's husband, Tom, picked that same day to retire from the NYPD after thirty-nine years. Peter had easily passed the physical for the FDNY, did well on the written, and secured a high spot on the hire list after deciding he did want to return to New York and start a career with the FDNY. His military background and his father's pedigree made him an easy fit with the FDNY.

Sarah brimmed with pride at the graduation ceremony. Her son had returned home. He had followed her advice. His career was secure for the next twenty years or more, if he wanted it. All she worried about now was him staying safe. But after being married to a cop for so long, that was something she had learned to live with, to not really think about. It came with the job.

She had watched this morning as hijacked American Airlines Flight 11 had crashed into the North Tower of the World Trade Center at 8:46 a.m., cutting through floors ninety-three to ninety-nine and sending a jet fuel fireball down at least one bank of elevators, exploding on several floors below, including the seventy-seventh, the twenty-second, the West Street lobby, and the B4 level—some four stories below ground.

Hundreds of people in the North Tower were killed on impact.

Thick, black smoke from the burning jet fuel enveloped the upper floors and roof. Those at or above the ninety-second floor who were not killed by the plane's impact were essentially trapped as the three stairwells in the building were impassable. They had no way to reach the street, and the doors to the roof, if they could reach it, were locked. The Port Authority of New York and New Jersey—the bistate government authority that had developed the site—had never considered a roof rescue, and there was no plan for one. Some people below the impact zone were trapped in elevators.

At 9:03 a.m., a second hijacked plane, United Airline Flight 175, crashed into the South Tower.

Thousands of workers began leaving on their own, if they could, streaming down the staircases that were not blocked by debris.

Within minutes of the first plane hitting the North Tower, the city's 911 system was flooded and overwhelmed with calls. Some of the 911 operators were ill-informed about what was going on at the scene and gave callers— some of them inside the Twin Towers and desperate for information—conflicting advice about what they should do. Some were told to evacuate if they could; others were advised to stay in place and wait for rescuers to reach them. Some civilians who waited did not make it out alive.

Now, as the morning dragged on, Sarah was getting frantic. Her husband tried unsuccessfully to calm her down.

"Look, he's a probie. I'm sure he's with someone who knows what they are doing. And he was a marine. He can take care of himself. Try not to worry. I'm sure he will get in touch as soon as he can. It's a little busy there right now, no doubt. You have to give him some space. He's on the job."

"How can you tell me not to worry?" Sarah said, trying to keep her voice in check, not really wanting to take this out on her husband. "Have you been watching what I've been watching? Have you looked out the window? The tallest buildings in the city just collapsed, flattened like a couple of pancakes. Every firefighter in the city is down there. How do we know he wasn't inside when they fell? He's not answering his cell phone, and no one at the firehouse is picking up the phone."

"I'm just saying, don't jump to conclusions," Tom responded, trying not to show how worried he was. "Nobody's cell phone is working right now."

Sarah knew her husband could be right. But she had a bad feeling, a mother's intuition, about the events she was watching unfold on TV. She knew her son. It didn't matter that he was a rookie, a "probie" in FDNY parlance, as he was still on probation for a year after graduating from the academy. It didn't matter that before today he had yet to be called to the scene of a major fire. There would be no holding him back. He would be in the thick of things, trying to help out.

"Tom, I know he's down there. You know he's down there. I just hope he's somewhere safe."

Friends, neighbors, and other community board leaders started calling the Murphys' apartment and dropping by.

Her best friend and neighbor, Kelly Regan, whose husband also was on the job with the FDNY, tried to reassure Sarah.

"Peter's with the best of the best. They will watch after him," Kelly whispered quietly to Sarah as they sat on the couch together in front of the TV, trying to absorb and process the horrific images unfolding on the screen.

After a while, Sarah stopped hearing it. She just stared at the TV, watching as the networks kept replaying the footage of American Airlines Flight 11 crashing into the North Tower at 8:46:40 a.m. and then United Airlines Flight 175 crashing into the South Tower at 9:03:11 a.m. And then the incredible, unbelievable sight of first the South and then the North WTC Tower coming crumbling down, collapsing almost straight to the street in a mushrooming cloud of dust and debris with people on the street fleeing for their lives.

The hours became a seamless, repetitive routine of waiting, calling, searching for any clue about what had happened to Peter. The first confirmation of her worst fears came late in the day when Captain Mike Sarno at Peter's firehouse finally picked up the phone and delivered the words she dreaded to hear.

"I'm sorry to report that Peter is among the missing," Captain Mike said softly into the phone. This was not the kind of news that the FDNY usually delivered over the phone. Normally, a detail of officers would be dispatched to the member's home to deliver the news in person. But the department's normal notification protocol on 9/11 was overwhelmed by the sheer number of missing and presumed FDNY dead.

Sarah held the phone so Tom could hear as they stood together in the kitchen. "His entire unit is missing—all five of them," said the captain of Peter's firehouse. "We are still searching. We don't know what happened yet. They could be in a space that was spared from the collapse. We have the top search and rescue teams in the city working, along with the dogs who are trained to find a scent in these types of conditions. We're not giving up. We're going to find him."

She didn't want to believe it, but, right then, Sarah knew Peter was gone.

After the call, Tom gathered his old NYPD gear—a flashlight, rain gear, boots, his NYPD jacket, a first aid kit, water, along with his NYPD badge and cap—and headed down to Ground Zero to help with the search.

He tried to comfort Sarah as he went out the door. "Try not to worry. We will bring him back. I am going to stay down there until we do. I'll sleep at the precinct. Cell service is still spotty, so don't worry if I don't call you."

Tom knew better than most that Peter's chances of survival were very slim if he was caught in the collapse of the North Tower. The best he could hope for was to find his body so there would at least be some closure.

Sarah tried to sleep but her rest was interrupted by a thousand questions. She wondered how this could happen to a probie. And she wondered how many other firefighters had perished. Dozens? Hundreds? No one seemed to know yet.

Who was to blame—not only for the death of Peter but for all of the FDNY members who were lost in the twin collapses? She got up and paced the floors of her darkened apartment, flipping on the TV but turning down the sound.

And she blamed herself now for pushing Peter into taking the FDNY entrance exam. He could have done any number of other jobs. He had the looks and the brains. Civil service was not his only option. Sarah had wanted him back in NYC, urged him to come back home, and she had gotten her wish—but now she was filled with regret and guilt.

She drifted off on the couch, the glow of the TV flickering images of the tragedy over and over as the news cycle repeated itself, hour after hour, throughout the longest of nights.

CHAPTER FOUR

SEPTEMBER 12

Gusts of wind coming off the choppy waters of the Hudson River stirred the fine, white powder of World Trade Center dust that was moving across lower Manhattan. Small circles of swirling clouds—mini tornado-like pockets of papers and World Trade Center remains—touched down along West Street. Juan Gomez positioned himself just north of what was left of the World Financial Center, beyond the police line. His brown Rockports and the bottom of his blue jeans already were a grayish white from walking this far, past the crushed, abandoned FDNY rigs and cars littering the streets near the WTC site.

He kept his NYPD-issued press credentials secure in his pocket, careful not to draw attention. His goal was to get past the police line, to get closer to what had already been dubbed "The Pile," the place where hundreds of firefighters, cops, ironworkers, and laborers were digging, mostly by hand, removing debris one bucket at a time, as they searched in vain for survivors. He waited, hoping to see someone he knew to walk him in. To his right, the cracked glass ceiling panels of the World Financial Center atrium loomed high above, like a sci-fi movie set in a scene where invaders had attacked downtown New York, piercing the Center's signature architectural element with a single blow. Except this was no movie.

As he surveyed the mountains of crushed concrete and steel, now essentially a burial ground for thousands who were assumed to have perished here yesterday, Juan momentarily found himself recalling the day nearly twenty years ago—very near this spot—where he had first proposed to his late wife, Linda, the mother of their three children. He had made up a story about needing to meet Linda inside the World Financial Center atrium, with its vaulted glass ceiling and palm trees, after work to meet some friends for drinks. When she arrived, he walked her outside to P.J. Clarke's, which had tables near the water on the Hudson River. There, in front of a hundred or so diners and tourists, he knelt on one knee and popped the question. Linda started crying and let out a scream of joy as the manager of P.J.'s—a friend of Juan's—snapped a photo, which to this day remained pinned with a metal magnet on the door of their refrigerator. It reminded him of their happy life together, before the breast cancer, before the surgeries, before the chemo treatments and relapse of the cancer that ultimately claimed his wife's young life.

Juan snapped out of his daydream as a man approached.

He was an official—someone Juan didn't know—who passed by. The man, wearing a tan one-piece contamination suit and a respirator, displayed credentials Juan didn't immediately recognize. Not NYPD or FDNY. Probably a fed from OSHA. Juan wasn't sure.

"If you are going to stay here, you better put a mask on," he told Juan before moving toward The Pile. Juan dismissed the advice but was grateful the guy didn't tell him to move along. Juan had covered many a fire. Was this so different? Besides, where was he supposed to get a mask from, anyway? Certainly not from his employer, the *News of New York*, the city's upstart tabloid newspaper. Lucky if they supplied you with a pad and a pen most days.

Another official approached, moving fast toward the center of the site. Juan ran to catch up to him. It was Mike Maldanado, the FDNY's six-foot-five First Lieutenant Fire Marshal and a longtime pal and source. Juan was relieved to see him alive.

Maldanado was more detective than firefighter. When he showed up at a fire scene, it usually meant "foul play"—the euphemism for arson or worse. His crew could tell you not only whether a fire was intentionally set, but exactly where in the building it began, what kind of accelerant was used, and what route the fire traveled throughout the building. Maldanado was a thirty-year man with the FDNY. Divorced with two daughters, Maldanado could leave the department anytime on a more-than-decent pension. He already put his girls through college—both at Ivy League schools. But he stayed because he had one of the best jobs in the FDNY. He was widely respected by the brass and by the press. And, lucky for the press corps, Maldanado enjoyed the nightlife, and he liked to drink. He was a regular at Elaine's, the Upper East Side watering hole for the city's political, journalistic, and artistic elite. After a few, Maldanado would banter back and forth on the big story of the day with reporters he trusted, like Juan, sometimes revealing key clues or insights. Such was the draw of Elaine's. It was a place where secrets openly were exchanged, and everyone knew it.

Today, though, Maldanado was all business and in no mood to talk. He no doubt had lost scores of close friends and colleagues in the attack. Juan knew to approach him with kid gloves.

Juan carefully circled ahead of him, momentarily blocking Maldanado's path to The Pile.

"Mike, how's it going?"

"Not today, Juan. Not on this one."

"Come on, man. I know you're super busy. I won't ask you anything. No on-the-record quotes. Promise. Just get me in."

Maldanado gave Juan one quick, eye-to-eye stare, as if to say, *You sure about this?* The two had known each other for ten years. Juan hoped Maldanado had enough trust in him at this moment to know he would never burn him. They had worked many a fire scene together.

"Keep your credentials in your pocket and stick close," Maldanado said. "Anybody says anything, I don't know you. Got it?"

As they turned a corner, a piece of the North Tower façade emerged in the distance. Smoke billowed from the pit. More debris dust kicked up. Reams of office paper, documents from the WTC Twin Towers offices, were scattered everywhere. Juan picked up one of the pieces of paper. It had the Port Authority of New York and New Jersey logo and looked like some kind of an invoice for consulting services. Juan wondered how it had survived the collapse, along with tens of thousands of other scraps of paper from the Port Authority and other firms that once occupied WTC space. Pieces of office furniture—file cabinets, desks, chairs—were mixed in with the twisted steel and glass from the Twin Towers. Somehow, they also had survived intact. None of it made sense.

Closer toward the center of The Pile, hundreds of private-sector construction workers—ironworkers, carpenters, operating engineers, laborers—assembled, waiting to be deployed in the search-and-rescue mission now in full swing on day two of the largest such operation in the history of the city of New York. They just showed up, Mike said, their hardhats on, carrying the tools of their trade, ready to help. Nobody called them. No overtime pay was expected for this job. They joined hundreds of city firefighters, including those who made it through the collapse, who also were on the site, looking for their fallen colleagues and missing civilians. Along with NYPD Emergency Services, they dug through the rubble by hand, forming long chains of bucket brigades, carefully lifting away the debris as they listened for any sounds of survivors.

The city already had ordered up a dozen more refrigerated tractor-trailers to handle the anticipated corpses. The trailers were lined up on a side street, near the crippled but still standing World Financial Center, which the city had designated as a temporary morgue.

"Chief, how many guys did you lose?" Juan asked Maldanado, testing the waters of their reporter-source friendship.

"I thought you said no questions. 'Promise.' Remember?"

"Nothing on the record, I said."

"We don't know yet. Some guys have been down here all night and are just reporting in, but it doesn't look good. We lost entire companies. Could be three hundred guys or more. And a lot of the brass are gone. I don't even know who the hell is running the department now."

"Three hundred? How is that possible?"

From covering the FDNY for so long, Juan knew his firefighting history. The largest loss of life for the FDNY in a single incident up until 9/11 occurred in October 1966 at the 23rd Street "Wonder Drug" fire when the floor of a building at Broadway and 23rd Street unexpectedly collapsed, killing a dozen firefighters. Other infamous fires—known within the department by their nicknames like Father's Day, Third Avenue Collapse, Black Sunday, Waldbaum's fire—also had claimed multiple FDNY lives, but nothing approached the scale of loss Maldanado had just described.

For the first time since they met up on West Street, Chief Maldanado stopped walking toward The Pile. He turned to Juan to face him, tilting back the front of his battered, white, chief's fire helmet just a bit.

"Look. This operation was a clusterfuck. You understand? They set up the command posts in the wrong place, too close to the buildings. The trucks arriving on the scene were riding heavy. Extra men hopped on board, not wanting to miss the fire. They sent too many guys into the towers with too much equipment to carry. And they didn't get them out in time. No one knew the buildings would come down like they did. Like I said, the brass got hit too. Chiefs, captains…I lost a lot of friends. And one more thing," Mike said, clutching his "handy-talkie" radio, the small, point-to-point black boxes most firefighters keep strapped on their left shoulders, near their hearts, where they can find it easily and push to talk with one hand while on the move. "Ah, never mind. I shouldn't even mention it." He tapped his radio nervously.

"Come on, Mike, what?"

"Nothing. I gave you enough. I gotta go. Keep safe down here, will ya? There's a lot of guys with heavy equipment and tools. They don't all know what they are doing. Watch yourself. And we never talked. Got it?"

"Roger that. Thanks. Can I call you later?"

"If you can find me, sure."

Then he was gone, heading deeper into The Pile of smoke and twisted metal.

Juan waited a moment, then saw where Maldanado was headed. A makeshift command center had been established under a white tent on the outskirts of The Pile. Juan recognized members of the mayor's NYPD security detail hovering outside, now heavily armed and brandishing automatic weapons, clearly departing from their normal procedure of concealing their guns to blend in as the mayor moved around the city.

Juan approached the tent. But before he even reached the security detail, the mayor's chief of staff, Mary Sullivan, spotted him and came walking directly toward him.

She did not look pleased. Mary was a statuesque, six-foot-tall figure with long, straw-colored blonde hair that she wore pulled back off her face in a tight ponytail. Not a stray hair escaped from the tight bun behind her head. The fair complexion of her skin and crystal-blue eyes telegraphed her Irish heritage. She cut an impressive figure in any room and emitted an air of no-nonsense authority. Mary had served two previous mayors (Edward I. Koch and David Dinkins). She was one of the few holdovers Giuliani had kept on when he defeated Dinkins in 1993. She knew how to push and pull the levers within the vast city bureaucracy to help her boss get things done, a talent every mayor appreciated. And she was fiercely loyal to whoever was in the mayor's chair at the west wing of City Hall.

"Juan," she barked at him. "What are you doing here? This is a restricted area. No press. You know that. How did you get past the police line?"

Juan did not answer her directly.

"Mary, I just need a few minutes with the mayor. My editors are looking for an update. Can you get me inside the command post?"

"Absolutely not," Mary said firmly. "You need to get out of here, or I am going to have to call the security detail."

Juan was not budging. Not without a comment from the mayor or confirmation of the number of firefighters lost. "Mary, I just learned that we may have lost as many as three hundred firefighters down here, and I need to confirm that with the mayor."

Juan was surprised to see Mary at Ground Zero. Among her many duties were to serve as the mayor's gatekeeper, scheduler, and protector. The mayor valued loyalty above all else, and Mary ranked as among the two or three top people whom he trusted implicitly. But Mary rarely left her office at City Hall, where she screened every meeting, every event, and every phone call before anyone reached the mayor.

Juan also knew that Mary's husband was a top FDNY officer in one of the elite rescue units. He hesitated at first to ask about him, afraid of the answer.

Juan saw that his question about the number of FDNY lost hit Mary hard. Her bulldog demeanor changed, and Juan sensed her guard was down.

"Mary, I hope your husband is okay. But I need to get the mayor on the record about loss of life among the first responders. If this number is right, it would be unlike anything the FDNY has ever experienced. You know that."

Mary suddenly started to sob.

"My Bill is among the missing, Juan," she said, turning away and covering her face. When she finally looked up, their eyes met, not as news reporter and government adversary, but just as two human beings, caught in a terrible scene.

"That's why I am here with the mayor," Mary continued. "They are searching, but they haven't found him yet. Off the record, your number is correct. In fact, it's likely higher, closer to three-fifty. The mayor is not going to come out to talk to you, but I heard them use that number. It's accurate. Do not quote me."

Juan had known Mary for nearly a decade. He had always treated her with respect, keenly aware that if he wanted access to Giuliani, she could either help him or block him. His years of taking the time to get to know her were now paying off.

"Okay, Mary. I'm truly sorry about Bill. I hope they find him and that he is all right. I won't use your name. Thank you. If there is anything I can do or if I hear anything about the rescue, I'll let you know. Stay strong."

Juan started to back off and walk back in the direction from which he came. He had what he needed, and he didn't want to push Mary any further, not now.

First, he leaned in to give Mary a quick hug, which she accepted.

"This has been a terrible day for everyone," he whispered in her ear.

In small but thoughtful ways, Mary had been supportive of Juan when he was losing his wife. She had inquired about Linda's care throughout her battle with breast cancer and offered on more than one occasion to get the mayor to call over to Memorial Sloan Kettering if Juan needed help getting in to see the best cancer specialists in the city. Juan had always politely declined these offers, but he appreciated Mary's interest and what he judged as her genuine compassion and concern. He never forgot it.

"When I lost Linda, you were always there for me. If you need a shoulder now, let me be there for you too, okay?" Juan said to her softly.

Mary nodded yes. Without another word, she turned and headed back to the tent where the mayor was meeting with FDNY and NYPD brass, reviewing the latest rescue and recovery efforts.

Juan needed to get back uptown to the newsroom. He knew the loss of so many firefighters would be a major component of tomorrow's 9/11 coverage, and now he had the story.

CHAPTER FIVE

Back inside the temporary command center at Ground Zero, Mary briefed the mayor on her encounter with Juan. Normally, a press officer would have been assigned to shoo Juan away, but Mary had volunteered when she saw him approaching the tent.

"I got this," she told the mayor. She needed a distraction from the grim reports coming from the FDNY commanders, and everyone inside the tent knew it. The mayor had not wanted Mary to accompany him to Ground Zero, but she had insisted. She was desperate for any news about her husband and the other firefighters, many of whom she knew personally from social events and friendships that had formed over the years as a result of Bill's role with Rescue 12, one of the elite units within the FDNY called upon in building collapses and other sensitive rescue operations.

Upon her return to the tent, Mary told the mayor that Juan already had the number of fallen firefighters, but she didn't know how he got his information. She told the mayor that she confirmed the number, as she knew the FDNY press office was about to release the information anyway. There was no sense in stonewalling Juan on this point. The mayor nodded his approval.

As she sat inside the mayor's specially equipped, white
Ford Explorer SUV for the short ride back to City Hall,
Mary thought about her last words yesterday with Bill,
words she now wished she could somehow take back.

It had been another beautiful fall September day. Not a
cloud in the sky.

Bill had come home late the previous night after picking up an extra shift on his side job. He didn't really feel
like working the overtime, but he couldn't afford to turn it
down either, not with the fertility bills piling up.

Mary was already in bed by the time he got home. She
had turned toward him when he climbed in beside her, hoping he would reach for her, but he fell asleep almost as soon
as his head hit the pillow. He was bone-tired from his regular tour at the firehouse and from the extra shift banging
nails on a construction site in Queens.

When she woke on the morning of 9/11, Mary was still
upset that Bill had turned down her offer of a quickie. Her
feelings were bruised, and it didn't help that Bill fell asleep
last night without so much as a good night.

She nudged him awake and decided to confront him.
The alarm clock read 7:00 a.m.

"Bill, what's wrong? Why are you so hands-off lately?
I feel like something is eating at you, and you are not
telling me."

Bill groaned. He wanted to sleep more. He didn't have
to be out the door for another hour.

"Come on, babe, I'm just tired," he said, rolling
back over.

Mary wasn't letting him off that easy. "No, it's more than that. You never want to fool around anymore. You don't even want to touch me."

Now, Bill was getting his Irish up.

"Mary, for Chrissake, all I do is work. I'm trying to pay these bills. I want to have a kid as much as you, but $20,000 a pop is really killing us. I can't keep up with it, even with all the overtime I'm picking up at the firehouse and on the side job. It's just too much. We're going to be in debt forever if you don't get pregnant soon. I don't know how much longer we can keep paying for the treatments."

Ah, Mary thought, *it's about the money. It's always about the money*. Not about what she was going through, about her feelings of inadequacy, of longing for a family. All Bill cared about was the stupid money.

Bill got out of bed and headed for the kitchen to make himself some coffee. Mary followed him, not wanting to let it go. His back was turned as he filled up the coffee maker with fresh water.

"You said you would do whatever it takes, remember?" Mary said, her tone now almost a scream. "Whatever it takes…that's what you said. I guess you didn't really mean it. I guess you really don't want to have a family. All you care about is the money."

She was near tears but held them back as Bill stopped making coffee and turned toward her.

"You can't be serious, Mary," he responded. "I've been busting my hump to make it happen, working the overtime and going to the doctor's office to…you know…. I've done everything you have asked, but it's never enough. No matter what I do, it's never enough, and it doesn't seem to be working. It's not your fault, and it's not mine. Maybe it was just not meant to be. Maybe we need to accept that."

Mary, pushing thirty-five, couldn't hold back any longer. She started sobbing and shaking. She sat down at the kitchen table.

She wondered if Bill was right. Maybe she would never get pregnant. Maybe she had waited too long to try, always putting her demanding career at City Hall first.

Bill came over and put his hands on her shoulders. There was nothing left to say. And he had to get to work at the firehouse.

He flipped on the news. The Fox 5 morning anchors were reporting that the polls were now open for the September 11th Democratic primary for mayor of the city of New York, which was to be held that day. It looked like a close race between the two front-runners, Mark Green and Fernando Ferrer.

"Go to work," Mary said as Bill went back upstairs to get ready. "I'll call you later after I hear from the doctor."

She heard Bill turn on the shower while he shaved.

When he came back down, dressed now for his shift, Mary was still in the kitchen, nursing her second cup of coffee and washing some dishes. She stood over the sink, keeping her back to her husband.

"I'll talk to you later," he said as he headed for the door.

Mary said nothing, giving him the silent treatment, her emotions a jumble of anger, hurt, sorrow, and regret. Normally, she always called out as he headed out the door, telling him to be safe. Not this time. Not on this morning—of all mornings—on the morning of 9/11.

As the mayor's SUV pulled back up to City Hall, Mary snapped back to attention. She got out of the car before the mayor with his security detail and helped to clear a path up the marble steps to the front entrance, where reporters routinely hovered, hoping to catch the mayor and other city officials for comment as they were coming in and out of the building.

The mayor sensed that Mary was shaken by the visit to Ground Zero. He called to her as they headed up the City Hall steps and motioned for her to walk with him. "How are you doing?"

"I'm fine." She paused, then admitted, "No, not really. Bill and I had a row yesterday morning before he left for work, and I never got to say I loved him one last time."

The mayor nodded but wasn't really sure what to say. "Bill knew you loved him. You were everything to him. I could see it when you two were together."

She wanted to believe that, but more than anything, she wanted yesterday morning back, so she could make it right.

"As soon as I hear anything about the recovery effort, I will let you know. Meanwhile, you should get some rest. And, Mary," the mayor said, pausing for effect. "We're going to get the SOBs who did this. I spoke to the president this morning again. He is going to come to Ground Zero. He is on this. This attack on America will not go unanswered."

CHAPTER SIX

arah could no longer take the endless stream of well-
meaning neighbors, friends, and relatives who came by
her modest, Pelham Bay home, many bearing trays of
food and cookies. She grew weary of the awkward greetings
and forced conversations. Some friends tried to be upbeat:
"They will find him."

"He could still be alive."

"Don't give up hope."

"Be strong."

Others just gave her a hug and silently looked at the
floor, avoiding any eye contact. It had taken on the trap-
pings of an Irish wake—except her son's whereabouts were
not yet known. Most of her friends and relatives now presumed Peter dead, although they would never reveal their
true thoughts when trying to comfort Sarah. She knew what
they were thinking, though. She had thought it, too, but
kept it buried, pushed it back. She would not give into that
feeling. Not yet. It had only been a week since the attack.
Her son could still be trapped somewhere under the rubble.
It was possible.

In the background at her apartment, the TV news coverage droned on, night and day, around the clock, showing the

planes crashing into the Towers, over and over again, and then live reports from the smoldering remains at Ground Zero. They kept the TV on but muted the sound. Sarah's husband, Tom, had spent most of the last seven days at the pit, coming home only once to get a new set of clothes and some rest. He spent every other waking moment working with his former NYPD and FDNY contacts at the scene for any word on the rescue effort, which now quietly had turned into a recovery mission, although it was becoming increasingly obvious to the first responders and to City Hall that there was not much even to recover in the way of bodies, at least not fully intact ones.

In the first days, Tom had even joined the bucket brigade of active and retired first responders who literally dug through the rubble with small shovels and by hand, filling up plastic five-gallon buckets with crushed concrete and glass, passing what they could remove from one man to another, carefully clearing away as much as they could until heavier equipment arrived. All this in hopes that a few survivors had somehow managed to stay alive in pockets of space created underneath 1.8 million tons of debris that had come crashing down upon them. Everyone working The Pile knew the chances of survival were slim, but they kept digging, hoping against hope for a miracle that never came.

Sarah could no longer stay home. She asked a friend to drive her the 21.7 miles from her Bronx home to downtown Manhattan so she could see the recovery effort for herself and visit the last place on Earth where her son had been.

In their nightly phone calls, Tom urged her not to come down to Ground Zero.

"It's too dangerous down here," he told her in as calm a voice as he could muster. "There's heavy equipment all over, and you wouldn't be allowed on the actual site. There's nothing you can do here."

Tom wanted to spare Sarah the pain of seeing it. He had been to many a crime scene in his twenty years with the NYPD, but nothing compared to the sheer destruction at Ground Zero. Twisted and crushed FDNY fire trucks and cars, hit by falling chunks of steel and concrete, lined the nearby streets like a scene from a horror movie set. Smoke continued to drift from The Pile. Men with crowbars, sledge-hammers, and cordless Sawzalls, designed to cut through almost anything, scrambled over the debris. Dump trucks and eighteen-wheeler open container rigs were lined up on West Street, waiting their turn to haul away the crushed remains of the city's tallest structures.

Sarah told Tom she couldn't stand idly by in the Bronx any longer.

"I need to be there. I need to see it for myself," she told her husband.

"I wish you would listen to me for once," Tom responded. "This is not a good idea. The guys from the FDNY are busy working The Pile. They are not going to have time to talk to you. None of the other family members are here unless they are on the job. You would just be in the way."

"I hear what you are saying, Tom," Sarah said quietly into the phone. "I just need to be near him. I know they won't let me on The Pile. That's okay. I just need to be as close as I can get. Do you understand? I need this."

There was silence on the line. Tom hesitated but then gave in.

"Okay. Call me when you get downtown. I will meet you at St. Paul's. But you're not going to be able to see much, and you can't stay long. I have to get back to The Pile."

Sarah had her friend drop her off at 14th Street, which was as far south as private vehicles were allowed to travel during what amounted to almost martial law downtown. Heavily armed National Guard troops were stationed at every major intersection and along the main avenues leading downtown. Sarah walked the rest of the way to the World Trade Center site. The smell of the pit grew stronger with each passing block she traveled, making her way past City Hall, down Broadway, reaching St. Paul's Chapel, which had become a refuge for first responders. They slept there on the pews and on cots in between shifts digging on The Pile. Hundreds of volunteers from across the city flocked to St. Paul's to serve meals, make beds, provide fresh socks, and comfort the first responders in any way they could as they worked twelve-hour shifts on The Pile. The fence around St. Paul's had become an impromptu memorial. Photos of missing loved ones, teddy bears, flowers, hand-made signs surrounded the perimeter of the church.

Sarah met Tom just outside the main entrance on Broadway.

They walked to the rear of St. Paul's facing Church Street, across from the eastern edge of Ground Zero. Miraculously, the church had been spared any damage during the WTC attack. Not even a single window was damaged.

When Sarah and Tom turned the corner past the church, the first broken tridents from the base of the WTC façade came into view, sticking up crooked into the air, twisted, shattered, like a bent memorial to the destruction. They stopped on Church Street, overlooking the giant pit of rubble, men and machines digging slowly through the remains of what had been one of the world's most recognizable structures, icons of America's economic might, freedom, democracy, and capitalism.

"This is as far as we can go," Tom said quietly, holding Sarah's arm.

A steady stream of first responders, NYPD personnel, laborers, and other rescue workers passed by them on their way back and forth from the church to The Pile. No one seemed to be in a hurry now. It had become a routine, almost like any other job. There were no live human beings being brought out of The Pile, only rubble.

One look made it clear to Sarah that her son was gone. She silently overlooked the scene, frozen, then collapsed into Tom's arms, turning away from Ground Zero. They embraced as the sun started to set over the grim site, the twisted WTC tridents and cranes piercing the sky behind them.

"Take me home now, please," Sarah whispered. "I understand. You don't have to say it. He's not coming back."

Soon, it would be time to bury her son, if they could find him.

CHAPTER SEVEN

SEPTEMBER 12

Juan made his way back uptown on foot toward the news-room, eager to confer with other reporters and editors covering the day's extraordinary events and file his story about the number of firefighters believed to be lost during the attack. It was still hard to comprehend. Firefighters of all ranks from houses across the city had been killed. Entire units were missing.

As he passed by the ash-covered office buildings, store-fronts, and crushed vehicles, he thought about his own loved ones, his three children—Jennifer, Chris, and Matthew—and how they have been handling it all. And he tried to work out in his head what he had learned while at Ground Zero. Juan kept focusing on the "how" and the "why" of the story.

The words of his FDNY pal Maldanado kept rattling around in his head. "This operation was a fuck up..." There still was little room or appetite at the paper for that kind of story. The tragedy was too fresh and too little was known about what really happened in between the time the planes hit the North and South Towers and when they collapsed. But it wasn't too soon to start reporting, to go down that road.

Just then his cellphone suddenly came back to life. He recognized the number immediately. It was his daughter, Jennifer.

Jennifer had just turned seventeen. She ruled the house, and she usually was very good at looking after her younger brothers: Chris, who at thirteen was entering the awkward stage between boy and young man; and Matthew, a sweet ten-year-old who liked airplanes, food, and baseball. Jennifer had long, straight, thick hair, a deep, brown color that complemented her dark eyes and model's face. She attended Bishop Loughlin Memorial High School, a coed Catholic high school in the Fort Greene section of Brooklyn, run by the Christian Brothers. The Brothers ran a tight ship. Girls were still required to wear plaid skirts and white blouses with navy blazers while the boys wore ties and khaki pants. On a reporter's salary, Juan could barely afford the $10,000 a year in tuition. But neither Juan nor his late wife Linda trusted the public high schools in Brooklyn, even the magnet ones or the increasingly popular charter schools.

"Where have you been all day? I tried to reach you," Jennifer said in a worried and annoyed tone that reminded Juan of his late wife's.

"I have been at Ground Zero most of the day," Juan replied, careful not to provide too many details. "I tried to call you, too, but the cell service was spotty. It's pretty bad down there still. The search is continuing, but I don't think they are going to find anyone at this point."

"We think five of our friends at school lost their fathers," Jennifer told her dad. "Three of them were firefighters, and the other two worked for Cantor Fitzgerald. They were on the top floors."

This was one of the situations when Juan missed Linda the most. Being a news reporter for a major tabloid in New York was a dream job for a journalist, but it also was a demanding job, one that could take a toll on a family. Sometimes, Juan had no choice but to be away from Linda and the kids. When a big story broke or he was chasing a lead or a source, it often meant working late, sometimes for days on end, until a story played itself out.

When Linda was alive, he never had to worry about what was happening at home. Linda took care of everything. She had her own career as a therapist in a school, but she had flexible hours, and the kids always were her first priority. It was an old school arrangement, but it had worked for Juan and Linda.

Now, with Linda gone, there was a gap. His job was no less demanding, especially when a story like 9/11 broke—the most intense story of his career. Juggling the needs of the story against the needs of his family was not easy. In his heart, Juan knew Jennifer was right. She needed him home and so did the boys, but he could not walk away from this story. He would have to lean on Linda's sister, Aunt Sue Ann, and other relatives and neighbors to fill the gap until he could figure out what had happened that caused hundreds of firefighters to perish.

"There's a vigil and a Mass back at school tonight for the students who lost someone, and I'd like to go. I

really want to be with my friends. Are you coming home?"
Jennifer asked.

Juan was torn. He knew it was important for Jennifer,
at her age, to be with her friends, especially at a time like
this. And at school he knew she would be safe and under the
watchful eye of the religious leaders and teachers there. But
there was no way he could get away.

"Honey, you know I can't leave work now. This is a
huge story, and the city is depending on us to tell them what
is happening down at Ground Zero, including the families
of your friends who lost people today. I am going to be late.
You have to stay home and watch your brothers. I'm sorry."

There was a pause on the line. Then an explosion
of emotion.

"This isn't fair," Jennifer shouted into the phone.
"You are never home. Mom would have been here, especially on a day like this. I'm going. Chris is old enough to
watch Matthew."

Juan thought about it for a second. "Not tonight. I'm
sorry. I need you to help out and stay home. I don't want
Chris and Matt to be home alone, not tonight."

"You are ruining my life, Dad," Jennifer shot back. "I'm
not Mom. This isn't my responsibility."

"Jennifer, I have to go now. I'm almost back at the newsroom. I will try to get home as soon as I file my story. Stay
put. Okay?"

"It's always about your stupid story," she said. "What
about us? What about your kids? Don't we matter more
than your story?"

She hung up.

Juan knew she was angry but that she would do the right thing and watch her brothers until he returned home. He would ask Aunt Sue Ann to stop over later. Jennifer was right. This wasn't fair. He was asking a lot of a teenager. But life was not fair. Cancer wasn't fair. 9/11 wasn't fair.

He needed to keep his focus on the story at hand and try to figure out how the FDNY could have lost nearly 350 men in one day.

On the far West Side of Manhattan, a few blocks from the backside of Penn Station, editors and cityside reporters at the city's most aggressive tabloid newspaper were pounding away on another day of covering what for most would be the most memorable and painful story of their careers. When Juan arrived, entering the football field-long *News of New York* newsroom, he surveyed the usual rows of reporters and editors sitting at battered, cluttered desks, some stacked with piles of newspapers, and the coffee-stained blue indoor/outdoor carpet that hadn't been replaced in years. The room was abuzz as usual at this time of day, as the first deadline for tomorrow's print edition loomed. Shortly after the attack, a huge American flag had been hung overnight near the news desk, just beyond the storied, four-sided wooden clock that had been salvaged from the *News*'s old newsroom on E. 55th Street in Midtown East when the paper's publisher, Kenneth S. Schwartz, III, moved the *News of New York* to cheaper quarters on the West Side, a move that the old *News* guard still viewed with resentment, believing it hurt the paper's stature and ignored the history of the place.

The appearance of the flag didn't surprise Juan. The city and the country had been attacked, apparently by a terrorist group, on our own soil. It was a natural response. But it also made Juan uneasy. Did this mean patriotism would trump honest reporting about the attack? Wasn't it the paper's job to remain neutral, even in this kind of situation—or perhaps especially in this kind of situation? The FBI and the city's Joint Terrorism Task Force had begun supervising the rounding up of dozens of "persons of interest" in Queens and Brooklyn, persons mostly of the Muslim religion.

What would the posture of the paper be toward City Hall as more became known about the city's response? No *News of New York* editor was seen as friendlier to City Hall than Billy Baldwin, the paper's fifty-year-old editor-in-chief who ultimately controlled the city desk and some three hundred editorial employees who prepared the daily report as well as longer range reporting projects. Baldwin was a British import, a chain smoker and heavy drinker who liked to frequent high-end strip clubs. His main interests seemed to be celebrity gossip and soccer, neither of which were considered mainstays to most of the *News*'s traditional readership of working-class New Yorkers who depended upon the paper to stick up for them and aggressively cover crime, courts, civil service, City Hall, housing, and labor issues. Baldwin was one of the many out-of-town editors that Schwartz had hired away from one of London's Fleet Street tabloids in a never-ending, misguided, and ultimately unsuccessful effort to juice up the *News of New York's* tabloid coverage and boost street sales of the newspaper. Schwartz was a bitter publishing and real estate rival of billionaire Mortimer Zuckerman, the owner of the more traditional tabloid in town, the New York *Daily News*, which enjoyed a larger readership than the feisty but financially struggling *News of New York*. The two tabloids and the *New York Post* were locked in a three-way circulation war, competing for every scoop and screaming headline, one of the last great newspaper battles in the country. Zuckerman's real estate empire also vastly eclipsed Schwartz's portfolio of NYC properties, a source of constant competition and irritation to Schwartz.

Given Schwartz's ties to City Hall, Juan wondered how aggressive Baldwin would allow the paper to be in uncovering what really happened in the hours and days after the WTC attack.

Shortly after he arrived in the newsroom, Juan got his answer.

He checked in with city editor, Mike McFeeley, who gave him a heads-up that Baldwin was looking for him. This usually meant trouble.

Baldwin saw Juan talking to McFeeley and summoned him to his corner office for a debriefing.

"Good luck," McFeeley told Juan. "And try not to punch him out, okay? You still got a mortgage to pay, right?"

Juan's relationship with Baldwin was a complicated one.

The *New York Post* recently had tried to woo Juan over with the promise of a two-step raise. While Juan had qualms about the *Post*'s conservative slant on the news, a 30 percent pay hike was serious money. Tuition money, as he called it, enabling him to pay for his kids' college expenses.

Juan had built his reputation by covering the mayor. Reporters who cover the mayor work out of a crowded room on the first floor of City Hall downtown, known as Room 9. They are corralled in the east wing of the building, steps away from where the mayor and his top staff are housed. Juan had broken a number of exclusives out of City Hall, and that had caught the attention of editors at the *Post*. Just as Juan was about to accept the offer, Baldwin unexpectedly stepped in, matching the *Post*'s offer and elevating Juan to investigations editor, the head of the *News of New York's* small team of investigative reporters.

All this made Juan's post-9/11 relationship with Baldwin all the more complicated. While grateful for the raise, Juan did not trust Baldwin. Like most reporters, Juan was suspicious of his editors. Baldwin, in particular, was an editor with very strong political views that often clouded his news judgement. The newsroom, as a whole, did not trust him.

Since the 9/11 attack, Baldwin had been sending signals to back off the FDNY aspect of the story. Juan's other editors—all of whom reported to Baldwin—had been able to deflect the pressure, giving Juan room to keep reporting. But now it seemed to be coming to a head.

As Juan walked into Baldwin's windowless office—known in the newsroom as the 'Ice Box,' partly because of the temperature, which Baldwin kept at a chilly sixty-five degrees all year, and partly because reporters seldom enjoyed their encounters there—other reporters in the newsroom kept one eye on the encounter, hoping for some fireworks.

"What's the latest from Ground Zero?" Baldwin asked Juan.

"Still smoldering. They haven't found any remains in days," Juan told his editor.

"Listen," instructed Baldwin. "We should focus our energies on who did this. It's clear it was terrorists. But which ones, who was responsible? How did they pull this off?"

"That's a tall order," Juan said, seeing where Baldwin was starting to go and not getting a good feeling. "There are overseas forces at work here. We can work our NYPD and FBI sources, but you know in this atmosphere they are not going to give up much of anything. What about the local angle? We lost hundreds of firefighters. And the air down there is pretty bad. They got guys working on The Pile, and the smoke is filled with toxins, my sources are saying. All that plastic and building materials make for an awful brew when it burns. The city's response could be the part of the story we own. Honestly, the *Times* is going to be able to do a better job on the international angles. We could zero in on what happened between when the first plane hit the North Tower and when the Towers fell. They had, like, an hour and a half to get out of there."

"No," Baldwin said, emphatically. "Don't go there. *Don't look back.* We have to stay focused on the search and rescue and the rebuild effort. That's the local part of the story. This creates a huge hole in downtown and in the city's economy. That's our part of the story."

Juan looked at Baldwin and was stunned. Three hundred dead NYC firefighters, a toxic waste dump in the heart of the financial district that was spewing smoke across downtown and into Brooklyn, and Baldwin didn't want to look back? Where was this coming from? Juan's antenna went up immediately, given Baldwin's well-known ties to City Hall. Could this be coming from the Giuliani people? Or was it coming directly from Schwartz?

Schwartz had picked up the paper in a distress sale as a sideline, a diversion, from his primary, profit-making real estate business. His firm, New York Properties, controlled some of the city's most prestigious commercial buildings. As a developer, he was always on the hunt for the next big project. In New York—where real estate is to the city what oil is to Texas—Schwartz needed City Hall. All zoning, land-use, landmark-preservation, and tax-incentive decisions ultimately came before the mayor or his commissioners. Schwartz knew it, and the mayor knew it. This upended the traditional relationship between the newspaper and City Hall.

As a leading commercial property owner in town, Schwartz and his fellow NYC real estate tycoons had billions on the line. If NYC became a less desirable place to work and live as a result of the 9/11 attack, the value of Schwartz's commercial holdings would plummet. Who knew when the market might recover? And what firms would want to locate downtown, which was destined to be a construction site for years to come under the best of scenarios?

Juan decided this was not the time to engage in a knock-down, drag-out argument with Baldwin. He had learned that Baldwin almost never reversed his decisions, regardless of the facts or arguments put before him. He was dogmatic. A stealth approach was best at this point. Juan would continue to report out the story of what happened and how it happened and build as strong a case as he could before making the case again. One thing was for sure—one part of this story, the story of how hundreds of FDNY members could wind up dead—wasn't going away, even if City Hall and Baldwin tried to wish it away.

But Juan knew he would need proof—hard evidence that the FDNY had royally screwed up the response and jeopardized the lives of its members. Who could help him piece that part of the story together? He needed some sleep. He needed to think it through. He needed to get back home and check on Jennifer and Chris and Matt. He filed his story and got a goodnight from McFeeley after his editor gave it a quick read. It was a solid piece of daily reporting. Nearly 350 firefighters missing and presumed dead. Cause as yet unknown.

"I'll call you if the copy desk has any questions. Go home. Get some rest," McFeeley said as Juan headed out the door. "We'll need you fresh tomorrow."

CHAPTER EIGHT

Inside City Hall, the mayor's chief political operative, Lou Amato, dropped into the office of First Deputy Mayor Peter Brezenoff before the 7:00 a.m. staff meeting. Both occupied coveted real estate inside City Hall, just a few steps from the mayor's office on the west wing of the building.

Mary Sullivan stuck her head in the office door.

"The mayor wants a quick update after your staff meeting and before he heads back down to Ground Zero again," Mary told Brezenoff. "What should I tell him? Twenty minutes good?"

"That works," Brezenoff replied. "I'll be right in as soon as it wraps up. Thanks, Mary."

Brezenoff knew that Mary had the mayor's ear and trust. They all depended upon her to make sure the office ran on schedule, day in and day out, and keep the staff in line and focused on the mayor's priorities. In City Hall, geography mattered. Her desk was located only a few steps away from the mayor's office and those of the deputy mayors. Her influence exceeded her years. She knew the mayor's routine and anticipated his every move. She looked up to him. A life-long Democrat, Mary had expected to be let go when Giuliani won office. But he had kept Mary at the seat of power, and she was grateful for that. So much of her identity was wrapped up in her position at City Hall; she wasn't sure what she would do if she had to find a job outside of city government.

At City Hall, the mayor's men were busy dealing with the most massive cleanup operation in the city's history. There were dozens of competing demands placed upon them, all urgent and requiring immediate attention. There were the FDNY and NYPD families who had lost members and the funerals still being planned. There were the families of the civilians still missing. And then there was the business community, worried about the impact of the attack on the future of downtown. In the backdrop of it all—unspoken most days—was what this all meant for the image of the mayor.

George Kelly, the mayor's press secretary, sat on the outside circle of the morning briefing of the mayor's top aides, who met each day in a City Hall basement conference room, which had been converted in the days after 9/11 to a mini command center.

Lou Amato had been arguing in the meeting to stick to his original game plan. "We keep the focus on the recovery and the cleanup. This was not the doing of our administration. The terrorists are to blame."

Lou's angle didn't sit right with George.

"Yeah," George said, interrupting. "But we have at least 3,000 dead, 343 of them New York City firefighters."

George dealt with the New York City press corps every hour of every day, ever since Rudy was first elected. He lived with the media beast and knew it better than anyone in the administration. Part of his job was to forecast for the mayor how quickly the press would turn on an issue and to make sure the mayor understood how it might play with the press—the unvarnished version. He doubted the story line that Lou was suggesting would hold for long. Then there will be hell to pay.

"The goddammed building collapsed on top of us, on top of the FDNY command center. Our Office of Emergency Management command center burned to the ground, located in a WTC building that we picked for it and then had to evacuate. How the fuck did we *not* know the buildings were coming down and at least get our people the fuck out of there? You can't blame all this on terrorists. A cornerstone of the mayor's legacy was to revamp how the NYPD and FDNY operate. They are supposed to coordinate response to a disaster like this through OEM. The NYPD had helicopters up but apparently didn't bother to tell the FDNY that they could see the towers leaning. They only radioed their own guys, most of whom got out in time. This is a fucking disaster on the response level. The press will eventually get to it. Not right away, but it's there for the picking. Juan Gomez of the *News* is already starting to ask questions. And that prick Wayne Barrett at the *Voice* will be all over us. And the *Times* smells Pulitzer. Kevin Flynn and Jim Dwyer of Metro know the FDNY and NYPD better than we do. We should try to get ahead of it. Appoint a commission to study the response. Ask somebody big to head it out. If we don't do it, somebody else will."

Lou fired back. "No. No internal investigations. Not now. It's too early. We have to stay focused on the rescue and the cleanup. If we start now with the who-knew-what-when approach, we will tear the FDNY and NYPD apart even more than they already are. Fuck the crazies and the press. The best way to stay ahead of this is to look forward. Focus on the search for survivors, the cleanup. Honor the dead. Rebuild. The city's future depends on what we do now. If we let them tear us apart with finger-pointing, we're dead—politically."

But George wouldn't let it go. "You're nuts, Lou. He's at 30 percent in the polls. The press is going to rip us apart once they realize how fucked-up the response was yesterday. We'll be lucky if we're not indicted."

Finally, the mayor's senior advisor, Peter Brezenoff, spoke up. Peter and the mayor had been friends since high school. The mayor—big on loyalty—trusted Peter like no other advisor.

"George, enough. We need you on this. You're right, we have tremendous exposure here. But Lou is right too. If we play this right, everything will fall in place. We're going with Lou's line: '*Don't Look Back.*' That's our overarching message. You've got to carry it—to your staff, to the agency flacks and to the press corps, as best as you can sell it. Call Baldwin at the *News* and tell him that's our position. Maybe he can get Juan to back off."

George nodded silently. He knew that once the debate was over and Peter came down on one side or the other that was it. That's how the Giuliani administration functioned.

If you couldn't live by those rules, you were out. No freelancing. No leaking on your own. Stick with the line.

The meeting was over.

After George left the room, Lou turned to Peter.

"How is Mary doing? She seemed pretty rattled after she came back from Ground Zero. I know she has a relationship with Juan."

Mary Sullivan's loyalty was unquestioned within the mayor's inner circle. Yet everyone at City Hall was painfully aware that her husband, Bill Sullivan, was captain of one of the FDNY's elite rescue units, and he was missing, presumed dead. When cops got in trouble, they called on Emergency Service Units. When city firefighters needed help—with a rescue, a collapse, or other dangerous situation—they called on the rescue units. The rescue guys were the most gung-ho of a gung-ho department. They were big. They were strong. And they came prepared with the latest equipment, and they knew how to use it. Bill's unit had been among the first to respond to the WTC.

"She just wants to know if there is any sign of her husband," Peter said. "You don't have to worry about her. She will not go off the reservation. I told her not to come in today, but she wanted to be here," said Peter. "There's been no sign of Bill. He hasn't turned up. He was last seen on the fifteenth floor of the South Tower. It doesn't look good."

"Let's talk to her together, if you have a minute," Lou said.

They walked over to Mary's desk, just outside the mayor's first-floor office and motioned to her to come into Peter's office.

After returning from Ground Zero with the mayor, Mary had tried to busy herself with the work at hand. She knew the pressures on the mayor and his staff were unprecedented. They had to manage the search and rescue operation, get the cleanup going, and deal with the expectations and fears of a shaken city. National and local media were hanging on the mayor's every word and clamoring for access to him. Mary helped him juggle it all, but, at the same time, she sought any clue, any hint of news about her Bill.

Mary admired Peter, who gave her a warm hug as she entered his office. Mary was aware that Peter attended Mass most mornings before coming in. Perhaps it was his Catholic school training. She saw how, in times of crisis like this, Peter took on an outsized role at City Hall. He had the calmness, the reassurance, and the right words of condolence that were priestly and genuine. He served as an alter ego to the mayor. Mary had seen the two work through many a crisis, but nothing like this. She worried about them both.

"We're still searching for Bill or his unit. We have everyone on it. We're not going to give up. Are you sure you wouldn't rather go home, back to Floral Park? I can have the PD give you a ride," Peter said as Lou looked on sympathetically.

"I'd rather be here," Mary said softly, holding back her emotions. "In case we hear something, I want to be close by."

"We understand," Peter said softly, holding Mary's hand now. "If you need anything, we are here for you. You know that."

She wanted to believe Peter, yet something didn't sound right. She had been around City Hall and around the FDNY long enough to know when the brass was up to something. She didn't say anything to Peter, though. She was not about to overstep her position, especially not now. All she wanted was news about Bill and his unit.

Though she tried to stay hopeful, she began to think of what her life would be like without Bill. Now, more than ever, the mayor and his senior staff seemed like her family, offering some stability in a world that had been turned upside down. Yet she wondered if they were being straight with her. She didn't want the sugar-coated version of what happened to Bill. She wanted to know the truth.

"Thank you, Peter. I know you are all doing your best."

CHAPTER NINE

SEPTEMBER 13, 2001

Juan came in early the next day. He wanted some quiet time in the newsroom before it got busy. He needed to plot out his next moves without distractions from editors, other reporters, and the phones.

At 8:00 a.m., he was the only one in the newsroom except the morning editor who was there to "open up." The a.m. editor checked the pressing stories of the day and made some early reporting assignments. He knew not to even think about assigning Juan to anything. Juan reported only to McFeeley and worked on special projects that the other editors on the city desk largely were unaware of until it was time to publish them.

Juan had been putting off making a follow-up call to Mary Sullivan. He knew from their encounter at Ground Zero that she was shaken up. There still had been no word about her missing husband. It was a bad time for her, and he knew he should leave her alone. But it was a call he had to make.

Mary picked up the call on the third ring. "I can't really talk now," she said softly, almost in a whisper.

"I just wanted to say again how sorry I am about Bill," Juan told her sincerely. "They still haven't found him yet?"

"Not yet."

"I know this is an awful time. Are you alright?"

"I'm holding up. I'm just hoping to hear something. The guys at Ground Zero haven't given up. They are still looking."

"Mary, I say this as a friend. You have to prepare your-self for what may come next. So far, they haven't found anyone down there. You know that.

"I know that, Juan," Mary said softly. "I'm just not ready to give up yet."

There was a long pause. From his years working sources on the phones, Juan had learned not to be afraid of some silence. Both parties sometimes needed to gather their thoughts. Dead air was okay during an interview.

Juan broke it first.

"Listen, I know this is the worst time, but can I come see you?"

"Why? Why now?"

"I can't talk about it on the phone. It's about what hap-pened down there."

"This is a really bad time," Mary said, whispering at this point into her cell phone, fearful the mayor or some other high-ranking administration official would walk by and overhear her. "I'm heading home soon, just to get some sleep."

Juan persisted. He had to get Mary alone, face-to-face, away from City Hall. That's the only way he would be able to convince her to help him.

"I'll meet you at the Triple Crown," Juan suggested, referring to a diner not far from her house in Floral Park, on Jericho Turnpike on the Queens-Nassau border, a spot remote enough that no one from City Hall or any of the other papers would spot them. "You have to eat something."

Once or twice before, Mary had agreed to meet Juan at this same diner. Mary felt comfortable there, sure she wouldn't be spotted by anyone she knew from City Hall. It was a forty-five-minute drive for Juan with traffic from the West Side, but well worth it if he could convince Mary to be a source on the story.

"Okay. But I can't stay long," Mary whispered into her cell phone.

"Eight-thirty okay?"

"See you then."

Juan checked himself out with McFeeley, letting him know he was going to meet a source without saying who or why or what the meeting was about. Juan had a good enough rep with the editors that he didn't need to check in on every detail. They trusted him; most of them, that is. He headed to his car, a 1996 Honda Accord, that he kept parked near the newsroom in the New York Press (NYP) parking zone on the south side of W. 33rd Street, across from the FedEx depot. Usually, heading out at night, you had to have your keys at the ready and make a beeline for your car. If you looked just a little lost or lingered too long on the street, the working girls who walked this still pretty-raw part of Manhattan would make an approach and inquire if you were out for a "good time," a line they used nightly with the truck drivers of the FedEx depot and any other potential Johns cruising the neighborhood. This night, though, the girls must have taken the night off. The street was deserted, except for the cars of other reporters. No tourists. No guys from Jersey looking to escape their suburban troubles and score a quick hookup.

On the drive out to Floral Park, down 34th Street, through the Midtown Tunnel, east onto the L.I.E. and then south on the Cross Island Parkway, Juan thought about how he was going to pitch Mary. This wouldn't be easy. She had helped him out before, letting him know about some of the infighting within City Hall on various issues, confirming some of his info about who was in the doghouse and who still had the mayor's ear. Most of it was harmless. He was careful to protect her, and she appreciated his caution. Her boss was, after all, a former federal prosecutor. He didn't take leaks lightly, especially from his inner circle.

Juan had learned early in his reporting career that people like Mary could be very helpful or put up roadblocks. He never made the mistake of ignoring them. They were the "gatekeepers," the people who controlled access to the high-powered people they worked for—and Juan needed access to. Most were incredibly loyal to their principles. Why else would they be there? Getting them to help you out was a tough nut to crack, one that typically took years of careful cultivation. He chatted them up, never seeming rushed, always remembering their names, birthdays, and inquiring about their families, their weekend plans. And he picked up on their signals—when it was a good time to try and bother them (and the men they worked for), and when it was not.

This pitch would be a direct appeal to Mary's conscience. Juan was counting on a basic presumption: that
Mary's loyalty to Bill and her desire to find out what happened to him would outweigh her loyalty to the mayor. It
was worth a shot.

Just then, Juan's cell phone, sitting on the front passen-
ger seat, came alive with a ring from his home phone. It was
his daughter.

"Dad, are you coming home?"

"Not yet. I'm going out on the Island to meet someone.
I will be back right after that. Is Aunt Sue Ann still there?"

"Yes, but I think she wants to go home. Can't you come
home now?"

"Sweetie, I wish I could, but I have to meet this person.
It's about what happened down at Ground Zero. I should
be home by ten. I'll see you before you go to sleep, okay?
Can you put Aunt Sue Ann on the phone for me, please?"

His daughter handed the phone over.

"Juan, are you coming home?"

"Yes, but not just yet. Can you stay a couple more
hours? I know it's a lot to ask, but this story is all over the
place. I have to meet someone."

Sue Ann knew not to ask too many questions. She would
stay, in memory of her sister. She knew Juan must be under
a lot of pressure at work in the wake of the attack. It was all
over the news, all the time.

"I'll stay until the boys are asleep and then I'll leave
Jennifer in charge. Ok?"

"Thank you, I really appreciate your help. You know
that, right? You are the best aunt my kids could ever ask for."

As night fell on City Hall, Peter had offered, again, to have the NYPD drive Mary home tonight to Floral Park. But she stuck to her normal routine instead. She hopped on the number 2 subway line from City Hall, and, within fifteen minutes, she was at 34th Street-Penn Station. Despite the shock of 9/11, the Long Island Rail Road had resumed service quickly, providing a reliable link in and out of the city.

Mary didn't even know exactly why she had spoken to Juan. Talking to him could only get her fired, she knew. And yet, there was something exciting about it, something about meeting him that broke her routine. It also gave her a certain power. Some of the men at City Hall were arrogant, totally full of themselves, and rude to her and the other staffers. She was able to let Juan know who were the good guys and who were the bad guys, at least in her eyes. It was payback of a sort. And, she convinced herself, she was actually helping the mayor by talking to Juan from time to time, although she doubted the mayor would see it that way. Some people close to the mayor took advantage of their positions, trying to boost their reputations, even at the mayor's expense. By setting Juan straight, she kept some of these self-serving players in check.

Mary had brushed off his initial advances. She knew what he was up to. She had been trained during her years at City Hall under Koch and Dinkins and then by the Giuliani men—some of the very best former federal prosecutors in the country—to never talk to the press. Give them nothing. They were only trouble. But Juan was persistent, more persistent than most of the other City Hall reporters, and Mary found him kind of charming in a roguish sort of way. Most of the men around City Hall were so straightlaced, adhering to Republican form. Dark suits, red ties, white shirts with button-down collars. These were very careful men. They often came out of the best schools in the country and were on the fast track. After a few years at the US attorney's office and then City Hall, they would be on to big jobs at big law firms and Fortune 500 companies. Juan had no such airs. He wore dungarees and no tie. His shirts were often open to the third button with no undershirt beneath. His brown, curly hair was a little too long. He could talk about almost any subject—the latest movie or Broadway play, the Yankees, the best, inexpensive restaurant to try in Chinatown or Little Italy, both within walking distance to City Hall. Also, Mary knew that Juan was close to a number of the top dogs in the administration. They trusted him. Said he was a tough reporter but one who wouldn't burn you. She heard the banter about him. It put her at ease a bit with him when he tried to chat her up. Slowly, he won her over. She would confirm small details or point him in this direction or that when he called her. He was always careful to call her on her cell phone as everyone at City Hall suspected their landline phones could be tapped at any time. She never told Bill about these encounters, or anyone else. It was her little secret. Her relationship with Juan gave her a feeling of empowerment.

She got off the Hempstead branch of the LIRR one stop earlier than usual—the Bellerose stop—and walked the few blocks up to Jericho Turnpike where the Triple Crown diner was located. It was a typical Greek, New York-style diner with booths and burgers, a rotating display case of gooey-looking desserts, a dish of mints and the newspapers for sale by the front cash register. The coffee was always hot, and patrons knew they could depend on a good, inexpensive meal—anytime of the day or night. Juan was already at the diner when Mary walked in, sitting in a booth by the back, away from the windows.

He got up and gave her a friendly hug.

"Thanks for coming. I really appreciate it. I know you must be exhausted. I wouldn't have asked you to come, but it's important."

He ordered a cheeseburger. She went for the Greek salad, always mindful of her calorie count, even now.

Juan didn't beat around the bush. "Something is not right about what went down at Ground Zero, and I think City Hall is already trying to cover it up. I need your help."

"What do you mean, cover it up? How can they cover this up?"

"I'm not sure yet. But some of my other sources—people inside the FDNY—are saying this operation, the response to the fire, was screwed up. Too many guys went up into the Towers, and they didn't get them out in time. That's why so many guys died."

"Well, isn't that kind of obvious?" Mary said. "Nobody knew the buildings were going to come down. If they knew, I'm sure they would have told everybody to get out."

"Maybe they did," said Juan, putting his cheeseburger down for a moment and looking straight at Mary. "Maybe they tried, but no one heard the warning."

"What do you mean?" Mary was confused.

"I'm not sure yet. I don't really know," Juan said. "A source inside the FDNY has been telling me to look at the communications. He was hinting at a problem with the radios but he's not coming clean. I covered the first bombing of the Trade Center in 1993, and I remember then the firefighters complained about their radios not working properly."

"What do you mean?"

"The WTC Towers were so tall; they had interference or something. I'm not sure. I just remember they had trouble talking to each other during the '93 attack."

"Wouldn't they have fixed that by now?" Mary asked logically.

"I don't know. You would think so," Juan said, though he was doubtful that the city could ever fix anything right. "Anyway, look, Mary, I need your help. You are on the inside. There are a lot of families, just like you, who are going to want answers. They are going to want to know what happened to their loved ones. I need you to keep your ears open and let me know if you hear anything about the communications not working at the WTC during the attack. Can you do that?"

Mary picked at her salad, not looking Juan in the eye. "I want to know what happened to Bill and the rest of the guys, too. You know I do. I'm on alert. But I can't betray the mayor. He's going to have a really hard time now keeping the city together. I don't want to make it any worse for him."

"I'm not asking you to do that. Just let me know if there's something you think I should be looking at as this unfolds."

Mary didn't answer. She separated the black olives and feta cheese from the greens on her plate, thinking over what Juan was asking.

"Just think about it."

The check came. Juan offered to give Mary a ride home.

"No. I don't want any of the neighbors seeing you."

"Right. Well, let me give you a ride up Jericho at least to Tulip Avenue. You can walk the rest."

Mary knew why he made the offer. The more time he spent with her, the better his chances of convincing her to cooperate.

Mary didn't say a word in the car. She wondered to herself whether she should trust Juan. He had played it just right. And now she was torn between her loyalty to the mayor and her desire to know what really happened to her Bill and the other firefighters at Ground Zero.

"I'll call you if I hear something," she said, getting out of the car and looking at Juan directly in the eye as she closed the door. "But you have to protect me."

"I'll never give you up. You know that. I've been doing this a long time, and I have never betrayed a source," Juan said. "I have your back. We both need to find out the truth."

CHAPTER TEN

OCTOBER 9, 2001

The FDNY bagpipers showed up early at the church, St. Benedict's on Otis Avenue, just off the Bruckner Expressway, the working-class Bronx neighborhood where Peter Murphy grew up and where his parents, Sarah and Tom, still lived in a modest attached house. This was the third FDNY funeral of the week for the bagpipers. Hundreds of funeral Masses in churches just like this one had been held throughout the city and on Long Island during the weeks following 9/11. Often, there were multiple funeral services on the same day. The record was sixteen.

Before the funeral, the guys at Peter's firehouse had come over with some of Peter's personal belongings—including his extra gear—a turnout coat with his name on the back, and his FDNY helmet. Sarah had lovingly placed them in Peter's old room along with the framed photo of Peter's FDNY Fire Academy picture with his helmet on, looking straight at the camera. She would visit him there, sometimes sitting for hours, going through his childhood trophies and other belongings that she had also kept in the room.

One fact she couldn't get past was the knowledge that she had convinced Peter to take the FDNY test, seeking for him a steady line of work and ties that would keep him in New York where one day she hoped he would settle down and raise a family so she could become a grandmother.

That hope was gone now. Lost in the ashes of the World Trade Center dust. She asked herself if she indirectly had caused her own son's death. What if she hadn't pushed him to take the FDNY test?

Her husband knew the pain she felt. On the morning of the funeral, he tried to comfort her.

"You can't blame yourself for this," Tom said quietly as they dressed. "He loved the idea of being part of the FDNY. It was a good fit for him, coming out of the Marines. This is the life he wanted. You just nudged him in the right direction. You did the right thing telling him to take the test."

Sarah looked at her husband as he put on the jacket to the one dark suit he owned and rarely wore. He was a good man, she knew, and he meant well. But Tom had stayed at the NYPD too long. It was steady work that allowed him to provide for his family, but the job had taken a piece of his soul. He didn't question the world the way Sarah did. And now, in the wake of Peter's death, he receded even further into a post-NYPD retirement funk with no real purpose to his days.

After thirty years of marriage, she still loved him, but she wanted more out of life. Peter's death had awakened in her a fire and a sense of mission. She would now channel all her energy into a quest for answers.

"I just have so many questions," she told her husband. "I know he loved the job and the firehouse. He told me so. I'm okay with what I did, pushing him toward the FDNY. What I can't understand is why this happened. He only had six weeks on the job. He just got out of the Academy. How could they put him in this position? And what really happened down there? Did he even get the word that the South Tower had collapsed? How could they lose so many guys? That's just not supposed to happen. I can't let this go, Tom, and I need you with me on this. After the funerals are over, I'm going to start pushing for answers. City Hall has got to be held accountable."

The FDNY bagpipers warmed up outside the white-brick Roman Catholic church as mourners started to fill the pews of the modest, one-story building that had served as the center of Catholic life for generations. Sarah arrived at the church wearing a simple black dress. She wore no makeup and displayed no jewelry except for her wedding band. Her short-cropped, still-blonde hair looked a little disheveled, because she had forgotten to comb it out completely. The NYPD blocked off the streets around the church to accommodate the hundreds of mourners who showed up to pay last respects to Peter Murphy, one of the only probies the FDNY lost on 9/11.

Two Bronx-based FDNY ladder companies had positioned their rigs on the street directly in front of the St. Michael's entrance. They extended their aerial ladders high above the street to form an inverted "V" and hung a giant American flag between them. Hundreds of uniformed FDNY members lined the streets leading to the church. Fire companies from Long Island, Westchester, and New Jersey also came to honor Peter Murphy's sacrifice.

As the bagpipe detail played the familiar and mournful notes of "Amazing Grace", Sarah walked slowly under the giant American flag and up the front steps of the church, passing the hundreds of mourners outside. She carried the large, framed photo of Peter in his FDNY helmet, an official photo all FDNY recruits take when they first come on the job. Peter's youthful, strong facial features and earnest expression jumped out of the frame. He clearly wore the FDNY helmet with pride.

Sarah wanted to remind the world what Peter looked like when he was alive—a strapping, vibrant, eager twenty-five-year-old, ready for action. Tom had gently questioned whether it was a good idea to bring the framed photo. But Sarah was determined. The TV cameras and news photographers set up outside the church to cover the funeral all zoomed in on Sarah as she made her way into the church with the photo.

Sarah felt her heart beating faster. She wasn't quite ready for the intensity of the moment, having so many cameras trained on her as she ascended the church steps. Tom held her by the arm, but she walked up on her own, steady and slow, looking straight ahead. The reporters and cameramen were respectful but unrelenting in their focus on her. She wanted them to feel her pain and to come to know, in some small way, what she had lost—her precious, young, strong son.

Sarah was savvy enough to know that by carrying the photo of her son up the steps and into the church that she was—to some degree—exploiting the death of her own son to gain attention. She was okay with that. She knew what she was doing. If this was what it took to get answers, she would do it, and keep doing it until the media and the mayor paid attention.

Inside the modest church, every seat in every pew was taken. Well-wishers filled the choir loft and stood along the walls of the side aisles. The last time she saw the church this packed was on Easter Sunday. Sarah and Tom made their way up to a reserved area at the front of the church. All eyes were trained on them as they walked up the center aisle.

Mayor Rudolph Giuliani, there to give a heartfelt eulogy at Peter's funeral Mass, embraced Sarah and Tom on the way into the church. He spoke about the sacrifice Peter and the other men of the FDNY and NYPD had made to try and save lives. He spoke of their heroism.

Sarah was grateful the mayor appeared at her son's funeral, but his words failed to soothe her. Her sadness and sense of loss were quickly giving way to anger.

The FDNY had assigned an officer to every family who had a suffered the loss of a loved one on 9/11. If they needed anything at all, the assigned officer was their contact. As she knew all too well, given Tom's long career, it was partly good grief counseling management and partly damage control. The department wanted to head off trouble from the families. They knew loss can turn to anger quickly—and that the anger could easily be directed at the FDNY and at City Hall.

In Sarah's case, no amount of handling was going to work.

Her son had vanished from the planet. Nothing was recovered, save his helmet. No body part. No DNA. No scrape of clothing or personal belonging. Her husband had joined the search at Ground Zero over the last four weeks, working his NYPD contacts. Still, not a trace of Peter ever turned up.

As the mayor spoke from the pulpit, Sarah could only think about the unanswered questions she had. She wanted to shout them out—right then and there in the church—and force the mayor to respond. "What happened to my son? How did he spend his final hours? How could this be?"

She held back, though, not wanting to embarrass Tom or make a scene. Not yet anyway.

But the questions swirled inside Sarah's head every hour of every day.

The mayor and his entourage left the service via a side entrance as soon as Peter's service was over. The press was camped out on the front steps outside the church, but the mayor long ago had established a policy of not commenting to the media at funerals. Both sides knew the rules. This day was no exception.

Sarah lingered outside the church to talk to friends, relatives, and a few of the other 9/11 widows who had come to her son's funeral to show their support. Sarah was deeply appreciative that they attended. They didn't know each other well, but they now had a shared bond that drew them together.

One of the widows, Maureen Riley, quickly approached Sarah.

"Sarah, we just want you to know that we are here for you," she said, giving Sarah a long embrace. Riley's husband was still among the missing, presumed dead. Three other 9/11 widows stood nearby.

"I know nothing will bring Peter back. I know that. But I just want some answers," Sarah confided to Maureen.

"We want answers too," Maureen responded. "We feel the same way as you. We can't move on until we know what happened down there. The mayor has been doing his best, but City Hall isn't telling us the truth."

Right there, outside the church at her son's funeral, Sarah and Maureen formed that most powerful of unions—a sisterhood pact—one born out of grief and unexplainable loss.

"Alright then," Sarah said, her mood picking up a bit. "Let's talk tomorrow. Right away. I don't want to lose a day."

"Okay!"

The other 9/11 widows, now in a semicircle around Sarah, nodded their heads in agreement.

Sarah's husband was standing nearby and overheard the conversation. He gently had urged her to move on, as had some of her closest friends from the Bronx. If she heard that phrase one more time, she was going to slug someone.

Now, outside the church, Tom tried again to put the brakes on what he saw as a possibly self-destructive campaign. He pulled Sarah aside. "I overhead what you were saying to the other widows. You have to start thinking about letting it go. There's nothing to be gained. It's not going to bring him back."

Sarah loved Tom. And the loss of Peter had brought them closer together. He did everything he could to find

Peter, to find out anything about him. He spent weeks at Ground Zero and hours on the phone. She knew he was hurting just as much as her. His long-awaited retirement from the NYPD, after thirty-nine years, had turned into this ongoing nightmare. It was not what they had planned.

"Tom, I know you might be right. I might spend months or years pushing for answers and get no return out it. I understand City Hall isn't going to respond to us without tremendous pressure. I get it. And I know you are trying to protect me, but I have to ask you to understand what I need right now. And that is answers. I can't let them just get away with this. Someone has to be held accountable."

If for no other reason, she wanted to make sure the FDNY and the city didn't just try and sweep this whole thing under the rug. With all the adulation of the FDNY and the outpouring of sympathy, it seemed like the city could get away with just about anything. No one wanted to say anything critical, at least not yet.

"And I know what this could cost us. It could consume us. I will try to keep a balance, I promise. But you know better than me that institutions like City Hall and the FDNY do not take to criticism, to probing, to second-guessing of how they operate. They will fight us tooth and nail. They have the lawyers. They have friends in the press. They have time on their side. But I do too. And I have one purpose—to find the answer of what happened to Peter and the other men."

She could see he wasn't happy.

"Tom, I won't let it go. I want them to admit what went on down there and make sure it never happens again. I don't want some other mother and father to go through what we are going through."

They entered the black limo the funeral home had sent to the church to be part of the blocks-long funeral procession. The limo lined up behind the fire truck from Peter's firehouse in Brooklyn that carried the empty, flag-draped coffin representing the still-missing Peter Murphy. There were no remains to officially bury.

CHAPTER ELEVEN

LATER, THAT SAME DAY (OCTOBER 9TH, 2001)

Among the 9/11 families, Mary would be considered one of the "lucky ones." Some of her husband's remains were recovered on October 5, 2001, near the base of the North Tower, along with those of several of the men in his unit. One surviving firefighter told Mary he had last seen Bill on a deserted 25th floor, checking to make certain no civilians were left behind.

The funeral Mass was held on a Tuesday at Our Lady of Victory Roman Catholic Church in Floral Park. Known simply as "OLV" among the locals, the church was a modest structure, flanked by a parish grammar school and a convent that once housed the nuns who taught at the school (but that had for decades been mostly deserted).

That day, burying one of their own, it seemed like the entire village turned out, along with half of the FDNY and representatives from nearly every fire company on Long Island. Most local fire departments on Long Island were staffed by unpaid volunteers, known locally as "vollys," a close-knit band of brothers and neighbors who operate local community firehouses as their own small-town clubs and hangouts. For a full-dress, line-of-duty funeral, they all turned out, packing the streets in uniform for blocks and blocks in every direction. The church was so full they had to set up loudspeakers so the overflow crowd in the small village green directly in front of the church could hear. Police blocked every intersection leading from the funeral home to the church.

Mary wore a simple black dress with a string of pearls that Bill had given her on their fifth wedding anniversary. She pulled her thick, blonde hair back into a single ponytail. She wore no eye makeup, mindful that it would likely get ruined today. Her sister, Diane, joined her in the front pew of the church, the same local parish church where Mary and Bill had been married.

Diane was considered the smart one in the family. Against great odds, she had finished college, graduating from NYU, and then attended NYU Law School, graduating at the top of her class. She worked for one of the city's top law firms and somehow juggled the crushing hours her job demanded with raising a family, including two teenage girls, an eleven-year-old son, and a husband who was also a lawyer. They lived in Westchester County, in tony Mamaroneck, a relatively short ride on Metro North to Grand Central and half an hour from Floral Park, assuming there was no tie-up on the Throgs Neck Bridge or on I95N.

Diane handed Mary a small, white handkerchief. They glanced at each other and leaned in for a brief hug. Diane never fully approved of Bill, but Mary knew that Diane had grown to respect Bill's work ethic and his devotion to her.

The two sisters would find a way to get through this, Mary thought. She was glad Diane was with her now.

As the mourners settled into their seats and they waited for the priest to start the service, Mary's mind wandered to the last time she was with Bill at his firehouse for the annual Christmas party.

Mary and Bill had both been looking forward to the get-together. Held on the first Saturday of December, it always was a highlight of the frantic holiday season. The spouses brought their children to the firehouse, where the men had been preparing for weeks. The men on duty that day would still have to jump on the rig if a call came in, but everyone else could stay and enjoy the party. Each FDNY house had its own holiday traditions and party, an event that was planned for and anticipated all year long.

The men cooked an elaborate meal using the firehouse kitchen. There were food runs days in advance, menu debates, Christmas lights and decorations to be hung, and a tree erected—all to impress the wives and the many children who attended, all part of the FDNY brotherhood and its largely Christian culture.

Bill was on duty that day, and he went in early to help with the preparations. Mary didn't mention it to Bill, but she had a doctor's appointment earlier in the day, and she arrived at the Brooklyn firehouse as the festivities were well underway.

There were more than twenty children in the house when Mary walked through the small entryway cut into one of the larger, red garage doors, opening up to the bays where the fire engine and ladder and rescue units were stored. The kids ranged in age from infants to teenagers. Some were dressed up in their holiday outfits. A half dozen or so of the boys and girls were crawling in and around the compartments of the fire trucks under the watchful eye of their fathers. It was the one day of the year they were allowed to do so as a group. They squealed with excitement as they each took a turn hitting the horn or turning on the emergency lights.

Tables, chairs, and a Christmas tree were set up on the first floor, in the living space where the guys normally watched TV and ate their meals. Mary greeted the other wives warmly with hugs. The women of the men from Rescue 12 shared a close bond. And they welcomed a chance to be together to catch up on gossip and survey how each of their respective children had grown and developed during the past year.

Nancy McMahon, the wife of the battalion chief over Rescue 12, pulled Mary aside. "How are you and Bill doing?" she said in a low voice.

Mary had confided in Nancy about the trouble they had been having. She wanted to talk to her, but this wasn't the place or time. "We're fine, doing fine," Mary said.

Just then the children started to gather around the shiny brass pole that connected the upstairs living quarters to the firehouse floor as a brass bell was rung from above, announcing the arrival of the Big Man.

"Ho! Ho! Ho!" bellowed Bill as he came sliding down the brass pole, dressed in an expensive, red-velvet Santa suit the house members had chipped in to buy years ago. "Merrrrrry Christmas!"

Mary's eyes lit up with pride, and she laughed and smiled as Bill gathered the children around him and sat in a special chair near the Christmas tree. She helped Bill hand out gifts to each child, who got a chance to sit on his lap and take a family photo. Bill played it perfectly, pausing with each child as if they were the only one in the room and taking time to listen to their special Christmas list wishes.

During a brief lull in the procession of children, Bill turned to Mary. He sensed something was wrong.

"What's happening? You seem distracted," he said.

"I went to the doctor today. I'll tell you later," Mary said as another child scrambled up on Bill's lap.

Bill now hurried along the remaining few children. He then quickly disappeared up into the second floor sleeping quarters to change out of his Santa suit and hurried back downstairs to find Mary.

"Come on," he said to her, pulling her into the vacant officer's room, just off the garage floor. He closed the door. "Tell me what the doctor said," he demanded.

"I didn't want to ruin the day for you. I know how much you were looking forward to the party," Mary said.

"Mary, come on, I don't give a damn about the party. Are you okay?"

Mary couldn't hold back any longer. She started to sob. Watching all the children play with each other today and being among all the young mothers just made Mary feel even more alone and upset.

Now, Bill drew her close and wrapped his large, 6'2" frame around her. "Tell me what's wrong," he whispered.

"The doctor says I have a cyst on one of my ovaries. It's not cancerous, but the ovary has to come out. He says we can still have kids, but he says it may be more difficult. He wants me to see a specialist."

Bill had a thousand questions, but he held them back, not wanting to upset Mary any further. He squeezed her closer and held her face in his large, strong hands.

"This is going to work out. Trust me. We will have a family if that's what you want. We will go see every specialist in the city to make sure we get the right answers and treatment."

Mary let herself exhale in Bill's arms, her emotions now out in the open. "I just want to be a mom, like the other wives. I want to give you a son and a daughter and watch them grow up. This news wasn't part of the plan."

"The plan now is to first take care of you," Bill said, reassuring her. "Your health comes first. And I will be there, every step of the way. We will get through this together, and no one in the family or the firehouse needs to know about it if you don't want to tell them. We are going to work through this."

The crowd in the church sat up in their seats as a familiar figure approached the pulpit.

Diane saw that Mary appeared distracted, and she gave her a soft elbow and a "pay attention" glance just as Mayor Giuliani was set to take the lectern. He had just arrived from Peter Murphy's funeral service in the Bronx earlier in the morning. Mary knew the mayor had one more funeral on his schedule for today after this one.

Mary broke out of her daydream and sat up straight, eyes on her boss.

The mayor lauded Bill's bravery and sacrifice on a day when his city and nation came under attack from terrorists.

The mayor had given this eulogy now dozens of times, but as he had known Bill and Mary for years, he was able to give it an extra personal touch, which Mary greatly appreciated. He talked about how the two had met, how Mary didn't fall for Bill at first but that Bill was nothing if not persistent, and how, eventually, he had won Mary over with his corny firehouse jokes, good looks, and towering physique and presence. Bill took over a room when he entered. Everyone seemed to want to talk to him, Giuliani recalled, even the mayor of the city of New York.

This line got a laugh.

Mary smiled too, grateful the mayor was there to honor her dead husband. The mayor concluded by speaking directly to Mary and to her family, talking about Mary's own dedication and strength of character.

"Bill would want you to honor him and his brothers, but he also would want you to move on, to keep going, to look to your future," the mayor told Mary. "As dark as this day is, there will be days ahead for you that will be bright. And know that we are all here for you and for your family and that we will never forget Bill's sacrifice."

A single bagpiper from the FDNY color guard unit—the Irish guard replete with kilts and sash—played "Amazing Grace" as Bill's casket was carried out of the church by his FDNY brothers and down the steps into a waiting FDNY truck from his company in Brooklyn. Overhead, the Floral Park fire department used their bucket extension ladder to hang a huge American flag, suspending it directly over the church steps. Mary walked silently behind, carrying Bill's helmet, supported by Diane on her right. Diane held her tight and close. The two looked straight ahead at Bill's casket, afraid they would lose it if they started making eye contact with so many family members and friends who filled the church. Directly behind them were the FDNY officers and other firefighters from Bill's firehouse.

Outside, thousands of uniformed first responders—FDNY, NYPD, Nassau and Suffolk County PD, and volunteer firefighters from across Long Island and the metro area—lined the streets in an honor guard.

Slowly, they made their way down the steps of the church.

Juan did not approach her. Mary saw Juan and acknowledged him with a glance. She was glad he came. She had been thinking about what Juan said at the diner. It seemed far-fetched. Bill had never mentioned anything to her about the handy-talkie radios he used every day on the job being faulty. If it was a big problem on the job, surely, she would have heard him talking about it to one of his pals, even if he didn't say anything to her directly about it. But maybe, as Juan indicated, it was something about the Trade Center, the height of the buildings, that could interfere with the radios? She didn't dare ask anyone at City Hall about Juan's theory. That would be too dangerous, especially if Juan ever wound up actually writing anything about it. She would then be suspected as a source of his. And suspicion alone would be enough to mark her as a scarlet woman inside the Giuliani camp. It was exactly what she had to avoid. No, she would wait, bide her time, and, as Juan advised, keep her ears open. After all, a lot of documents came across her desk on the way to the mayor's. She had access to almost everything he saw, including reports from the NYPD and the FDNY. Every meeting with every city commissioner from every department went through her. If something was up, sooner or later, she would catch wind of it.

Juan's theory raised a series of questions, questions that kept her up at night. Did Bill really sacrifice himself trying to get others to safety? Was he the hero everyone was making him out to be, including the mayor, now that he was dead? Or did he just not hear the order to evacuate? Surely, if he was told to get out, he would have tried to save himself and his men. Did the order come too late? Or was he too high up the in the North Tower and just run out of time?

After the funeral, after the burial, after the last of her well-meaning relatives and neighbors bearing trays of food had departed, Mary dialed Juan's cell phone number.

"Thanks for coming today."

"I hope it was okay I came. The mayor was there, so I figured that was good cover. How are you holding up?"

"Not bad. The service was really nice, wasn't it? The mayor did a good job and so did Bill's brother. I'm just overwhelmed by everyone coming over and wanting to help. There's really nothing they can do. I just have to get through this. My neighbors didn't want me to spend the night alone, but I shooed them all home. I couldn't wait to have a moment of peace in my own house."

"You don't find it hard, being there without him? I know what that's like," Juan said, and she knew he was referring to when he lost his wife last year.

"When I am alone, sometimes I feel like he is still with me," Mary confided to Juan over the phone. "It's weird. But with all his stuff around, I feel him. His uniforms. His work clothes. His equipment. His tools in the garage. I sense him. I talk to him at night sometimes. I think he is guiding me, still."

Juan understood. "I know what you mean. I talk to Linda about our kids all the time. When one of them is having trouble at school or acting out, I ask her what I should do. It sounds silly, I know, but it helps to have that conversation. I feel her too. And I ask her to help me keep the family together. I think it works."

"Listen, I've been thinking a lot about what you said at the diner," Mary said, getting back to business. "I'm starting to think the only way I can get past this all is to help you find the answers to what happened. I need that closure. I need to know if Bill really was a hero or if the city screwed him somehow and that he didn't need to die. I owe it to Bill to try and find out. Do you really still think that maybe they didn't hear the order to get out?"

"I'm starting to piece it together," Juan said, not letting on that he really wasn't much closer than when they had met at the Triple Crown. "I've got another source saying they had problems with the radios. Nothing specific, though. I'm still tracking it down. I need a document, something that explains what happened. All I have now is kind of second hand. Not enough to go with."

Mary paused for a moment, weighing the risks again of helping a reporter track down what could be an explosive story with implications for her boss and mentor. "I'll be back at City Hall in a few days," Mary said. "I'll see if there is any email traffic on this or memos coming across about it."

"That would be great. But be careful. This is as sensitive as it gets."

"I know," said Mary, thinking she did not need to be reminded of how fast she would be fired if anyone at City Hall ever found out. Bill's death—the most painful thing she'd ever gone through—did suddenly give her some financial independence. She was surely going to be the beneficiary of a sizeable settlement from the various 9/11 funds set up to compensate victims' families, in addition to Bill's FDNY pension. She could afford this risk—and it was one worth taking.

"I'll call you once I get back to the Hall. It's better if I call you."

"Okay. And listen," Juan said sincerely, "Call me if you just want to talk. It doesn't have to be about the story. I'm around."

"That's very sweet, Juan. I appreciate it. What helped you get back on track after you lost Linda?"

"Work got me through. I threw myself into the next story. I still think about her every day. But you move on. You have to. The alternative is paralysis. It's good you are going back to work soon. I found that was the best thing."

Mary thanked Juan for his advice and hung up the phone. She started to drift off to sleep and, instinctively, she reached over to Bill's side of the bed for a good night nudge. But all she felt was his empty pillow.

CHAPTER TWELVE

A few weeks had passed since Sarah visited Ground Zero and Peter's funeral. She was starting to realize—for the first time since Peter went missing at the WTC—that she had been thinking only of herself. Her visit to The Pile and, especially to St. Paul's Chapel, brought home to her how much hurt there was out there across the city. She wasn't the only one who had lost a loved one.

The entire FDNY family was in crisis. Her city was on its knees. And what had she been doing? Nothing. Sitting in her house in the Bronx, worrying at first, and then wallowing in her grief at the loss of her beloved son.

Now, alone again in her bedroom, Sarah lay in bed as the first rays of sunlight hit the windows. She hatched a plan. No more self-pity. She would continue to grieve for Peter. That would never change. The loss of a son, especially one as young and promising as Peter, was a loss that would be with her every hour of every day. She suspected she would never be the same, never get past that loss. But now she realized she had a larger purpose: to find out why he died and to be a voice, if needed, for other 9/11 families.

She had no idea how to go about it.

As she lay in bed, thinking of what she saw at Ground Zero, thinking of the volunteers and the first responders, the FDNY men and women who were still working, still going about their jobs of helping others, even in the face of having lost so many of their friends and coworkers, she was ashamed. Instead of thinking about her own loss, her first instinct should have been to help them during this siege.

Her inaction, her paralysis, stopped today.

She knew what to do next. She dressed and went straight to work—in her kitchen. She gathered up all the trays of food that her neighbors had brought over after Peter's funeral. There were so many well-wishers with food, she had to freeze most of it. Now, she double-wrapped them carefully in tin foil for the ride to Brooklyn. And she made a tray of her own lasagna, a dish that was Peter's favorite, one that she made for him every time he came home from the Marines or from one of his far-flung adventures rock climbing, scuba diving, or running a marathon.

She was headed to Peter's firehouse. She wanted to talk to his colleagues, to the men who had been with him since he graduated from the FDNY Fire Academy, and to the firefighters who had been at the WTC—at least those who had made it back alive.

During the drive from the Bronx to the Brooklyn Heights section of Brooklyn, where Peter's firehouse stood, one of the oldest companies in the city, located in a nearly hundred-year-old, flag-draped, two-story brick structure, she realized how little she knew about Peter's life since he joined the FDNY.

Mothers were not allowed to visit their sons at work, especially those who worked for the FDNY. The culture of the firehouse was insular and male-dominated. What happened at the firehouse, stayed at the firehouse. So, it was no surprise that Peter told her little about his day-to-day life with Ladder 389. Sarah was used to this. Her husband rarely brought home problems from his shifts with the NYPD. When she asked Peter about how it was going at the firehouse, he would break into a big smile and say it was going great. He loved being one of the guys, and it was clear to her that he felt at home with the FDNY as he did when he was in the Marines. It was another brotherhood, and he seemed to fit right in. She was happy that he was happy. And that's all she really needed to know. His decision to join the FDNY was the right one.

But now, in the wake of his death, she needed to know more, to probe more deeply about his work, to understand how someone with his athletic ability and survival skills, honed in the Marine Corps, could have been trapped inside the WTC, unable to make it out.

She parked on the street near the red, front double-doors of Peter's firehouse. The flags out front flew at half-mast. Purple and black bunting had been draped over the front of the firehouse, above the garage doors where the engine and truck were stored at the ready, waiting for the next call.

A makeshift memorial had been built to one side, spilling onto the street. On a piece of plywood, there were five photos of the men from the house who were missing and, at this point, presumed dead. Lieutenant Kevin Callahan's photo was on top and, underneath, in a pyramid form, were the headshots of the four other men who did not return from the fateful 9/11 run: Mike (the Termite) Sullivan, Patrick (the Irish) Barry, Sal (the Eggplant) Esposito and Peter (the probie) Murphy.

Candles, flowers, personal notes, and handmade posters surrounded the photos, which had been wrapped in plastic. As she paused at the memorial, what hit Sarah was how young these men were as a group, all in their prime. They were not supposed to die that day.

It was clear there had been an outpouring of concern and sympathy from the local community. Sarah tried to keep her emotions in check as she gazed at her son's photo and those of the other men. But the questions swirled around in her head: *Why would God take them? And why like this?* As a Catholic, Sarah believed in the Almighty and that most people were good. But this tested her faith—to her core. How could such evil exist? How could something so senseless be allowed to happen, robbing these men and their families of their time together? These good men were not coming back to the firehouse, not today, not ever.

The firefighter assigned to the house watch desk was responsible for greeting any visitors who knocked on the small wicket door built into the larger apparatus doors of the firehouse. He recognized Sarah as she approached and came outside immediately to greet her.

"Mrs. Murphy," he said. "Why don't you come inside?"

Sarah snapped out of it.

"I brought some food. It's in my car. Can you help me?"

"Of course," said the firefighter, who Sarah didn't recognize. "Let me get some of the other guys out here to help."

Within a few seconds, five other guys came out to greet Sarah and help her bring in the trays of food. They escorted Sarah up to the kitchen, where the rest of the men on duty joined them.

The kitchen was the center and soul of any firehouse. It was where meals and bonds were made, beefs got resolved, and the problems of life and the world and the political biorhythms of the city of New York government and of the FDNY were endlessly debated and "square-rooted"—looked at from every possible angle. Firefighters, after all, did sometimes have a lot of time to kill in between calls.

When firefighters invited someone into their kitchen, it was more than just a gesture of hospitality, it was a sign of acceptance.

Sarah was given a seat at the head of the table. Overhead, behind her, hung a rack with dozens of well-worn aluminum pots and pans of all different sizes. A giant, cast-iron, eight-burner gas stove was to her left.

The men had been working for weeks down at Ground Zero. Most had barely been back to see their own families. They were physically tired and emotionally drained. Like Sarah, they had not fully processed what had happened to their colleagues, and they didn't quite know what to say to the mother of "the probie" for whom they all felt responsibility.

Only one of the men at the kitchen table, Joe Demma, had been on the 9/11 run with Peter. He was the "chauffeur" of the ladder company. He sat right next to Sarah but didn't make eye contact right away.

Captain O'Reilly spoke up first to break the ice.

"Mrs. Murphy, we all want you to know that Peter had immediately become one of us in this house. Even though he had only been with us a short time, he had become an indispensable member of our family and of our company. He was on his way to becoming an outstanding firefighter. He was physically strong with great endurance. He listened and learned quickly. And he had an infectious smile and the kind of personality that we all were drawn to. He had the kind of leadership abilities you hope for in a recruit. I could see it almost immediately, and I knew he would one day be in command. He was a beautiful young man, and you should be very, very proud of him."

Now, it was Sarah's turn to say something.

"Thank you, captain. And thank you all for taking Peter into your hearts so quickly. He didn't tell me much about the firehouse, but it was clear to me he loved being here, being a part of the FDNY. I'm grateful to you all.

"When I visited Ground Zero, I came away with a purpose. I want to learn as much as I can about what happened. I think I owe that to Peter…and to all the other members of the FDNY who aren't coming back. I'm hoping you can help me. That's one reason I am here."

Firefighter Demma spoke up next.

"Mrs. Murphy, I was with Peter on the 9/11 run, and I am the only one who came back. My heart aches for him and for our other brothers we lost. I can't explain it. I wish I had answers, but I don't. We responded to the WTC call like hundreds of other guys. It was obviously the biggest fire we had ever been at, unlike anything we had seen or experienced. There was a lot of confusion at the WTC. Peter went in with the Lieutenant and the other guys. We know they started to climb the stairs. We had radio contact with them for a little while, but then the radio channels were so clogged with traffic we couldn't reach them and then the radios just went dead. They next thing I saw was the South Tower coming down. We had civilians dive under our rig with us just to try and escape the debris. Then, we all moved farther north to get away from the cloud coming at us. A little while later, the North Tower came down too. We didn't really know what was happening inside. We could only hope Peter and the other guys somehow made it out or found a safe place to shelter."

The other men looked around at each other, searching for the right words to try and comfort Peter's mom.

"Lieutenant Callahan was one of the most experienced firefighters in Brooklyn," said Captain O'Reilly. "I'm sure he was watching out for Peter. We all look out for any probie. If there was any way of getting out of there, anyway at all, I'm sure the Lieutenant would have found a way."

Sarah paused. This wasn't going to get her anywhere, she thought. She decided not to put them on the spot, to ask the questions she really wanted to ask: *How could you let my son get killed? Why didn't you protect him?*

The captain offered to show Sarah where Peter slept in quarters and to open his locker. She put her hands on the cot where Peter had last slept when doing a "24"—a round-the-clock shift. She sat on the bed, stroking the blanket, feeling her son's presence, and pausing, her head in her hands.

Sarah declined the offer to go through Peter's locker. She wasn't ready for that, not yet.

She emerged from the bunk room to find a dozen firefighters in their light blue FDNY uniform shirts lined up on each side of the hallway leading back to the kitchen in a sort of honor guard for her. They all saluted as she walked down the hallway. She was touched by the gesture, which was as much for Peter as for her. They presented her with Peter's backup FDNY helmet.

She accepted the helmet and went down the line, shaking the hands of each firefighter.

"Thank you all very much. You are now members of my family. You carry memories of my Peter. If there is ever anything I can do for you, please let me know. And thank you for sharing your thoughts and emotions with me today. It was very comforting to me to hear your recollections about Peter."

When she returned to her car, alone and out of sight, she let herself cry a deep, long sob, clutching her son's helmet in her lap. It was her first really good cry since Peter went missing.

Peter's own colleagues seemed to know little about what actually happened on 9/11. Or were they just trying to shield her from the facts? She couldn't tell. She found it odd and disturbing that they seemed unaware of what happened inside the WTC Towers. The FDNY was as good as the NYPD at putting up roadblocks to outsiders who wanted information. Letting others second guess how they operated was not something they took to kindly, not even from the mother of one of their own. The FDNY knew how to circle the wagons.

Either way, Sarah realized now that she would need to find her answers elsewhere and that she would need help doing it.

CHAPTER THIRTEEN

Juan was dog-tired when he finally got home to his Brooklyn apartment after Bill's funeral. He had been chasing leads all day after the service but not really advancing the story. At least he scored one breakthrough—Mary had agreed to help, to keep her ears open at City Hall. That was a major development that hopefully would bear fruit.

As he parked his car and walked the block to his house, Juan thought about his talk with Mary after Bill's service. He felt her pain, her loneliness. He had not delved into all the details of the real ache he felt from losing his wife—the aimlessness, night after night, with an empty bed and no mother for his three teenage children. He was trying to offer Mary some encouragement. She would discover the pain soon enough, all on her own, as he did. He went six months before he could even think about touching any of his wife's things. Her clothes and jewelry still occupied the same space in their tiny bedroom. Only when her sister called to help him did he begin to clean out her closet, donating most of it to the St. Vincent de Paul Society, keeping some of the jewelry as keepsakes to give to their children when they were older.

At night, Juan often dreamed about Linda and their life together, before the cancer claimed first her breasts and then her young life.

He knew the families of the 9/11 victims, like Mary, were now feeling the same loss, asking the same deep questions, that he did when he lost Linda. How could this be happening to us? Why me? There were no real answers and no real solutions except to keep going, to keep living.

As he put his key into the lock of his second-floor apartment door on Atlantic Avenue, near Henry Street, he heard some muffled noises from inside the living room. First some low groaning sounds and then, as he opened the door, the sound of multiple sets of feet quickly hitting the wood floors near the couch. The lights were low, but he saw the bare back of his daughter—her shirt off and bra undone—scrambling to put her shirt back on. Next to her was Tony, a local boy she had met in middle school, who was always hanging around. Tony also was struggling to find a sleeve of his plaid flannel shirt to put his arm through. He caught Juan's glance and hurried to clothe himself. At least they both had their pants on, Juan thought as he entered the room and confronted them.

"What's going on here? I thought you were watching the boys, and instead I find this? Tony, you better collect your things and get on home right now."

Juan was trying to stay cool. *How would Linda want him to play this?* he thought. *Don't overreact, she would say. She's just seventeen. That's the problem. Don't yell, she would advise.* But if he didn't yell, the next time her pants likely would be off, and God-knew-what would happen next.

Once Tony scurried out the front door past him, Juan yelled at his only daughter in a voice stern enough to get the message across, but in a tone quiet enough so as to not wake the boys.

"What the heck were you thinking? This isn't how Mom and I raised you. I mean you are doing this right here in our house, with the boys asleep upstairs? What was going through your head?"

"I'm sorry, Dad," Jennifer said, sheepishly, looking at the floor. "We didn't do anything."

"It didn't look like nothing to me," Juan shot back through clenched teeth. "You get pregnant, then what? You are only seventeen. You have to be the one to put the brakes on. You know that, right? A boy will always want to go all the way. I wish your mother were here."

With that last line, Jennifer looked up and gave Juan a stare. It seemed like minutes were going by as the two glared at each other in silence.

"I wish Mom was here too, because you *never are*," Jennifer said, her voice up two octaves. "You are always running around the city worrying about a story instead of us. We need you to be home! I get it. The city is burning up. But how do you think that makes us feel? We're scared too. At least Tony was here."

"Don't start this," Juan said, firmly. "You know I have a job to do, and this is an all-hands-on-deck situation at the newspaper. You're old enough to know that. I asked Aunt Sue Ann to look after you. And I expect you to act your age and take some responsibility now. I need your help watching the boys sometimes. You know that. I'm sorry too that Mom isn't here, but there's nothing I can do to fix that. I still have to go to work. I have to pay the rent. And you have to carry your weight around here, not fool around with Tony behind my back in my own living room!"

"You just don't get it," Jennifer shot back. "All those people dying? One minute they're here and then they're just gone. Forever. Just like Mom. Why do things like this happen to us? It isn't fair."

Jennifer stormed past Juan and up the stairs to her room. She said nothing more. This wasn't over, Juan thought. But he didn't know how to make it better. He knew Jennifer was at least partly right. He should be home more, especially for her. She had taken Linda's loss the hardest of his three children. These past few weeks had been especially hard on everyone, and he was mostly absent.

He went into the kitchen and flipped on the 11:00 p.m. news. More reports from Ground Zero. Channel 4 had covered Bill's funeral. Their Long Island-based reporter, Greg Caroll, was doing a stand-up in front of the church, then his report went to a voiceover as they rolled tape from earlier in the day during the service, showing Mary following the casket as Bill's fellow firefighters carried it up on to the fire truck for the ride to the cemetery.

Juan chugged down a cold Corona Light and quickly ate some cold cuts left in the fridge. Over the TV news, he heard Jennifer sobbing quietly in her room upstairs. He left her alone for a while so they could both cool down. Then he headed upstairs and gently knocked on her door. She didn't answer.

"Honey, I'm sorry I yelled," he said quietly through the door. "You know I'm just worried about you. I like Tony, but you have to be careful. You can't let a situation get out of control."

Still, no answer.

Juan decided not to push it.

"Get some sleep. We'll talk in the morning. I'm going to try and be home more. I promise."

As he lay in bed, trying to go to sleep, he thought about abandoning the radio story. Maybe it was too much work at too high a cost to his family. He could kill it himself. Baldwin didn't even want him to pursue the story. And McFeeley wouldn't really care if he dropped it either. He could just go on to something else, not related to 9/11.

Then his thoughts went to Mary and to Bill and to Maldanado and to all the other friends from the FDNY he came to know over the years. What would they say if he ignored the story, if he took the easy way out?

Instead, he resolved to make a hard, quick push to get the story. And then he would spend some more time with Jennifer and the kids. He knew what he was doing professionally wasn't fair to them. He would make it up to them once he wrestled this one to the ground. He hoped it would all be worth it. Yet, he had to wonder if it really was.

CHAPTER FOURTEEN

NOVEMBER 5

After 7:00 p.m., when the mayor headed back up to Gracie Mansion or out to an evening appointment, City Hall started to quiet down for the night. Most of the reporters in Room 9, the press area, had filed their stories for the next day's paper or for the 6:00 p.m. broadcasts and were checking out with their editors before making one last call to the mayor's press office to make sure there were no newsworthy events involving the mayor that evening that they had to worry about covering.

And the mayor's staff could rest a little easier once he had left the building and his NYPD security detail gave them the all-clear-for-the-night signal.

As was her custom, Mary did not leave the building right away. She needed this time to prepare for the next day, to line up any last-minute additions to the mayor's schedule and to go through his emails and correspondence to be certain she didn't miss anything critical.

She also kept a watchful eye on the staff, attuned to the biorhythms of the place. It helped that her cubicle was so centrally located, steps from the mayor's office and from those of the first deputy and the other deputy mayors, that she could hear most conversations, especially when the deputies left their doors open, as they often did to get some air circulating in the centuries-old building they inhabited. Sometimes, the first deputy would even crack open a window and light up a cigar in his office, knowing no one would dare call him on it.

Mary's ears perked up this evening as she overheard Peter talking to Lou Amato.

"Who is Sarah Murphy, and what does she want?" Lou asked Brezenoff.

"She lost her son, a probie...she's teamed up with a professor from John Jay, a guy from their fire science program. They're calling for a full investigation. She's getting some traction with the *News*."

"Have we tried talking to her?" asked Lou, whose job included trying to head off public dramas that might hurt the mayor's image and political fortunes.

"We back-channeled. She's on the community board in Pelham Bay. Apparently, she's uncontrollable at this point."

"I thought the FDNY had people assigned to every widow and relative," Lou said, referring to the plan the FDNY brass put in place, with City Hall's approval, in the wake of the attack.

"They did. Her husband was on the job with the NYPD, a detective. He's retired, though. This was their only son. She doesn't understand how a probie could be put in harm's way. She's pushing for release of the 9/11 tapes. She wants to hear if her boy was on the tapes. She wants to know where his unit was last seen. She's only the tip of the sword.

There will be other families calling for the same thing. Maybe we should try and get ahead of this and appoint our own team to investigate. At least then we could try and keep a lid on it."

"No, it won't do any good," Lou said. "Then we'll get accused of trying to whitewash the whole thing. We just have to try and stall this, until we get the site cleaned up. In a few months, it will be the next guy's problem—probably Bloomberg, the way it's looking now."

"Yeah, but any investigation will come back to us," Brezenoff said, "whether we are in office or out. And the next guy, if he's smart—and Bloomberg certainly is smart—may pin any problems about the response on us."

"Bloomberg won't do that," Lou countered. "He wants our endorsement. And he wants to move toward a cleanup and rebuild as quickly as we do. I think he is good to his word. I just want to get past the next couple of months without any subpoenas coming our way. I'm going to call over to the *News* and see if we can put a damper on this story."

Mary knew who Lou would call at the *News*. He would go straight to Billy Baldwin, his editor of choice whenever he felt a story wasn't going favorably toward the mayor. Ideologically, Baldwin had been in sync with almost all of the Giuliani administration's front-burner issues—the crack down on street crime, including the squeegee men harassing motorists for money at the East River crossings; the get-tough approach with the city's municipal unions; the effort to reduce the size of the city government bureaucracy; and the then-revolutionary idea that able-bodied welfare recipients should have to work for their benefits.

Lou knew Mary was still at her desk, and he asked her to dial Baldwin's number and connect them.

Mary had the number on speed dial.

"*News*," answered Baldwin's secretary, Delores.

"This is Lou Amato calling from the mayor's office," Mary said. "Lou would like to talk to Billy. Is he around?"

"Let me get him for you, Mary. How are you all holding?"

"Very well, Delores, thank you for asking. These are some tough days, but we're all getting through it together."

"Here's Billy."

Mary transferred the call. Lou answered, hitting the speakerphone button so Peter could listen in. Mary, too, could hear most of the conversation from her desk. Lou didn't bother to close his door. The smoke from Peter's cigar was getting to him, and he needed the circulation.

"How is it going there?" Billy asked, with genuine concern.

"We're getting through it, Billy, thanks for asking. The hardest part is dealing with the families. They want answers and, frankly, off the record, I don't have a lot of good news for them."

Lou decided to get right to the point. He had fed Baldwin tips for years, carefully cultivating him. As a result, Baldwin often enjoyed exclusive access to City Hall's top secrets—a powerful tool that allowed Baldwin to appear "in the know," passing on the best inside gossip to the *News*'s mercurial owner.

"That's why I'm calling you. One of the family members—the mother of a probie who was killed—is holding a press conference outside my office in a few minutes. Sarah

Murphy. She's teamed up with some professor from John Jay. They're calling for full inquiry into the response. I can't have a full-fledged investigation unfold, not now, not while we are still searching for remains and trying to piece the FDNY back together. As I've mentioned to you before, we have to look forward and not look back. That's just what the terrorists would prefer, that we concentrate our energies on finger-pointing and engaging in the blame game instead of figuring out how to prevent the next attack. That's where our energies need to be. We must look ahead. Just don't give her a lot of play, if that's possible. If the *News* makes her into a crusader, the rest of the media will follow."

"Lou, I can never say what the value of a news story might be until it comes across my desk. But from what I heard at the morning news meeting, it doesn't sound like much of a story to me. One mother and a CUNY professor calling for an investigation isn't likely something to worry about. It will probably make the paper, but I would say toward the back of the lineup. Certainly, it is not page one material in my book. We have bigger fish to fry."

"Thank you, Billy. It's great comfort to know we have an editor at the *News* who has good common sense."

"While I have you on the phone, what is the status of the recovery effort?"

Mary leaned in a little closer. She wanted to hear Lou's update about the Ground Zero recovery. She was not surprised to hear Baldwin push Lou for more details. Billy Baldwin knew how to work the Giuliani men. He might be in the tank with them, but he was still enough of a newsman to know how to cut a deal. If he was going to shit-can the

Murphy-calls-for-an-investigation story, he sure better get something out of it so he could at least boast to a few select editors that he cut a good deal.

"We're just about ready to call it, Billy. It's hard for the families to hear, but at this point, we aren't going to find any more remains. We are moving into the cleanup phase. Some of the families would have us in search-and-recover mode for another month or more. Off the record, we can't afford any longer to slow down the cleanup effort. This is some of the most valuable real estate in the entire city. The sooner we get the mess cleaned up, the sooner we can rebuild. The real estate community is already knocking on our door. They know that the viability of the entire downtown area is at stake, maybe the viability of the city's entire economy. If we don't move ahead with the cleanup soon, it potentially could hurt the metro region for years to come. We simply can't afford it. We can't take that risk."

"Can I use any of that, Lou? Essentially, what you are saying is, at this point, the city's primary focus will be on the cleanup, and the search for victims is—essentially—over. Is that right?"

"That's correct. Of, course, we will still look for remains. But the chances now of finding anyone alive are zero."

Mary slumped back in her chair, careful not to let out an audible gasp. This was not really new information to her, but she was shocked to hear Lou put it so bluntly.

"That's big news, Lou."

"That's why I'm giving it to you, Billy. I know you will be able to treat it in the proper context."

"So, we can go with it, then?"

"Yes, just don't quote me directly. Use me as a source close to the mayor."

"Got it."

Mary knew Lou was good at covering his tracks. By staying on background, Lou was giving the mayor some wiggle room if, say, the families went ballistic about City Hall calling an end to the search and rescue effort. This way, the mayor could backtrack off his own administration's leak if he had to, depending upon the reaction.

"Okay then, we have a deal," Lou said. "And I don't have to worry about that Murphy-investigation story?"

"The story you just gave me is much, much bigger, Lou," said Baldwin. "You just knocked that Murphy story to the back of the paper."

"Good. I appreciate that, Billy. I really do. And I won't forget about it, either. It's times like these when you find out who your friends are. Can I ask about one more item?"

"Surely."

Mary started to pack up her belongings for the night. It was getting near eight o'clock, her normal time to leave the office, and she didn't want Lou or Peter to think she was hanging around just to listen in on the call. But then she heard Lou mention Juan. She lingered a little longer, pretending to pack up her briefcase.

"What's Juan Gomez poking around on? I hear he's asking around about the radios," Lou asked Baldwin.

"The radios?" Baldwin seemed genuinely surprised at Lou's question. Could he honestly not know what his star investigative reporter was up to?

"Something about whether the radios that the firefighters were using weren't working right on the morning of the attack."

"That would be a big story, Lou. I didn't know he was on to that. Let me check it out. Is it true? Were the radios screwed up?"

"Off the record, I don't know yet. I have my own people looking at it. I just don't want some half-baked story on this at this moment. The families are already on edge. It wouldn't be right to base a story on tidbits from here and there."

"I'll check into it," Billy told Lou. "And, if you want, I can promise I'll run it by you if Juan has something we think is worth printing."

"Fair enough. Thanks again."

Mary had heard what she needed to know. She gathered her belongings and headed out the door without saying anything to Lou or Peter. She said good night to the lone remaining NYPD officer manning the security desk on her way out, as was her custom. Walking to the subway, she could barely contain her disgust. She wanted to let out a scream.

Lou was trading on information about 9/11 just like it was any other story. It made no difference to him, Mary realized. Information was power, a commodity to be used as a means to an end. In this case, Lou's goal was to try and reel in the 9/11 families, put a damper on Juan's probing of the faulty radios, and contain any damage to the mayor.

Mary was no virgin to this kind of information horse-trading. She had seen it done countless times by Peter and Lou and by the mayor himself. They were expert at pulling the levers of power to advance their interests. This time, it hit home. This time, they were trading up on the dead bodies of 9/11 victims, on the memory of her dead husband.

This time, it was personal.

CHAPTER FIFTEEN

Sarah now started each day working the phones for at least three hours. She stayed in touch with the other 9/11 family members, some of whom also were seeking answers from City Hall, and she sought out allies in the broader FDNY community. Sarah's background as a member of her local community board—the most basic and grassroots form of government in New York City—now came in handy. She knew how to get people together and organize toward a goal.

Sarah had sought and received meetings with the FDNY brass and with City Hall. They were polite and sympathetic, but they went nowhere. She decided that the only way she was going to get answers was to make some noise. It was the only kind of pressure City Hall understood.

Tom had gotten in touch with some of his old NYPD contacts on the faculty of John Jay College on the West Side of Manhattan, the CUNY institution dedicated to criminal justice studies and issues relevant to first responders. Tom's buddies recommended a member of the faculty who was an expert on the FDNY who might be able to help Sarah get some answers.

On a dreary day, a Monday, Sarah and Professor Glen Costello, the CUNY expert Tom's pals had recommended, gathered with a few other relatives of the FDNY missing and dead at the southernmost tip of City Hall Park, within sight of the City Hall steps but far enough away that the NYPD detail assigned to guard City Hall would not hassle them. A light drizzle started to fall. Umbrellas went up, but the small crowd did not disperse. They were waiting for a few more TV cameras to arrive. Juan Gomez showed up from the *News of New York.*

Sarah had hoped he would come. The professor had some contacts at the *News* who he reached out to in advance of the press conference. He had spoken to Juan about Sarah and her quest for answers. Costello walked Sarah over to introduce her to Juan as the other reporters and cameramen set up equipment and readied themselves for the start of the press briefing.

Sarah went right over to him. "Pleasure to meet you, Juan. I am a fan of your work," she said, shaking his hand. He was shorter than what she imagined. But his dark, Latino features made up for it. He looked frazzled and disheveled, though. It was clear he didn't know who she was.

Costello stepped in. "Juan, this is Sarah Murphy, the woman I told you about, the mother of the probie who was killed on 9/11. She's from the Bronx. She's the reason we are here."

Sarah could see Juan's demeanor change. He dropped the guarded look reporters put up when dealing with random members of the public, unsure of their intentions.

"Yes, good to meet you as well. The professor has told me a lot about you. This is pretty brave of you to step forward like this. I'm sure City Hall and the FDNY can't be happy about it."

"I'm done worrying about what the FDNY brass and City Hall are thinking," Sarah responded. "I'm here to try and get answers."

Juan liked her directness. "Me too. I hope we can work together."

Costello motioned to Sarah and Juan that it was almost time to start the formal briefing.

Juan didn't know if much would come of this briefing. But he was willing to help Sarah and the 9/11 families by trying to give them some ink.

The press conference was scheduled for 11:00 a.m., prime time for a media briefing. The professor and Sarah were not all that experienced with the press. They had enlisted a local PR guy to help—pro bono. He at least knew enough to make sure they got today's press conference on the Associated Press Daybook, a not-for-publication listing issued the night before to news editors around the city alerting them of the next day's possible newsworthy events, including all public appearances by the mayor. Each item on the AP Daybook carried a one sentence description, just enough for an editor to decide whether it was worth it to assign a reporter:

11:00 a.m.—City Hall Park—Sarah Murphy, mother of 9/11 victim FDNY probie Peter Murphy, and CUNY Professor Glen Costello are joined by other 9/11 relatives and advocates to call for a full investigation into the city's 9/11 response and to urge the mayor to release tapes of all 911 calls and internal FDNY radio traffic from the morning of the attack.

No organized group of 9/11 families at this point had publicly called for an investigation of the city's response. Others, including the mayor's critics, had thought about it and had privately agreed it was needed. But no one dared do it out in the open, on the record. Not while the funerals were still happening. It seemed premature. Feelings were still too raw.

Sarah had weighed these considerations but rejected them. It was important to start an investigation now, while events and memories remained fresh. She was amazed that no one else was pressuring the city for a full-scale, independent probe of what happened on the morning of 9/11. She could hardly believe that 343 firefighters had perished, not to mention the nearly 2400 civilians, and no one was calling for an investigation.

Outside City Hall, as the drizzle became a steady rain, Sarah Murphy gathered herself for this moment. In addition to the print reporters, four TV cameras—Channels 4, 2, 7, and NY1—had arrived, along with the two major all-news radio stations in town—Newsradio 880 and 1010 WINS. This was more coverage than she and the professor had hoped for. She had spoken before community groups in Pelham Bay and had granted a few interviews to local Bronx reporters in the past, but those engagements were nothing like this. When those TV cameras flicked on their portable lights and stuck six microphones in your face, there was nowhere to hide. The professor quietly went over the talking points with Sarah, just out of earshot of the reporters. They had now been joined by relatives of a few other victims' families as well as a couple of recently retired FDNY officers who believed a full investigation was needed.

"Are you ready for this?" the professor asked her. They both knew she would be the focus of the journalists' attention. "Are you sure you want to go through this? There's no turning back once we go on the record. City Hall will come after you, you know that?"

"I'm ready, more than ready," Sarah reassured him. "The mayor needs to hear this, and so does everyone else in this city."

Sarah stepped forward toward the cameras. The cameramen closed in on her, forming a tight semicircle around her. The reporters thrust their handheld microphones with their station logos toward her face. The print reporters stayed just outside the circle, holding their tape recorders as close as they could while juggling notebooks and pens, ready to jot down her best quotes.

From under her raincoat, Sarah revealed a framed eight-and-a-half by eleven portrait of her dead son, Peter Murphy. It was the same one she brought to his funeral. All the cameramen recognized the image.

The TV camera crews zoomed in on the photo and then pulled back to show Sarah holding it, her face a solemn testimony to the pain and loss she and the other 9/11 family members were experiencing as they searched for answers.

"This is my son, Peter Murphy. He was a 'probie' for the FDNY. He was last seen going into the North Tower of the World Trade Center on 9/11. He had only six weeks on the job. He went to work. He answered the call. He never made it out of the building. I want to know why. Firefighters are not supposed to die when they fight a fire—especially not probies. Every firefighter takes a risk going to a fire scene. But they aren't supposed to die. When they do, it means mistakes were made. Three hundred forty-three men died inside those Towers, including my son. That means something went horribly, horribly wrong. And we can't blame it all on the terrorists. I want to know what happened to my son. Why didn't he get out in time? The city of New York, the FDNY, and the mayor need to be held accountable for what happened after the planes hit the buildings. The response to the attack was their responsibility. We need to know what mistakes were made so they don't happen again. There's only one way we are going to get those answers and that's with a full and independent investigation."

The story ran deep inside the *News* the next day, on page seventeen, with a small, two-column headline: "Family Members Call for 9/11 Investigation." Juan's story quoted Sarah and the professor. The mayor's office issued a terse statement, noting that it was too early to launch an investigation while search and rescue and recovery efforts were still ongoing at Ground Zero (even though they were about to be suspended.). The NY *Times* did not cover the press conference. The New York *Post* ran a short item. The TV stations, though, gave Sarah's story good play on the evening news, and NY1 put it into the news cycle, airing it that afternoon and repeating it every hour. The image of Sarah holding a framed portrait of her dead probie FDNY son while standing in the rain outside of City Hall was irresistible for the local TV news, and some stations led their broadcast with Sarah's call for a formal investigation into the city's response.

The press briefing had worked. Surely, City Hall was paying attention. Sarah, the community organizer from the Bronx, was now playing in the big leagues. *Not too shabby*, Sarah thought to herself as she rode the subway back up to the Bronx. *Not too shabby at all.*

Sarah and the professor got together the next day to recap and plot strategy. They were pleased with the outcome of the press conference. For Sarah, it was a huge step, publicly challenging the FDNY and City Hall. She never imagined herself in such a role. She came from a civil service family. Her husband was drawing a city pension via the NYPD. Going public was not something you did, especially not when you came out of one of the uniformed agencies like the FDNY. You did not wash your internal laundry in public and you did not dare to take on the mayor of the city of New York.

"Thanks for your help," Sarah said to the professor as they shared a bagel and coffee in Ellen's Café near City Hall. "I couldn't have done it without you. But is that it? What happens now? Will City Hall just ignore us?"

The professor did not want to misrepresent how hard this fight would be. He had been involved in other battles involving government agencies. It was never easy. They rarely yielded if they did not have to, and this administration had a reputation for toughing it out, no matter what.

"They will ignore us if you let them. You have the moral high ground. You now have the media's attention. You are only asking that the facts come out. And you are a mother, advocating for her son and the other families who suffered a loss. You have a strong case. But you have to keep the pressure on. You have to show up. Not just one time like yesterday, but every time there is an opportunity to be heard. Your voice and the voices of the other family members must be a constant part of the public conversation now. If you go home and give up, City Hall wins."

Sarah understood what the professor was saying. She vowed to stay in the fight.

"I'll do this for as long as it takes," she said. "They are not going to get away with it. Not this time."

CHAPTER SIXTEEN

The only editor at the *News* in whom Juan had confided about his faulty radio theory was Mike McFeeley, the city editor. McFeeley instantly spotted the dangers in pursuing a story line like the one Juan suggested. He agreed that Juan should do so very quietly. He would try to help him when the time came, but, in the meanwhile, he officially didn't know anything about it.

"Sarah Murphy is reacting out of the loss of her son, but what she is saying makes some sense," Juan told McFeeley. "Probies are not supposed to die at fires. Neither are three hundred firefighters. Something went terribly wrong down there. And City Hall is doing their very best to deep-six it all. They are trying to keep the focus on the recovery, the cleanup, and the terrorists. They don't want anyone looking at how the FDNY and NYPD handled the response to the attack."

"You'd better get some more sources on this, or it's going nowhere," McFeeley advised Juan in his usual no-nonsense fashion. "This one is a career-ender if you get it wrong. It has to be locked down tight or else we'll both be out of a job."

Juan knew McFeeley was right. He had been working his contacts, pulling out all the stops, and pressing for information. In addition to Mary, Juan had enlisted Professor Costello up at John Jay. Juan had grabbed him after the press briefing in City Hall Park and told him what he had been hearing about the radios. Costello said he would check with some of his contacts within the FDNY.

Costello was himself an expert on the kind of radios the FDNY used. He had written about some of the FDNY's communication problems in trade journals that covered the fire apparatus industry. His sources in the FDNY were already buzzing about all the problems the guys encountered on 9/11, not least of which was the radio communications.

Juan dialed the professor's number up at John Jay.

"Professor Costello here."

"Hey, prof. Juan here. I wanted to follow up on our conversation after the press briefing. Have you heard anything about the radio issue?"

"You are definitely on to something. Everyone in the department knows the radios are old, and they don't have much bandwidth. At a big fire, with so many units responding, everybody gets on at the same time, and they tend to step on each other's transmissions.

"Mysteriously, every time the department tried to update the radios, the same contractor was the only one to submit a bid," the professor said. "Some of my sources in the department suspect some kind of collusion between the contractor and the city, but they don't have any hard proof."

Prof. Costello thought the only way to get to the bottom of whether the radios had failed during the 9/11 attack was a full-blown, very public investigation of the city's response. That's why he had decided to help Sarah Murphy. As the mother of a probie killed on 9/11, he knew she could draw the kind of media attention to the issue that would be needed to pressure City Hall.

But Costello, too, had to be careful. He worked for a university that was dependent upon City Hall and Albany for much of its funding, so he had to be cautious about stepping too hard on political toes. Academic freedom wasn't really free, not when you were talking about taking on the sitting mayor of the city of New York. The moral outrage of the 9/11 families was the best bet to applying pressure to City Hall. By keeping victims' family members like Sarah out front on the issue, he could stay pretty much in the background.

Juan knew Costello was a sharp political player in his own right. He suspected he knew a lot more than he was letting on about. He also knew he wouldn't have aligned himself with Sarah Murphy unless he had a larger motive.

CHAPTER SEVENTEEN

DECEMBER 15, 2001

Mary waited until the mayor had left the building for his 11:00 a.m. appointment uptown. He was meeting with some real estate bigwigs who wanted to discuss the future of downtown, post 9/11. They were already pressing for the Port Authority and the city to rebuild at the WTC site. The mayor had to balance the concerns of the family members—who wanted the recovery to continue until all the missing were found—against the real need of the city to clean up the debris, start repairing the damage to the PATH and WTC transit stations, and begin thinking about what would replace the WTC Towers in the years ahead.

She walked alongside the mayor as he left his corner office, went through the gate leading to the City Hall rotunda area, and down the steps of City Hall, where a fully loaded, specially equipped, late-model Ford Explorer was waiting, its engine running, tinted windows rolled up tight. Mary made sure the mayor had his briefing book and talking points. She reminded one of the advance guys to keep him on schedule; he had a 12:30 p.m. lunch uptown and a 2:00 p.m. back at the Hall. "Don't let him run behind," Mary admonished. "Give him the sign when it's time to move on. Break in, if you have to."

As the mayor's entourage pulled out of the City Hall parking lot, heading toward the FDR Drive, Mary walked past the NYPD security checkpoint at the parking lot entrance and into City Hall Park. She walked toward the southern tip of the park—which the mayor had lovingly restored, complete with working, gaslit streetlights—and dialed Juan's cell phone.

"Can you talk?" she asked.

"Yes, I'm just walking back to my desk."

"Listen, I can't talk long now. I'm on my lunch break. But I need to see you. Can you be at the diner tonight? Eight o'clock?"

"I'll be there."

The rest of Juan's day was a blur. He made a round of calls to his FDNY sources. Spoke to the professor. And he poked his head in McFeeley's office and told him he was meeting a City Hall source tonight about the radio theory. McFeeley nodded but said nothing at first.

Juan was used to McFeeley's non-reaction reactions. It was one of his editing skills. He used it to test reporters.

"Are you still chasing that? Is it going anywhere? What else do you have going?"

"I just need a few more days on the radios. It's going to pay off. My gut tells me it's there."

McFeeley didn't bother looking up. He simply took another long drag on his Marlboro, still staring at his computer screen, and mumbled, to no one in particular, "Your gut is going to get us in trouble."

Juan knocked on the outside glass of McFeeley's office wall on his way out the door of the newsroom and gave him a thumbs-up sign as an acknowledgment. He knew there was a lot on the line. He was excited about Mary's call and the meeting. If anyone could help move this along, it was going to be her.

She was already seated in the back of the Triple Crown when Juan got there. She still had her work clothes on, so she must have come right from the train station. She wore a navy-blue blazer and matching skirt with a slight slit up one leg. Her white blouse was unbuttoned slightly, revealing a small gold cross with Bill's FDNY house number on it. Her thick, straight hair was pulled back in a tight, short ponytail.

"Thanks for coming," she said, getting up to greet him with a quick hug. As she settled back into the booth, she took her blazer off and folded it carefully, placing it on the seat next to her.

"I'm glad you called," Juan replied. "How are you doing?"

"I'm okay, really."

They ordered quickly, the usual salad for Mary and a cheeseburger for Juan. Mary waited for the waitress to disappear into the kitchen before speaking. She was serious about her words being confidential; she had even checked on the way into the diner to make certain the other booths near them were empty and that there were no other patrons she recognized.

"I heard something you should know about. The mayor had a big meeting with the police and fire commissioners a few days ago. They didn't look happy going in, and they looked even worse coming out. I heard it was very heated."

"Do you know what they said?"

"No. But I found something afterward that made me even more suspicious. It was an email from one of the fire commissioner's staffers—the first deputy—saying they had been interviewing all the guys who had been at Ground Zero on 9/11 and that most of them never heard an order to evacuate."

"Did you get a copy?"

"No, I didn't dare make one. I wasn't even supposed to see this one. They are routing FDNY stuff around me now because they think it will just upset me, so it's going to the mayor now either by hand or through Peter. I just saw this one open on my coworker's screen for a moment while she stepped away, and I answered her phone."

"You've got to get a copy. This is very significant. Did it say anything else?"

"There was a whole report attached to the email, but I didn't have time to even open it. I overheard Peter on a phone call with the radio manufacturer later on, asking them some pretty pointed questions."

"Like what?"

"Something about a 'repeater.' Where was it installed? How many were there? I don't even know what that means, though."

"You sure you heard right? A repeater?"

"That's what he said. A repeater. It was a long call, and Peter was pretty steamed. I couldn't hear the guy on the other end, but it wasn't a pleasant exchange."

"I'll check with some of my other sources. They might be able to shed some light on this 'repeater.' But you have to try and get your hands on that report. Can you do that?"

"It's not going to be easy," Mary said. She put her head into her hands for a moment. Juan took the signal. She had worked all day and was tired. He knew not to push her anymore tonight.

"You took the train here? Let me drive you home."

"I left my car at the station. Drive me there, please."

Juan felt a kinship to Mary that went beyond a reporter's normal urge to protect a source. He felt a chemistry, but he repressed his instincts in this regard. It was too soon after Bill's funeral to even think about approaching the subject. And getting involved with a source was never a good idea.

Journalists deal with death, mayhem, and destruction on an almost daily basis. It's part of the job. They report on murders, fires, rapes, riots, serial killers, child beaters, corrupt cops, and self-serving politicians; they often see the worst elements of humanity in the toughest parts of town. The newsroom veterans—like the cops and prosecutors they often cover—often think they know how to deal with tragedy without bringing it home or internalizing it. Those instincts kicked in for Juan when his wife died. He only took off a week from work, mostly so he could be there for his kids, at least initially. But he couldn't mask her loss forever. It took a toll. He sought out assignments that would keep him late at the office, depending on his wife's sister and neighbors to look in on the kids when he wasn't around. Sometimes, it hurt to be home with nothing but the TV to distract him. His kids needed him, but they also had their own lives, their own friends from school, and the neighbor-hood. They didn't want to hang out with Dad too much. The loss of their mother was not a topic they discussed. But it loomed over every activity, every birthday, every holiday. He wondered if all their lives would be better if he started dating again and found someone to help fill the void.

"This is fine, thanks," Mary said as they approached the small parking lot of the LIRR's Bellerose station. "You can let me out here. I'll be in touch as soon as I have some-thing else."

CHAPTER EIGHTEEN

DECEMBER 16, 2001

The next day when Juan got to the office, his first call was to the professor at John Jay. If anyone would know what a "repeater" was, it would be him.

"Need your help on a technical question," Juan said, skipping the usual pleasantries and chitchat. "What's a 'repeater?'"

"That's an easy one," replied Prof. Costello. "The radios the FDNY uses are more than fifteen years old, and the technology they operate on is even older. They basically are great if you are in a house fire and need to talk to the guy in the next room, but they suck in high-rise fires. The signal they use isn't strong enough. To get around this, in some buildings the FDNY put in 'repeaters.' They basically are devices that boost the radio signal so that it can go farther. The cops have them installed all over the city for their radios because they are always communicating with central dispatch. The FDNY, though, hasn't caught up with the NYPD. I think they put them in a couple of places, and I'm pretty sure the Trade Center is one place they installed one after the 1993 WTC bombing. Why are you asking about the repeater?"

"I'm not sure yet. There may have been a problem with it," Juan said. "That's what I'm hearing from a source. Does that make any sense to you?"

"If the repeater wasn't working that would explain a lot," the professor replied. "That would mean the handy-talkie radios the guys carried as they went up the stairs probably weren't working, at least not in terms of being able to communicate with the brass manning the command center in the lobby or nearby. That would mean they were being sent up blind with no way of being updated on the overall situation from the command post."

"But you said the cops had repeaters all over the place? Wouldn't their radios still be working, even if the FDNY repeater at the WTC wasn't?"

"Yeah, but you are forgetting a critical issue," the professor explained. "The FDNY radios and the NYPD radios are not what they call 'interoperable.' They are not on the same frequency. Essentially, they can't talk to each other, especially if they have separate command posts, which is what happened on 9/11. I'm hearing the cops were not present at the FDNY command post in either the North Tower or, later on, when they moved it to West Street."

"Wait a minute, run that by me again," Juan said, wanting to make sure he got it correct. "The cops and the FDNY radios can't talk to each other?"

"That's right, not directly," the professor repeated. "And if the FDNY repeater at the Trade Center wasn't working, the FDNY brass had no way of talking to those units they were sending up into the Towers.

"You have to get that confirmed. If you can nail down that the repeater wasn't working, you've got a hell of a story," the professor said.

This would explain what Mary had overheard at City Hall. Juan tried to absorb what he had learned from Mary and the professor. By now, he had spoken to enough other ranking FDNY officials who survived to know that an order to evacuate was given. But if the repeater wasn't working, it's likely many, if not all, of the 343 dead FDNY firefighters never heard it. This was front-page news—if he could confirm it. This cast the rescue operation on the morning of 9/11 in an entirely different light than that portrayed by City Hall. Instead of brave firefighters who willingly sacrificed their lives trying to evacuate civilians from the Towers, it was just as likely that many of the firefighters simply didn't know the buildings were about to come down and that it was time to abandon the effort and get out, as quickly as possible. It would also help explain, at least in part, why the NYPD lost only twenty-three men on 9/11, compared to the FDNY's 343. The cops got the word to get out; the firefighters didn't.

It was time for Juan to brief McFeeley. With the door to his office closed, McFeeley listened as Juan laid out the entire story.

"Even if what you are saying is true, how are you going to prove it?" McFeeley asked. "You've got no hard evidence. No memo. No report. No high-ranking official on the record supporting this. It's still a theory. We'll never get this past Baldwin. City Hall will have a cow if we run a story that says, essentially, the 343 firefighters might have lived if their radios worked."

Juan knew McFeeley was right.

"I'm not saying we have enough for a story yet, but it's there," Juan said. "The story is there."

"So go get it," McFeeley barked. "Get somebody on the record. Get a document. Get something. Look, Baldwin is already asking me what you are up to. He's starting to get suspicious. I can't stall him forever. You better hurry it up."

Juan went back to his desk in a corner of the newsroom. He considered his options. He could wait for Mary to get a copy of the report or email, but that could take days or weeks, if it happened at all. He could try and get a ranking FDNY official to go on the record, but that would be career suicide, and no one was in much of a mood to say anything negative about the FDNY, not even the usual union critics, not in this atmosphere, when the funerals were still playing out. He could try and bluff it out of Mike McLaughlin at the FDNY's public information office.

As deputy FDNY commissioner for public information, McLaughlin knew everything going on inside the FDNY. He was a trusted source. He ran a small but critical unit, tracking every media call and every FDNY job, including Emergency Medical Services (EMS) runs that might warrant media attention. His office did this twenty-four hours a day, seven days a week, from a small command center on the third floor of FDNY headquarters in Brooklyn. McLaughlin had done ten years in the firehouse. He studied English at St. Francis College in Brooklyn and had written for one of the weekly Brooklyn newspapers before joining the FDNY. His uncle—an FDNY battalion chief—was his hook inside the department. He helped him get a start at the FDNY press office. Now, he was running the place. The post put him in the upper management ranks of the FDNY. He dealt with the commissioner every day, sometimes three or four times in one day, and enjoyed unfiltered access. Any FDNY commissioner worth his turnout coat knew the importance of staying on top of what the press was asking about, what stories they were covering. If for no other reason, the commissioner might need to give the mayor a heads up about a negative FDNY story about to be published.

McLaughlin was regarded as one of the best press guys in the city. The press corps respected him and, for the most part, genuinely liked him. He had a way of getting inside reporters' heads. He took the time to get to know them. He went drinking with them. He hung out at Elaine's, the Upper East Side watering hole favored by boldfaced names in the entertainment, political, and media arenas. He knew who in the press corps was going through a rough time at home; who had young kids; who had a drinking problem; who liked to bet half their paychecks on the ponies; who felt they were underpaid and bucking for a promotion; who liked soft, feature stories; and who liked to do only hard-hitting ones. Above all, McLaughlin knew the importance of "feeding the beast"—the media beast. Every day was an opportunity. Some days the beast would get you, and some days the beast might help you. Nothing personal. Just business. Since he became such a good source to so many key reporters around town, McLaughlin also knew his value, although he rarely overplayed his hand. On occasion, if he felt a reporter was being unfair or hitting his boss or the department too hard, he would impose his own brand of punishment. He would simply tell the errant reporter that he was "going to 'yups' and 'nopes.'" That meant that no matter what the reporter asked, he would only get a "yes" or "no" answer (at most) from the entire FDNY press office and FDNY brass. Reporters found this tactic amusing but also dreaded it. They rarely could afford to be on the "'yups' and 'nopes' list" for long—frozen out of the juiciest department and City Hall gossip and not receiving any tips on potential stories. Luckily, McLaughlin was not the vindictive type and rarely held a grudge for more than a day or two.

The 9/11 attack was unlike anything the department— and the FDNY press office—had ever experienced. With so many chiefs and firefighters lost, the entire command structure was under incredible stress. The media had gone crazy, flooding Mike's unit with a volume of calls that it could not keep up with. McLaughlin decided early on to service the "beat reporters" for the papers first—the reporters who covered the FDNY on a regular basis—and then the regulars from the main TV stations. Everyone else would just have to wait.

Juan dialed McLaughlin's private Blackberry mobile number, known to only a few, select reporters.

He'd run the bluff to see if McLaughlin would confirm that the repeater was not working on the morning of 9/11, rendering most FDNY radios useless in the upper floors of the WTC. This was within the bounds of accepted journalistic practice. Juan had at least one source who had heard something about repeaters. And he had another—the professor—explaining how big a deal it would be if it wasn't working on the morning of 9/11. It was worth a try.

"Hey, I need to ask you something on the record, and I need an official response. Okay?"

"Do my best," said McLaughlin, knowing this couldn't be good.

"I'm hearing there were radio problems on the morning of 9/11 inside the Towers," Juan said in his most confident tone. "I'm hearing that a device called a 'repeater' that was meant to boost the signal inside the Towers wasn't working. Can you confirm this?"

"I need to get back to you," McLaughlin said, trying to stall for time. "What's your deadline on this? Do you have it good enough to go with?"

"I've got a source," Juan said, avoiding McLaughlin's question. "Why do you have to get back to me? Don't you know if there was a repeater at the WTC and if it was working? Isn't that something you would know by now?" Juan knew he was pressing pretty hard, but given the gravity of the story, he had no choice.

"I know there was a repeater at the WTC. I can confirm that," McLaughlin said. "After the '93 bombing, they installed one at 5 World Trade Center. That's where the repeater antenna was located. I don't know if it was working or not. Maybe it was damaged in the attack. I have to check.

"Juan, can we talk off the record for a second?" McLaughlin asked.

"Sure," Juan replied.

"Are you sure you want to go in this direction?" McLaughlin asked. "Say it's true. Say the repeater wasn't working. I think I know where you are going with this. If the repeater malfunctioned, it stands to reason that the guys' radios weren't working properly and that maybe they didn't hear any order to evacuate. But there is another possibility you don't seem to be considering. The repeater is controlled by a switch at the fire command console in the lobby of the WTC. Somebody has to remember to turn it on. Off the record, we are not sure that happened.

"Think about the consequences of your reporting, please. Right now, everyone's a hero. The families of guys who died believe their loved ones died as part of a rescue operation. They responded on the morning of 9/11, and they did their jobs. They helped as many people as possible escape. Isn't that the better memory for everyone to have? Why are you messing with that?"

"Their families deserve to know what really happened, Mike. You know that," Juan said. "The city deserves to know what happened."

"Just think about it is all I'm saying," McLaughlin repeated. "I know you got a job to do, but just think about the implications of what you're doing."

"I am, Mike. I am. Can you get me an answer or not?"

"I'll get back to you."

The bluff had worked, at least part of the way. Juan now had confirmation that there was a repeater at the WTC. He now knew the location—5 World Trade Center. But he still lacked the critical piece of information—was it working on the morning of 9/11?

McLaughlin, off the record, had raised a tantalizing and very newsworthy possibility: In the confusion and mayhem of the moment, someone in the chain of command in the lobby of the North Tower might have missed a critical step, checking if the repeater was turned on, thereby jeopardizing communications with hundreds of men who were already in the smoke-filled Tower.

Juan needed to get back in touch with Mary and brief her on what he had learned. He needed to push her to see what else she could find.

He reached her on her cell.

"Hey, can you talk?"

"Let me walk outside and call you back in five minutes."

Ten minutes went by before Juan's phone rang.

"What did you do?" Mary asked. "McLaughlin came over to talk to Peter. He looked pretty agitated. I heard him say that you had called and that you were on to something before they closed the door to Peter's office."

"It's about the repeater. It's about what you heard the other day. There was a repeater at the WTC, and it was designed to boost the signal of the handheld radios. But it looks like maybe it wasn't working on 9/11. The repeater system has to be turned on in the lobby. It's possible no one thought to flip the switch in the confusion of the moment."

Mary went silent on the line.

"You mean Bill never got the word to get out? Is that possible? How could they screw up the communications on such a big fire? This is hard to believe. And now City Hall wants to cover it all up? I can't get my head around this."

"I know it's a lot to take in. But, yes, that's what we are talking about. That's what I need you to help me confirm."

"I called McLaughlin about it directly and asked him to comment. I imagine he's checking with City Hall before he gets back to me. Keep your eyes out for that memo and let me know if you hear anything else, okay?"

"I'm working on it. They seem pretty worried about something over here. You must be getting close."

"Yeah, but I don't have enough to go with, although I didn't tell them that. I still need that memo, something more to confirm it." Juan's phone clicked, signaling another incoming call. "I have to go; this is McLaughlin trying to get me."

"Juan," said McLaughlin in his most official tone. "I can't comment on your question about the repeater. It's all part of the ongoing FDNY review, part of the after-action report. You'll just have to wait until that's complete."

"And when will that be?" Juan asked. "Two years from now?"

"There's a lot to look at, as you can imagine," McLaughlin said. "That's all I can tell you."

"So, you are stonewalling? That's your official answer?" Juan asked, his voice rising in frustration. "Do you really think you're going to get away with this?"

Juan knew the FDNY could get away with it. Their investigation would drag on, and they could hide behind it for a very long time. The public would move on and forget, as would most of the media. Unless he broke the story.

"Let me ask you one more thing," Juan said, now going for broke. "Can you confirm that the responding units turned the repeater on?"

"I'm not going to comment. You have my answer, Juan," replied McLaughlin before hanging up.

Juan was back to square one, more or less. He still had no confirmation that the repeater was the issue that caused the FDNY radios to malfunction on the morning of the attack.

He was depending on Mary to unearth some evidence that would allow him to move forward with the story. The story was really riding on her.

At the same time, he knew the pressure was mounting inside his newsroom to shut him down. He didn't know how much longer McFeeley could fend off Baldwin and Schwartz, who were feeling the heat from City Hall.

It was a chess match, and right now, he was at a stalemate.

CHAPTER NINETEEN

Back in the Bronx, Sarah had turned her kitchen table into her own command center. Each morning, she flipped through her well-worn address book, crammed with phone numbers and notations for the hundreds of elected officials, staffers, and community and civic leaders she had befriended over the years as a local community board leader. She worked her way down a list of those she thought might be helpful in her campaign.

Her pitch was simple and straightforward.

"I'm having a meeting, and I would like you to come," she would say, over and over. "We need to get the attention of City Hall and of the FDNY to get to the bottom of what happened. Only if we speak as one will we be able to get anything done."

Her first call that morning was to Juan. She dispensed with any pleasantries and got right to her ask.

"I want you to come speak to my group. I want you to update them on what you have found."

"That's not something I normally do, Sarah. I'm an investigative reporter, remember? When I find out something that is newsworthy, I put it into the newspaper, not report it at a community meeting."

"I know, but I'm not asking you to break any news. I just want my group to hear from you directly. Fill them in. Share with them your insights based on what you have already found and reported. You will make some new friends, some new sources. It is not going to hurt your reporting."

"I guess I could do that. I do need help. I've sort of hit a dead end."

"Okay, then. I will send you the time and the place. And thank you. This group really appreciates what you are trying to do. More than anyone, we want you to get to the bottom of what happened."

Now, Sarah had some new energy and a meeting to organize. She worked her list of widows and other family members of 9/11 FDNY victims she had compiled from friends at the FDNY and newspaper accounts. Many of the names of the 343 firefighters who were missing and now presumed dead had been released. A contact at the Uniformed Firefighters Association, the union representing frontline FDNY firefighters, had been helpful in providing her with phone numbers for some of the families.

Throughout the rest of the city, post-9/11 life was mostly back to normal, even though it was just three months since the attack. The subways, LIRR, and Metro North were up and running. People had returned to work, as they had been urged to do by Mayor Giuliani. In Midtown, the streets were crowded with the crush of daily commuters and even some tourists. Most businesses and schools were reopened. The lights on Broadway were back on. The New York Stock

Exchange, closed for six days, began trading activities again on September 17 and never looked back. Major League Baseball, having suspended games for six days, resumed play in New York City with the first post-9/11 contest at Shea Stadium on September 21 as the Mets took on the Atlanta Braves.

Walking along Fifth Avenue, near St. Patrick's Cathedral, it looked like any other busy, Christmas-shopping season in NYC. It was easy to forget that the site of the worst attack on American soil—just three-and-a-half miles south—remained an active crime scene with workers carefully removing the rubble, shipping it to Fresh Kills Landfill on Staten Island to search for human remains.

Sarah was not celebrating Christmas this year. No tree would go up in her home. Instead, she worked. She contacted the widows of the men from Peter's Brooklyn firehouse first, specifically the wives of the men who had perished along with Peter on 9/11.

She set the meeting for a Thursday night in the St. Agnes Parish Hall in Rockville Centre, the seat of the Catholic church on Long Island, where many of the lost firefighters lived with their families in either Nassau or Suffolk County.

A friend of Sarah's from Rockville Centre helped her arrange for the space through her church contacts. Once the church officials heard that Sarah was organizing a meeting of the 9/11 families, they offered meeting space for as long as the group wanted. A local bakery heard about the gathering and offered to supply free coffee and Danish. The Rockville Centre volunteer fire department leadership said they would be on hand to set up chairs and tables and to greet the family members and offer any assistance they could.

As word of the meeting spread, Sarah's phone rang constantly. Some local media asked if the meeting was open to the press. Sarah politely told the reporters it was a private meeting but that—at some point in the future—the group would welcome coverage.

Within a few days, more than fifty family members of 9/11 first responders had signed up to attend, almost all of them the wives of lost FDNY firefighters. Many of these family members had not yet buried their dead. They were still waiting for the recovery effort to unearth remains of their firefighter husbands, brothers, and sons.

More than a dozen widows were present on the night of the meeting. Several of them had brought photos of their lost FDNY members with them.

Sarah greeted each of them as they walked in and found their way to a group of metal folding chairs in the center of the large room, which doubled as a gathering place for parish events, parties, bake sales, and the like. She was sure to have a friend collect their email addresses at sign-in, making future communication easier.

Juan stood nearby, sipping a cup of black coffee, eyeing the crowd as they filtered in. He wondered if this was a waste of time and if the group would be hostile. Sarah had asked Professor Costello to attend as well and present his insights. Juan felt a kindship to Sarah and the professor. He respected what they were trying to do, but he needed to stay neutral and to not be seen as being in any way part of their group of advocates.

Sarah opened the meeting with a brief welcome, stating her objective clearly.

"My son was a probie, and he died on 9/11. They call him a hero, but I don't know if that's true," she told the other mothers and wives. "I want answers. I want to know what really happened to him. He was in the North Tower, and I'm not sure if he ever got the word to get out, even after the South Tower fell. The guys at his firehouse said it was chaos at the Trade Center. They couldn't hear each other on the radios.

"I've asked Juan Gomez here tonight from the *News*. He's been reporting on the radio issue, and I think he can provide us with some insight." She turned the floor over to Juan.

Juan kept his remarks brief. He avoided speculation but did tell the group that he was working on a story about the possible radio malfunctions. He was still doing research and couldn't say anything definitive yet, but, he told the crowd, it was possible the repeater system designed to boost the radio signal inside the Twin Towers did not work on the morning of 9/11. That was his working theory.

"I can tell you there are more questions right now than answers," Juan said. "Three hundred forty-three firefighters are not supposed to die. That much we know. There was a lot of chaos at the scene that morning. I am trying to verify what went on inside the buildings among the first responders. And I need your help. The city doesn't want it all to come out. They think you can't handle the truth."

It didn't take long for a flood of emotions to pour forth.

"We need some answers," said Cathy O'Rourke, whose husband, Pete, had been a battalion chief in Queens. "If what you are saying is true, that means my Pete never got the word to get out? I have to believe he would have tried to save himself and his men if he knew the building was about to come down. City Hall owes us the truth. The FDNY owes us the truth."

"I want to know what really happened down there," said another widow. "They are calling them heroes. But they are dead. We don't really know what went down inside those buildings. And it sounds from what you are saying like City Hall just wants to sweep it under the rug."

A third widow stood up. She was from Ronkonkoma. Her husband's remains had not yet been found.

"I heard the mayor and the real estate guys are already talking about rebuilding down at Ground Zero. This is sacred ground, and all City Hall seems to care about is how fast we can clean it all up so they can start to rebuild."

Suddenly, a man in his forties with a handlebar mustache with a clean shaven, bald head, and muscular, tattooed arms stood up to speak. He looked every bit the FDNY firefighter.

He looked right at Juan. "I can tell you your theory is correct," said the man. "I was there, in the North Tower. Our radios were not working. There was too much traffic. Most of the time all we got was static."

Juan's ears perked up. "I would love to talk to you after the meeting if you are willing."

"I am here and many of my brothers are not, so yes, I am willing. It's what happened, and people should know what went down."

Sarah looked at Juan. She caught his signals to wrap up the meeting. He didn't want to lose the chance to interview this firefighter. It could be a major breakthrough.

A few of the women lingered after the meeting broke up to speak with Sarah one-on-one. A core group of about six widows, including Sarah, had deemed the meeting a hit. Meanwhile, Juan zeroed in on the firefighter who had spoken up about the radios. They huddled in a corner of the room, out of earshot of the others.

"Are you certain the radios weren't working?"

"As sure as I am standing here talking to you."

Juan was glad he had come. The firefighter not only went on the record, but he also offered to put Juan in touch with other firefighters who had survived the collapse of the WTC who could help verify the communication problems, based on firsthand experience. Members of the FDNY, like the NYPD, rarely aired their internal secrets in public. But this was different. Too many guys had died for the survivors to remain silent for long.

It was the breakthrough Juan had been hoping for.

CHAPTER TWENTY

Mary exited City Hall down the front steps and found a quiet corner of City Hall Park, a few yards away, to make her call to her sister, Diane Mancini. Mary always looked up to Diane. She had a logical mind and a kind way. But friends, relatives, and colleagues knew not to cross her. She could cut you down in a phrase or two. She was loyal to her friends, but you didn't want to be on the other side of an argument with her.

Since 9/11, the two sisters talked at least once a day. Diane wanted Mary to move in with her family for a while after it became clear Bill wasn't coming home, but Mary decided to stick to her routine and stay in Floral Park.

Before she went all-in with Juan and risked everything she had worked for at City Hall, she wanted to run it by Diane.

Diane picked up Mary's call on the first ring.

"Hey, sis. How are you feeling today?"

"Good. But a little confused," Mary replied.

"What does that mean?" Diane asked. The two knew each other so well, they could sense what the other was thinking, picking up signals in a word or two.

"Where were you last night? I tried to call you at home and got no answer," Diane said, her lawyerly suspicion and sisterly instincts on the rise now.

"I was out. That's why I am calling you. I stumbled onto something at City Hall, something that shows Bill and the other guys maybe didn't have to die on 9/11, something that will look pretty bad for City Hall and the FDNY."

"What do you mean?" Diane asked, sounding worried about what her sister was getting into.

"I've been talking to a reporter at the *News*. He's poking around on the FDNY and 9/11. He thinks the reason Bill and the other guys were killed is because they didn't get the word to evacuate the Towers. He says the radios weren't working properly. I think he's right."

Now Diane's antenna had gone way up. She worried her sister was being taken advantage of at her most vulnerable time.

"Let me get this straight. This reporter is investigating the city's response on 9/11, looking at how the FDNY handled it, and you are talking to him without the mayor's okay. Are you crazy? Do you want to lose your job?"

Mary suspected this would be her sister's reaction. Nevertheless, she felt she needed to hear it, even though she already pretty much knew what she intended to do.

"If the people you work with at City Hall find out about this, you are not only out of a job—they will go after you. And you need them to be with you now that Bill is gone. You want to hang on to that house in Floral Park, right? You need your job. And, if they find out you are talking to the *News*, they will not only fire you but also blackball you all around town. You won't be able to find work after they kick you out of City Hall. You will be radioactive. They will label you a rat, a whistleblower. No law firm will hire you. No major corporation. No company that does business with the city. No CEO will ever trust you to be their right hand."

Diane paused to let her words sink in.

"I know. I know you are right," replied Mary. "But I feel I have to do this. If I can help find out what really happened down there, it will be worth it. Bill would want that," Mary replied.

Diane cut her off. "Bill would want you to stay safe and take care of yourself. Do you know how this is going to look? What if your friends found out, your neighbors and all the people who came to the funeral? This is not good. You have to cut it off, right now. It sounds like he is preying on you. He knows you're vulnerable right now. He's using you, Mary. Wake up! Reporters like him will do anything to get a story. He wants a big headline and a big story with his byline on it. He'll get a raise and a pat on the back from his editor, and you'll get fired. You know that. You are just a way into City Hall for him. You should know better. You have been around."

Now Mary was eager to get off the phone. She loved her sister, and she knew she was right on one level, but on another level, Mary was determined to help Juan get to the bottom of the story.

"This reporter isn't like that. He really just wants to get to the truth. He thinks the families deserve to know what really happened, and I agree with him. Bill would want the truth to come out, especially if Bill and his men never got the word to evacuate. Bill wouldn't give a damn what City Hall wanted. He would do the right thing, and now I have to do it for him.

"Sis, I have to get back to work. Love you. Thanks for the advice. I will be okay. I'll let you know what happens."

"Just be careful," Diane said, getting in one last warning. "And don't let this Juan character ruin your life just so he can get a front-page story. It's not worth it."

CHAPTER TWENTY-ONE

DECEMBER 16, 2001

City Hall wasn't the only powerful entity worried about Juan's inquiries.

High above the grid of Manhattan's streetscape, in a thirty-fifth-floor conference room at 270 Park Avenue, overlooking dozens of other black, glass-and-steel skyscrapers of Midtown East, the city's new employment center for the powerful finance, insurance, and real estate (FIRE) sectors, a small circle of the city's highest-paid legal talent from Lipton & Stillwell had assembled. They were there to counsel one of the firm's biggest clients on an escalating crisis.

The Fire Response Radio Corp. (FRRC) had grown from a small, Midwestern radio supplier founded in the 1930s to one of the federal government's key contractors during World War II to one of the country's most successful, privately held telecommunications firms. As America prospered following WWII, so did FRRC. The firm had expanded from radios to TV components to sophisticated radar systems and, during the last decade, had ventured into cellular and fiber-optic technology. FRRC retained its close ties to state, federal, and local governments. More than a third of its operating revenue came from contracts with local agencies like the FDNY that still depended on radios utilizing old-fashioned, two-way radio frequencies as their primary mode for communications in the field.

The last time the FDNY had put its $40 million radio contract out on the street via a Request for Proposals (RFP), entertaining bids from other firms in search of better technology that would work in high-rise buildings like the World Trade Center Towers, FRRC had beaten back all competitors. The firm hired the best legal talent and retained the most expensive City Hall lobbyists. FRRC also employed two of the FDNY's highest-ranking retired officers, including one who had helped write the specs for the radio contract while he was still on the job. And, during the campaign season, FRRC had maxed out on campaign contributions to every elected official who had anything at all to do with awarding or overseeing the new contract—from the mayor to the city council speaker to the chair of the Council Committee on Public Safety.

Peter Wedley III, the firm's third-generation owner, was not a man to leave anything to chance, not when a $40 million piece of business was at stake. Wedley was as driven a man as his father had been, and he had pushed the expansion of FRRC to new heights, riding the wave of demand for cellular wizardry while retaining strong links to customers still dependent upon handheld, point-to-point radios like the ones used by first responder agencies across the country.

Unbeknownst to the high-priced lawyers assembled this morning in the conference room overlooking Park Avenue, Wedley also kept a "black ops" budget on the side to help in retaining or winning multimillion-dollar radio contracts like the one up for grabs at the FDNY. As a privately held firm, FRRC was able to secret away millions into virtually untraceable offshore accounts that were controlled by Wedley and a small circle of his long-time FRRC confidants. These accounts did not appear anywhere on the company's books. And Wedley was careful not to discuss their existence or purpose, even with his attorneys. He was old school that way. While he presided over a billion-dollar empire built on making communications easier for his customers, he eschewed using any of this technology for his own, most important communications. He never used email, which he knew lived forever on someone else's server and was easily obtained by law enforcement authorities. He also avoided discussing sensitive business issues via cell phone, aware that it left a digital date and time stamp that also could be traced. And he created a series of shell companies he could funnel cash to when he needed to grease the right wheel during an RFP process like the one the FDNY had undergone just prior to the 9/11 attack to replace its two-way, handy-talkie radios that firefighters used in the field. Fire departments were often not run by the most sophisticated or business-savvy individuals. Most heads of department were trained as firefighters who had risen through the ranks, doing well on civil service tests and cultivating the right connections inside the department. Even as they rose through the ranks, some of them still operated as if they were in a local firehouse with frat-house rules when it came to personnel and procurement decisions. Some could be approached to help sway a vote on a selection committee when a contract was up for renewal. A well-timed, all-expense paid trip to a Caribbean Island or a discreet cash contribution to a child's college fund was not out of the question.

But none of this was on the agenda for this morning's meeting with the Lipton & Stillwell lawyers.

"There's going to be a focus on the radio communications inside the Towers sooner or later," Wedley advised the attorneys. "I want us to be ready for the onslaught. We advised the FDNY that our radios, as currently configured, might not work in a situation like the one we saw unfold on 9/11. We were very clear. We offered them additional software and hardware specifically designed for high-rise fires, but they did not request it in their final response back to us after we won the RFP. I want you to dig out all the correspondence on this topic and have it ready for when the subpoenas start to fly."

Stillwell's team took notes. Arthur Lipton, the named partner, who billed at a rate of $1,200 an hour, had represented the FRRC firm going back thirty years to a time when Peter's father had run the show. He knew many of the firm's darkest secrets. And he suspected that the firm sometimes operated "off the books" in its attempt to gain and retain business. He normally wasn't about to go poking around where his advice was not sought or ask questions that might produce troubling answers. But, on this occasion, he felt obligated to pull Peter aside after the meeting broke up for some one-on-one, off-the-record counseling.

"Peter, you know how hot this one will get. The national spotlight burns brightly. Congress will get involved. There will be official inquiries. Nothing can shut it down once it gets going. As your friend and attorney, I hope FRRC has proceeded with the utmost caution in its past dealings with the FDNY on this issue. If there is something you think I should know, now is the time to invoke the attorney-client privilege. What you tell me stays with me. I can only try and protect you and the firm if I know what the other side might find once they go digging."

Peter nodded politely.

"Don't worry, Arthur. I appreciate the concern. But we've got nothing to worry about on this. The city screwed it up all on their own. They could have opted for the better technology, but they decided to save a few bucks, and they got what they paid for. You can lead a horse to water, but you can't make them drink. I wish for the sake of the 343 dead firefighters that they had listened to us, but we have a clear conscience on this."

The meeting with the lawyers was over. But Peter Wedley knew that now his real work for the day would begin. He took the express elevator to the lobby, where a driver was waiting. Peter handed the driver an address in Queens, far off the path of high-priced Park Avenue lawyers and consultants. The driver knew the address. He took the Midtown Tunnel, heading east to the Long Island Expressway, exiting at the Queens Blvd. ramp, heading south.

Peter's driver took a right turn onto the Queens Blvd. service road and headed south for less than half a mile, making another right on to 63rd Drive, heading west, past a small row of local stores to just before the Long Island Rail Road (LIRR) overpass, where he pulled off onto a dirt patch that LIRR workers use to access the right of way. Across the street, in a nondescript, one-story red-brick building facing the tracks, an auto body shop shared space with SPD Inc., a one-man private security firm with no internet address or website, no listed phone number, and no known mailing address.

Peter pushed the small doorbell outside SPD's grey, steel door. He looked up into the lens of the security camera and was quickly buzzed in. Inside, he was greeted by SPD's owner, former NYPD detective (first grade) Michael Kazimir, a twenty-year veteran who was one of the first Russian-born members of the NYPD to make the rank of first grade detective. In the '80s and the '90s, his Russian came in handy on the job. The FBI and even the CIA from time to time had asked him to be assigned to special task forces that were tracking Russian mobsters who—like other ethnic mobsters before them—needed ways of washing the cash they earned from drug, gambling, and extortion rings by investing in legitimate businesses.

After he retired in 2000, Kazimir set up shop in Rego Park, home to thousands of Jews, some of whom had fled Nazi-occupied Europe during WWII. Some of Kazimir's colleagues on the job had their doubts about him, unsure whether he was really working for the NYPD or also funneling back information about investigations to the Russian mob he was sworn to take down. Now, in his mid-fifties and just getting by on his NYPD service pension, Kazimir found himself sometimes taking work from those at least affiliated with known mobsters he once chased, fueling speculation among his former colleagues about his true loyalties. Kazimir himself had qualms about some of the work he took on. But he didn't ask too many questions of his clients, especially if they were willing to pay him in cash. As for the whispers among his former colleagues on the NYPD, none of it bothered Kazimir. He would do what he needed to do to make a living. No one from the NYPD was offering to pay his kid's college tuition. His NYPD pension barely paid the rent.

"What brings you out to the great borough of Queens?" Kazimir asked Mr. Wedley. Kazimir had been most useful to the FRRC firm when the NYPD radio contract had come up five years earlier, and Kazimir—still on the job—had pulled in a few favors to get himself on the internal NYPD selection committee that handled the task of screening the vendors who wanted the contract. Kazimir had made sure FRRC stayed in the bidding for the NYPD contract. And Wedley had shown his appreciation back then, secretly funneling a series of small jobs from his vendors to Kazimir's start-up security business. Offshore accounts in Kazimir's name also were established to seal the deal.

Kazimir's wood-paneled office was unassuming, except for the numerous plaques and framed photographs covering the walls behind his desk and on either side. A number of them bore replicas of his distinctive NYPD gold shield and chronicled his years with various NYPD special units like the NYPD-FBI Joint Terrorism Task Force and the NYPD Intelligence Division.

Wedley got right to the point.

"I need some surveillance work done," Wedley said, placing a thick, white envelope squarely on Kazimir's desk. Inside was $50,000 in cash—small bills. "There's a reporter for the *News of New York*, Juan Gomez, who is sniffing around a story about the FDNY radios inside the Trade Towers not working. He seems to be getting some info from a Pelham Bay community activist, Sarah Murphy. She lost her son, a probie, and she won't stop until she gets answers. I need you to follow him. Find out who else Gomez is talking to, who are his sources."

Kazimir looked inside the envelope but then put it back on the desk and pushed it back a little toward Wedley.

"I don't follow journalists. You know that's awfully risky," Kazimir told Wedley. "You are asking for trouble, especially in this atmosphere. Anything to do with 9/11 is front-page stuff."

"I know," replied Wedley. "That's why I need you for the job. No footprints. That's just the down payment. There will be double that when the job is done."

It was a tempting offer. Most of Kazimir's clients paid late, and he had to chase after his money. The $50K up-front Wedley was offering could help make a serious dent in the college fund for his two teenage daughters. Still, Kazimir hesitated. If he got caught tailing a journalist, it would likely be front-page news, and his reputation and business would take a beating.

"For something like this, I'd need $200K up-front, plus expenses. This isn't going to be easy, and we can't get made. If we get made, I could be out of business. There's a lot of risk involved."

"Okay. Deal," said Wedley, pulling out a second cash-stuffed envelope and dumping it on the desk. He had come prepared for this type of negotiation. Two hundred thousand dollars was a small investment in an effort to shut down this story, which threatened to derail any future hope FRRC might have of renewing business with local governments and winning new contracts with the city. If it came out that FRRC was somehow responsible for the deaths of 343 FDNY firefighters on 9/11 because their FRRC radios had failed—even if it wasn't true—that would be a disaster from which the company might never recover.

"I'll let you know what I find," said Kazimir, taking the envelopes and dropping them into the bottom drawer of his desk. "No emails on this. I'll call you. Use this phone." Kazimir handed Wedley a "burner" phone, a disposable cell phone with a prepaid number of minutes that was virtually untraceable. Drug dealers used them for that reason, but they came in handy for this type of business as well. This way, there would be no record of contact between Wedley and Kazimir.

Kazimir didn't need to brief Wedley on the types of technology he would have to employ to tap the cell phones and landlines of the *News* reporter. The less Wedley knew about this, the better. But Kazimir was already going through in his head what he would need to do. He would place some physical surveillance at Juan's home and office, but the more critical information was likely to come via his cell phone conversations and email traffic. He would have to subcontract this work to a group of Russian hackers he knew and trusted. They worked efficiently and in the shadows from a location in nearby Kew Gardens.

Wedley headed back into the city, happy to leave Queens behind, but confident that he would now have a leg up on what this reporter was finding. How he would counter the story was another matter, but—as in any conflict—good intelligence was the key first step to a winning strategy.

CHAPTER TWENTY-TWO

Sarah was eager to reconnect with Juan following the meeting she had organized in Rockville Centre. They didn't get a chance to say goodbye at the end. Juan walked out with the firefighter who had offered to help Juan. Sarah wanted to know how it went.

Juan answered on the first ring.

"How's it going?" Sarah asked. "Did that firefighter help you? I had never seen him before, but I heard from one of my friends that he worked in Brooklyn. I think he was at the sister house to where my Peter worked."

"He was very helpful. He was in the North Tower. Not only did he confirm that none of the radios worked in his company, but the other guys he knew who survived complained of the same thing. He has already put me in touch with three other guys who confirmed it. And now they are putting me in touch with other men who also were there. Thank you for getting me to that meeting. Honestly, I wasn't sure about going, but you were right. It was a big help. I still need more evidence that the FDNY knew about the problem, even before 9/11. But I'm working on that. It will come. And now I have some evidence, some on-the-record interviews with firsthand witnesses to confirm the radio problem. It's a major breakthrough."

"I'm glad to hear it," said Sarah. "The families and the surviving firefighters are starting to realize that we have to press this case ourselves. The FDNY and City Hall are not going to help."

"So, what's your game plan?" Juan asked.

"We are getting stronger by the day," Sarah said. "More widows and families are signing on with us. The elected officials are not going to be able to ignore us forever. They are going to have to deal with us. I'm going to keep pressing our case. We want a full and fair investigation. And if we can't get it from the city or state, we will press Washington. The professor wants the city council to hold hearings on the radio and building code. You know the port authority was exempt from the current NYC code. They didn't have to adhere to the standards other developers had to follow when it comes to building skyscrapers. If they did, it's likely the buildings could have withstood the impact of the planes. And the people in the Twin Towers would have had more ways of getting out.

"We have plenty of avenues to go down, and we are not going away."

"Okay. Well, keep me in the loop. I'm pressing on with the radio angle. Hopefully, I can get a story in the paper soon."

"Okay. We'll stay in touch."

Sarah hung up, excited that Juan seemed to be making good progress on the radio story. She turned to her husband to relay the news.

"Tom, did you hear that? Juan got some firefighters to go on the record about how their radios didn't work in the North Tower. He says he is getting close to publishing a story in the newspaper."

Tom did not look up from the kitchen table, where he was reading the *New York Post*. "Good, then maybe you can get off this crusade. Let Juan do his job. Let City Hall do their job and leave the FDNY alone. It's enough already. It's all you talk about, day and night. I really can't take it anymore."

Sarah went over and grabbed the *Post* out of his hands and threw it on the kitchen floor.

"I don't know why you even read this rag. It's just a mouthpiece for Giuliani. And why are you always telling me to give up? I'm not giving up. Not until the truth comes out and we know for sure what happened to Peter. You should be helping instead of sitting around complaining about what I am doing."

Tom went silent. He picked the *Post* up off the floor, flipped it over to the sports section, and kept reading.

Sarah moved into the other room. She reviewed her scrapbook where she kept all of Peter's childhood photos, awards, school certificates, US Marines medals, and his FDNY probie photo. It soothed her to go through the book, which she did often.

She hoped Tom would come around one day to her way of thinking, but she wasn't letting him dissuade her. She was doing this for Peter, and nothing was going to stop her.

CHAPTER TWENTY-THREE

Kazimir had his assignment, and he wasted no time putting his plan in place. If it went as it should, Juan wouldn't ever know his every move was being tracked.

He paid a visit to his Russian hacker friends in Kew Gardens, just up the road north on Queens Boulevard.

The three hackers were gathered in a small, dark, nondescript conference space filled with tech equipment and double-screened monitors at every workstation. Wires ran everywhere. On the wall were a series of fifty-five-inch flatscreens on which they could mirror any important tracking information any of the hackers wanted to share with the group.

"I need full surveillance on Juan Gomez. He's our target. Lives in Brooklyn and works on the West Side. He's a reporter for the *News*, so be extra careful. We can't get made. But we need a dump on his cell for the last six months and to tape every incoming and outgoing call he makes.

"And I need his landline at work too."

The Russians didn't even look up. Within minutes, they had an exterior shot of Juan's home up on the flatscreens, photos of his three kids, the *News* building where he worked, his cell phone number, and his landline number at the *News*.

"Can we get into his computer at work?" Kazimir asked.

"It won't be easy," one of the hackers answered. "They have a pretty good firewall in place. His home computer might be quicker to access. We'll let you know."

Juan had laid a digital trail for the hackers. He kept a published home phone number, and his cell phone number was on every email he sent. He wanted to make it easy for potential sources to reach him, so he was pretty transparent about where he lived and how to reach him. His approach meant it was also easy for the Russians to find him.

Within a half an hour, the hackers had accessed Juan's home computer and cell phone. With his online credit card and bank accounts, they had a full profile of Juan's habits, including the bars and restaurants he frequented, the property he owned, his typical routes to his office and home, and a list of his most frequently called numbers.

"I need to know who he is talking to most often, especially since 9/11," Kazimir instructed. "Break out any repeat phone numbers."

Again, it wasn't hard for the hackers.

Sarah Murphy's phone popped up and so did a phone number downtown. Juan had called the number at least twice a week since 9/11 and sometimes more often. Usually, the calls were after five in the afternoon or before eight o'clock in the morning.

"Zero in on that number. Where is it located?"

The hackers did a reverse directory search that allowed them to put an exact location to the phone number.

"It's at City Hall," a hacker said. "Looks like it's inside the mayor's office."

The early morning and late-night calls were a tip-off.

"He's talking to someone there who doesn't want others to know they are talking to a reporter. He's calling before most people get in to work or after they leave."

The hackers now cross-referenced the number with a list of city officials from the Green Book, the city of New York's official directory, which lists every agency and major official inside the 200,000-person city government, including the office of the mayor and every deputy mayor. The number traced back to the office of the first deputy mayor. The hackers couldn't be certain who within the first deputy mayor's office might be picking up that extension, but they knew that it was someone very close to Giuliani who was having regular contact with Juan.

"Okay. This is good intel. We need boots on the ground now too. I need a team on him 24/7, at work and at home. If he meets anyone outside the office, we need photo surveillance. We need to find out who inside City Hall he's talking to."

Kazimir activated a second team for the surveillance, also all Russians he knew from the mother country. They were experienced and effective. Again, he warned them of the sensitive nature of this new assignment.

"This guy is a journalist. We can't get made. Take extra men if you have to, but do not make him suspicious. I need eyes on him around the clock."

This would be an expensive undertaking, but Wedley was paying top dollar. The budget was virtually unlimited.

"And don't engage with him. We're just trying to find out who he is talking to. That's all. That's our assignment."

CHAPTER TWENTY-FOUR

DECEMBER 17, 2001

Ever since her early days working as a young staffer on the advance team for Ed Koch at City Hall, Mary Sullivan had learned to keep a certain office routine that helped her boss stay on schedule and her in his good graces.

She arrived early, typically by 7:00 a.m., before the rest of the staff or her boss. She opened the office up, gathered the morning newspapers, made a copy of the mayor's private schedule for the day, and checked critical emails coming in and made copies of the most important ones. All of this material she laid out on the mayor's desk before his arrival so he could start his day as soon as he arrived at City Hall. If there was an issue that was particularly pressing, she would call him in his car on his way downtown from Gracie Mansion. His security detail always gave her a heads-up when he had left the mansion and was en route to City Hall. That way, she could alert the rest of the staff of his imminent arrival. No one at City Hall liked surprises. Everyone appreciated being kept in the loop, even about the smallest details, when it came to the whereabouts of their boss, the mayor of the city of New York.

As part of her routine, Mary also cleared the mayor's outbox, a mahogany, two-tier tray with the upper marked "out" and the bottom one marked "in." Any document in the "out" box either had to be routed to someone else in the administration, put into the day's mail, or FedExed or filed away. The mayor trusted Mary with the most sensitive of documents. His faith in her was unquestioned. She knew instinctively what to do with most of the documents that crossed his desk, and she often anticipated his desires.

Mary, meanwhile, tried to conceal any trace of her growing curiosity about the events of 9/11 and her suspicions—fueled by Juan—that City Hall was engaged in a cover-up. She did not want to lose the mayor's trust or her job. Not yet, anyway. Not until she found out as much as she could about what really contributed to her husband's death.

On this day, Mary was scrolling through the mayor's overnight emails. Commissioners who had permission to communicate directly with the mayor knew better than to put sensitive material that was potentially subject to the Freedom of Information Law in an email. As a former federal prosecutor, Giuliani's City Hall was particularly strict about not wanting to leave any kind of a paper trail on any topic involving potential litigation or that could become a news story.

The email Mary spotted this morning had the earmarks of a CYA communication. Surprisingly, it came from Mike Maldanado, the first lieutenant fire marshal of the FDNY, a thirty-year veteran of the department. The email was unusual for a number of reasons, the first being that it was against protocol for someone of Maldanado's relatively low rank at the FDNY to write directly to the mayor. Any communication coming from someone in Maldanado's position should be routed through his superior, in this case the chief fire marshal, and then via the fire commissioner. While a high-ranking FDNY official, he did not have a direct reporting line to the mayor's office. The second flag that caught Mary's attention was that the email was marked "Urgent" and "Confidential."

Mary knew the mayor would want to see the contents of this email as soon as he arrived at City Hall. She printed out the body of the email as well as the attachment, which was a memo addressed to the mayor that Maldanado had placed into a pdf file format so that its contents could not be edited or altered by any recipient. Maldanado did not copy anyone else on the email, not even his direct boss or the fire commissioner. It seemed as if he was trying to get the mayor's attention without burning all his bridges with the FDNY. His letter contained no direct threats, but the unstated implications of his actions were explosive.

Mary read the memo quickly and with great interest. It stated:

Dear Mr. Mayor:

I write this memo after much consideration and with a heavy heart. After more than thirty years on the job, including the last ten as the city's first lieutenant fire marshal, I hereby tender my resignation effective immediately.

I can no longer serve in an administration that appears to want to cover up, rather than uncover, the reasons why 343 of my colleagues perished on 9/11. The underlying reasons are clear to me, having investigated the command and control aspects of the fire as part of my official duties post-incident. The communications between the command posts established in the lobby of the North Tower and other locations were either nonexistent or woefully inadequate throughout the incident, resulting in hundreds of firefighters entering the Twin Towers without clear assignments or a means of receiving updated commands from their supervisors or of communicating conditions they were finding on floors as they searched in attempt to rescue any occupants who had not self-evacuated. When it became clear that the men were in imminent danger, even after an evacuation order and "Mayday" signal had been issued by chiefs on the scene, many were unable to hear the order on their handy-talkie radios. The FDNY's leading structural expert on the scene knew and communicated to other commanders that given the force of the impact and intense heat generated by jet fuel, it was possible the upper floors of the buildings could collapse. Despite this warning, many of the FDNY members in the Twin Towers were not notified or did not hear the warning of this possibility. It is my official finding that many of the deaths of 343 FDNY firefighters on 9/11 were caused by a breakdown in communication, command, and control, starting at the highest levels of the FDNY. At the root of the problem was the lack of effective radio communications. Despite numerous official warnings about the difficulties of radio communications in the World Trade Center Towers following the 1993 bombing of the WTC, the city repeatedly failed to adequately address the issue. While certain upgrades in equipment at the WTC were made, the basic radios used by FDNY members on 9/11 failed them.

Problems with the FDNY's VHF radios have been well-documented. The outdated VHF radios have only six usable channels. This translates to 450 radios for every channel, guaranteeing overcrowded airways even if the signal inside the Twin Towers had worked as intended. In many cases, it did not. The radio repeater system installed by the port authority (on the roof of 5 WTC) after the 1993 bombing that was designed to boost the radio signal inside the Twin Towers to enhance FDNY radio communications failed to work properly. Whether it was due to human error (they needed to be turned on at the command post by pushing two buttons) or because of system malfunction remains under investigation. In either case, the FDNY radios and systems those radios depend upon to work, including the repeater systems, are obsolete. The FDNY radios also are not interoperable with the NYPD radios, which transmit on the superior UHF frequency. Critical information about the status of the WTC possessed by the NYPD from helicopter vantage point also was not transmitted to the FDNY command post or to FDNY members.

My attempts since 9/11 to bring to light the problems with the department's radio system have been frustrated at every turn. My intention is not to embarrass the FDNY or your administration. However, I feel that we owe it to the 343 men who died on 9/11 to have a full examination of the facts that contributed to the worst loss of life in the department's history. We cannot hope to improve our operations unless we are able to examine what happened in an unvarnished manner without any fear of reprisal. Please see attached a copy of my final, full report on the aftermath of the 9/11 fire and building collapse that led to the deaths of 343 FDNY members, thirty-seven port authority police department members, and twenty-three members of the NYPD.

It is with great regret that I leave the department at this time. However, I believe I can no longer effectively serve in my position given the constraints placed upon my investigative authority—under which I am sworn to investigate the cause of any fire resulting in the loss of life or property.

Sincerely,

Mike Maldanado
First Lieutenant Fire Marshal

Mary made two copies of the email, letter of resignation, and the final report—one for the mayor's desk and the other for Juan.

She placed the copy for the mayor on the very top of his morning briefing papers. She then went to the ladies' room a few steps from the mayor's first-floor office, carefully checked each stall, and then called Juan on his cell phone.

"I've got it. Maldanado just sent the mayor a letter of resignation, citing the radio failure and cover-up by the administration as his reason for leaving. He documented everything. It's all there, just as you said. He detailed it all. I made you a copy. Get down here as fast as you can. I'll meet you in the park."

Out of habit, Juan took notes furiously and could barely get in a question.

"They will try to keep this quiet and immediately suspect you if you leak it. Are you ready for what's next?" Juan wanted to make certain Mary knew the gravity of her decision. The Giuliani crowd played hardball when they suspected disloyalty in their ranks. It would get ugly.

"I know what I need to do. This has to come out. I owe it to Bill. I want to make sure he didn't get killed for nothing. And I owe it to the other families. City Hall can't sweep this one under the rug. They will try and make it look like Maldanado left on his own for some BS reason, like to 'spend more time with his family.' And Maldanado won't go public on his own. This is the only way. I'm ready."

Juan cared for Mary and wondered if she really knew what a shitstorm she was about to unleash, but he wasn't about to stop her. He agreed that the larger import of this story overshadowed all other concerns.

"I'm on my way," Juan said. He didn't bother to call the newsroom. McFeeley didn't get in until 10:00 a.m. or so, and he was the only one Juan could trust.

Juan thought of his next steps as he rode the E train downtown. Mary didn't know about his source relationship with Maldanado, and he would have to keep it that way for now. Once he had the letter and memo in hand, he would call Maldanado and try to get him to go on the record or at least verify on background that he had written the document and sent it directly to the mayor. He suspected Maldanado would not go on the record, wanting to preserve his reputation within the FDNY and not be viewed as a whistleblower by his colleagues. Even though he was in the right, there were many inside the FDNY who believed it was never appropriate to go public with something like this, even in the face of these extraordinary circumstances and loss of life. The NYPD was not the only uniformed service with a code of silence when it came to talking to outsiders, especially to the press.

His next move would be to seek an official response from the FDNY press office, the fire commissioner, and the mayor's office. But those calls could wait until the last moment. Juan knew that the second the mayor's people knew he had the document, they would try furiously to shut down the story, pulling out all the stops. He would have to be ready to go and wait to make those calls until right before deadline.

He normally would also seek comments from the 9/11 families, but with this kind of exclusive, the fewer who knew the better, so he would have to limit those calls as well. He would call Sarah Murphy, of course, to add her voice to the story.

The memo, along with the firsthand accounts of the firefighters he had interviewed about the radios not working, would make it an airtight story.

It would be a blockbuster, impossible for the rest of the NYC press corps to ignore. The trick would be to get it past Baldwin.

Juan met Mary at the lower end of City Hall Park. Normally, they wouldn't meet so close to City Hall as they risked being seen. But time was critical at this point.

They met near the park's central fountain, just a few dozen yards from the steps of City Hall. By prearrangement, Mary came from the east around the fountain and Juan came from the west. They met like two Cold War spies, one not acknowledging the other.

No words were spoken. Instead, they both circled around the fountain once and then headed south, down Broadway, a few feet apart, until they were out of sight of City Hall, and it was safe to talk.

Mary had thought about what her sister Diane had said. She decided to confront Juan. His reaction would tell her a lot about his true intentions.

"Juan, before we do this, I have to ask you something. I want you to be straight with me."

"Mary," Juan said. "You can ask me anything."

"Are you just using me, just to get the story?" she asked. "Before you answer, I want you to know something else that I haven't told you. Something pretty important. Something very personal."

She stopped walking and turned to face Juan.

"I'm pregnant with Bill's child. I hadn't even told him. He died on 9/11 not knowing he was going to be a father. It was too early. I was saving the news until I was sure because we had tried before and it didn't work out, so I wanted to be sure this time.

"I don't even know why I am telling you this," Mary continued, averting his glance, "but I feel like we are getting in pretty deep together on this story, so I wanted you to know. And I have to know if you are just using me to get at the mayor."

Juan didn't know exactly what to say. He had been confronted before by sources who suspected his motives. But never quite like this.

Mary seemed to be tearing up and her body was trembling. He tried to calm her. "That's wonderful news, Mary. I'm so happy for you. You will have Bill's child to remember him by.

"As for your question—yes, I am using you. But only to get to the truth, not to hurt the mayor or anyone else. And, frankly, you will be using me, too—to get this information out to the public because you know how important it is.

"What matters to me is the story. That's the only thing that matters to me. That and protecting my sources."

Mary seemed to accept Juan's words. She passed a copy of the Maldanado letter to Juan in a plain manila envelope.

"Okay. I just wanted you to know that it's not just me on the line anymore. Soon, I will be a mom. I have to look out now for the two of us. But I think this is what Bill would have wanted. He would have wanted the story out there."

Juan did not open the envelope. Instead, he held it by his side.

"Mary, I have to be straight with you. After this comes out, you won't be able to go back to City Hall. You know that. And the Giuliani folks will treat you like a traitor. You will lose your job and any references you might need from them to find another. You have to be ready for that. Like you said, you will be a mom soon. How are you going to survive?"

"I know. And I will be okay. Between the 9/11 fund, Bill's life insurance, and his pension, we will be okay. Money won't be an issue. I do need to work, though. But I will figure something out. I appreciate you being honest. But I know the risks. And I am ready to make this move—for Bill and for all the FDNY families.

"You've got what you need, run with it."

CHAPTER TWENTY-FIVE

J uan and Mary took separate routes toward City Hall.
Juan walked on Broadway and then up Park Row
toward the old Surrogate's Court, just north of City
Hall on Chambers Street, south of Foley Square. Mary
crossed Broadway so they wouldn't be seen together as they
approached City Hall.

There were still some old, wooden telephone booths at
the Surrogate's Court, on the first floor, just off the main
lobby that Juan used from time to time to make calls that
required privacy. He couldn't risk having a conversation
on the street that could be overheard, and yet he couldn't
wait to make the call until he got back into the newsroom.
It would take all their coordination and smarts to get the
story in tomorrow's paper. And the deadline for tomorrow's
paper was only hours away.

Juan quickly read Maldanado's letter and the attached
report. It was as significant as Mary indicated. The report
laid out in a detailed chronology how many Mayday alerts
were issued from the command posts at the WTC on the
morning of the attack with exact times. It also included
summaries of reports from surviving FDNY members who

said they never heard the orders to evacuate the North Tower, even after the collapse of the South Tower. This was confirmation of information Juan had gathered on his own from the firefighter he met at the meeting of 9/11 widows that Sarah had organized in Rockville Centre.

This was particularly troublesome. One could reasonably argue that most of the FDNY chiefs on the ground that day had no way of knowing that the South Tower was going to come down like a pancake, but there was no excuse for keeping any firefighter in the North Tower once the South Tower had collapsed. Any firefighter who didn't get out of the North Tower either didn't hear the evacuation order, ran out of time, or simply ignored it, which would be foolhardy once you became aware that the South Tower had collapsed.

Maldanado's report also summarized the department's efforts over the past decade to upgrade the quality of its handy-talkie radios that all firefighters were issued, an effort that intensified after the 1993 bombing of the World Trade Center when jihadists planted a fertilizer bomb in a rental truck in the parking garage underneath the WTC complex. As Maldanado detailed, the effort to get FDNY members better radios, ones that would actually work inside highrise towers like the WTC, ultimately went nowhere due to funding concerns and normal government inertia.

But Maldanado's memo also contained another bombshell. He had referred the radio issue to the city's inspector general (IG) after he received allegations that the city's bid to replace the radios had been rigged. (The contract ultimately went to FRRC, the firm that had been supplying the FDNY handy-talkies for more than a decade.) Maldanado's report did not identify the source of the allegations except to say that he believed them to be of sufficient credibility that they warranted the referral to the city's top internal investigator. The IG, though, had no power to prosecute and, as with many mayoral administrations, it was where such allegations often went to quietly die.

The IG was appointed by the mayor, and few allegations ever resulted in action, at least not action that got reportedly publicly or that resulted in the type of indictments Giuliani was known for when he was the US attorney for the Southern District of New York. Since these allegations were now being repeated in Maldanado's official report to the mayor, they were totally reportable. Juan need only cite the source: a report to the mayor from the city's first lieutenant fire marshal.

Juan pumped some quarters into the old pay telephone inside the courthouse and dialed the city desk.

"It's Juan. Give me McFeeley."

"He's in a news meeting."

"Pull him out. Right now."

Seconds later, McFeeley picked up.

"We got it. All of it. One of the FDNY's top brass put it all in a report and letter of resignation directly to the mayor, and I have a copy. The radios malfunctioning. The missed Maydays. Even allegations that the radio contract was rigged. He lays it all out."

McFeeley asked a series of questions that editors are trained to ask. "How do we know the document is real? Can you get Maldanado to confirm and go on the record that this is why he resigned? Are the allegations in the report credible?"

Juan answered each one to McFeeley's satisfaction. He would be trying to reach Maldanado next, as soon as he got off the phone with McFeeley.

"Don't come back to the newsroom," McFeeley advised. "Baldwin will be all over you the moment you walk in the door. Get a hotel room. You can work out of there. Start writing. We don't have much time. I will alert the boys that it's a go for tonight.

"And, Juan, the stakes are as high as they get with this one. Take all precautions. Be careful. Make sure you are not being followed. Baldwin will stop at nothing if he realizes we are going around him, and who knows who else has a stake in seeing that this doesn't get published? If the FRRC people really are dirty, we don't know what they might do. Once this hits the paper, their whole company could be toast. If any lawyers or cops show up at your door, get out of there fast."

Juan knew McFeeley was right. He needed to be extra careful.

"Got it. And, Bill, thanks for backing me on this."

McFeeley brushed him off. "Get to work. You've got the Wood," using the old tabloid term for the front-page headline that screams at its readers each morning on their way to the subway. Harking back to the days when each page of type was set in metal in rows by hand, the large, front-page letters were made of wood, thus the term for any front-page tabloid story.

Juan called Mary. "Can you talk?"

"I can listen," she replied in a low voice.

"This is everything you said. It's a bombshell. We are going to try and get it in the paper tomorrow if we can get it past Baldwin. I can't go back to the newsroom. My editor wants me to work out of a hotel room, and I think that's a good idea. Can you meet me uptown at the Sheraton? The unions have some pull there, and we might need their help with security in addition to getting this published. I'm not going to use my name to check in. I'll call you back with the room number."

Mary hesitated for a second on the phone. She knew when she walked out of City Hall this time, it would be for the last time. She would miss working with the mayor and the excitement of being in the center of his universe. She had been with him for nearly eight years. But it was time to turn the corner. And she couldn't stomach the idea that City Hall would try and cover up what happened to Bill and the other firefighters.

"I'll be there in half an hour."

She packed up a few things, including a photo of Bill in his FDNY Rescue 12 gear that she kept on her desk and discreetly put them in a canvas bag she kept under her desk for when the farmer's market appeared each Thursday near City Hall. Everything else she left behind, not wanting to raise suspicions. She told Peter Brezenoff in an email that she wasn't feeling well and was going home.

She walked out the front door of City Hall, past the security detail, and down the wide marble steps that served as a stage for New York politics. A group of city council members was holding a press briefing on the steps, calling for more careful handling of the debris being removed from Ground Zero to allow for more time to search for human remains. After all, there was an election coming up in November, and these members needed to get their names out there. If only the reporters covering that briefing knew what she and Juan now knew. They would be surrounding her with their cameras and microphones and tape recorders. She thought what that would be like and then hoped she would not have to ever face the cameras. She hoped to remain Juan's anonymous source, although she realized the chances of that happening were slim.

Mary hopped on the number 2 uptown subway on her way to meet Juan. Her mind drifted to thoughts of Bill and to Juan. For the first time in her usually very organized life, she didn't know where she would be tomorrow. It was a strangely liberating feeling. After so many years of taking orders from her lawyer-trained bosses and spending her work life trying to advance their objectives, she was finally standing up for herself and emerging from the shadows.

The train screeched to a halt at 42nd Street, and Mary decided to get out and walk the ten or so blocks up to the Sheraton at Seventh Avenue and 53rd Street. She emerged in Times Square and, for once, enjoyed the crush of tourists who still filled the streets, largely oblivious to the continuing cleanup mission ongoing downtown at Ground Zero. She was glad they were still coming to the city.

At that moment, walking uptown, Mary was proud of what she was about to do. If her name ever surfaced, she knew she would be branded as a whistleblower in the media and as a rat, a turncoat, by the most extreme partisans within the Giuliani administration. She would be dead to the mayor—her most powerful patron. Her remaining friends in City Hall would be barred from talking to her. She never would work in government again. And her prospects in private industry would be dramatically diminished. No sector that did business with City Hall—like the real estate industry or the huge NYC nonprofit community— would touch her. She would have to find an employer with no connection or concern about City Hall, and they were generally few and far between.

In a few months, though, Rudy would be out of City Hall, having come to the end of his term-limited mayoralty. Who knows, maybe that guy Bloomberg could actually win. And then it would be an entirely new gang downtown. Either way, she wasn't turning back. Not now. This was her town, too, and "Giuliani time"—a term the mayor's critics coined to conjure up his sometimes-harsh policing tactics and conservative social service policies—was drawing to a close.

Her husband had died trying to defend this city. She was about to crash and burn her carefully crafted government career, but she was happy to do so if it meant the truth would come out about what happened downtown on 9/11—not just for her husband, but for all the first responders who found themselves trapped and out of time when the Towers fell.

CHAPTER TWENTY-SIX

Juan dialed the cell phone number he had for Maldanado, which he had in his favorites on his cell. Maldanado had been a trusted source for many years. Juan was not surprised to learn that Mike had written a memo laying bare the 9/11 dysfunction and putting it squarely on the mayor's desk. He was a straight-shooter and loved the FDNY and its collection of misfits, square-rooters, hard-chargers and, yes, genuine heroes (on occasion). Like so many others who served in the FDNY, the department had become family to him and a second home, a place where he grew up professionally and in so many other ways. He was closer to many of the men he served within the FDNY than his own, flesh-and-blood brothers.

But Maldanado knew the FDNY much more intimately than the strangers who had suddenly discovered the heroism that some of its members displayed on 9/11. He saw the malfunction, the bureaucracy, the petty rivalries both within the FDNY and with other city agencies, especially with the NYPD, that routinely hampered operations. From reading Maldanado's memo, Juan quickly realized that 9/11 had pushed Mike over the breaking point.

When Maldanado saw Juan's number light up on his cell phone, he hesitated at first to pick it up. Juan let it ring and hoped Mike would answer. He needed him to answer.

They hadn't talked since the day after 9/11, when they met at Ground Zero on the way to The Pile.

"Hey, haven't heard from you in a while," Mike said. "What's up?"

Juan did not let on right away that he had the memo Mike had written to the mayor. Juan knew Mike had his entire career on the line now, including his pension.

They talked about the funerals they had attended and how the department was doing in the wake of losing so many of its best men.

Finally, Juan got to the reason he called.

"Mike, I have the report and your letter of resignation to the mayor," Juan told him, always mindful that his deadline was looming. Juan needed Mike to at least acknowledge that what he had in his hand was authentic, that the resignation and report did indeed come from him. He hoped the shock value of his first question would pay off. And it did.

"How the hell did you get ahold of that?" Mike replied, genuinely alarmed and surprised. Mike paused, trying to absorb the implications of Juan's question and the reality that his report was in the hands of a reporter and now would become public.

"I only handed it in yesterday. Are you going with it in the paper? This is really going to put me out there. I didn't plan on it going public, at least not right away. Can't you sit on it for a while? I haven't even heard back from the mayor's office or the FDNY brass. There's going to be hell to pay on this, you know, and I am at the bottom of the hill when you-know-what starts flowing."

"I know how sensitive it is," Juan responded. "But you know this is dynamite. And I suspect you knew that when you wrote it and dropped it on the mayor's desk. It will be in the paper tomorrow—and on the front page. I wanted to call in part to give you a heads-up, to tell you to get ready for the shitstorm that is coming your way. I can't delay publication, not even for you. It's too hot. And I'm having problems of my own at the *News*. Between you and me, City Hall is trying their best to keep this all quiet, as you know. They are putting pressure on the paper. That's why your report and letter, frankly, are so important. It's impossible to ignore. I'm working with an editor now to get it all in the paper tomorrow. I'm afraid of what might happen if we delay and the mayor's people get wind that we are ready to publish. You understand?"

Juan had what he needed. Maldanado not only had not denied the document was his, but he had also confirmed that he had written it and given it to the mayor's office. That was a confirmation, good enough to satisfy McFeeley that the document he received from Mary was authentic.

He pushed his friend and longtime source for more.

"Do you want to say anything on the record? You might as well. Your name is going to be all over this whether you go on the record with me now or not. We are quoting extensively from the letter and your report. The public, including your colleagues, are going to wonder why you did it, why you broke ranks. Others will question your motives, especially if you don't speak up yourself."

Juan was giving him the hard sell, and they both knew it.

"Off the record, I'm not surprised that City Hall is giving your paper a hard time on this one. That's par for the course. That's one reason I put it all in writing now. I think I said everything I wanted to say in the report and in my letter to the mayor," Maldanado told him. "If you have a copy, have fun with it. I'll just add one thing—*on the record*."

There was a long pause. Juan had learned a long time ago to give a source like Maldanado time to think before speaking. Silence was not necessarily a bad thing in an interview like this one. He let it be.

Finally, after what seemed like an hour but was really only a minute, Maldanado came back on the line.

"You can use this from me," he said. "I think the public deserves to know what really happened at the WTC on the morning of 9/11 and why so many of our guys in the FDNY died. No one could have foreseen this kind of an attack or that the buildings would come down like a couple of pancakes. But I think the evidence is also clear that our losses could have been a lot fewer if we had better communication during the 102 minutes it took for everything to unfold. That's a long time. Different decisions could have been made—better-informed decisions—if only everyone involved in the operation had all the information available to them at the time."

Juan was momentarily speechless. For the first time, one of the highest-ranking members of the FDNY had admitted that poor communication contributed to the deaths of at least some of the 343 firefighters who perished on 9/11.

"You are saying this for the record, right? I am recording, and I want to be sure you are saying what you want to say. It's going to go straight into tomorrow's paper, assuming we get it all past the editors and publisher."

"Be well and safe, my friend," Mike said. "I know what I am doing, and it needs to be done. I'll see you around town."

With that, he hung up.

Juan's next call was to Sarah Murphy.

"Sarah, it's Juan Gomez of the *News*. I'm right on deadline for tomorrow's paper, but I wanted to give you a call. Mike Maldanado, one of the highest-ranking officers in the FDNY in the fire marshal's office, has resigned and sent a letter directly to the mayor with a report outlining his initial findings into causes that contributed to the deaths of the 343 firefighters who perished on 9/11. He was assigned to investigate as part of his fire marshal duties. He cites lack of radio communications as a prime cause. He lays it all out. Do you want to comment?"

Sarah had been preparing dinner for her husband. She wasn't expecting a call like this. But she knew Juan and she knew what this meant. Finally, there would be official investigations. There would be hearings. City Hall wouldn't be able to sweep it all under the rug, not after this.

"Juan, I haven't seen the report you are talking about, and I don't know this Maldanado fellow. But it certainly sounds very significant that a ranking officer of the FDNY would go on the record about one of the root causes of why we lost Peter and so many other men from the department on 9/11. I hope his coming forward will be a turning point and that more information will now start to come out about what really happened down there with the radios and communications on that morning. I believe most of the men from the FDNY never heard the order to evacuate. That's the only logical explanation why we lost 343 men, including my son. They were brave guys, but they were not fools. They don't go to a fire scene expecting to get killed. If they are given fair warning, they drop what they are doing, and they save themselves and their fellow firefighters—unless they are helping someone who is trapped. They wouldn't leave civilians behind who needed help. But most people on 9/11 self-evacuated. I don't think the firefighters were given a fighting chance to get out on 9/11 due to the radios malfunctioning. Now, you say this Maldanado is confirming it. I'm glad he stepped forward. It takes a lot of courage to do that in this atmosphere. He is a brave fellow. I'd like to meet him and shake his hand."

That was a meeting Juan would like to arrange someday. 9/11 mom and FDNY whistleblower. It would make for a good photo! He filed it away.

"Does that help your story, Juan?"

"Yes, yes…very much," Juan replied. "I'm just still taking notes. I want to make sure I got it all. Thanks, very, very much, Sarah. I really appreciate it. I couldn't have kept this story alive without you. You have been relentless. Pick up the paper tomorrow. I think you will want to read this one. And I will tell Maldanado you'd like to meet him. I've got to go now and finish filing this story."

"Take care. I'll look for your story tomorrow. Good luck," she said. "And, Juan, keep digging."

"Sarah, you can count on that," Juan replied. "Maldanado has just opened the door. The floodgates are about to swing wide open on this. And it all started with you and the professor. You got the ball rolling."

CHAPTER TWENTY-SEVEN

Juan was in the zone now, typing away furiously on his laptop. His notes were spread out on the bed in the room McFeeley had rented for him on the 16th floor of the Sheraton Hotel in Midtown. The story was coming together.

He was careful to save frequently and back up his work by sending emails to his Yahoo account, just in case the laptop crashed. He also was copying the story to a flash drive.

His concentration was interrupted by a knock on the hotel room door. Juan wasn't expecting anyone, not yet. He froze, not sure whether to answer.

"Maintenance," a man with a thick Russian accent said. "We are here to check your AC unit."

Juan did not immediately reply. He closed his laptop and gathered up his notes, ready to try an escape if he had to.

Again, the man knocked.

"Maintenance. I have to come in the room."

Juan looked through the peephole. The man had a grey uniform on and held a toolbox. He had an ID badge clipped to his breast pocket. He looked legit.

"Okay. Hold on," Juan said through the door.

Juan undid the deadbolt and unhooked the security chain. He opened the door a small crack, still ready to slam it shut if he didn't like what he saw or heard.

"I didn't call for maintenance. My AC unit seems to be working fine. Can you come back another time?"

"It will just take a minute, sir," the Russian replied. "Sorry to disturb you. The units down the hall are not working, and it's all one system, so yours will likely stop blowing air soon if I don't check it."

Juan remained skeptical but let the man in.

"Thank you, sir. I will be out of your way very quickly."

The Russian went over to the window unit, took off the cover, and pretended to check one of the valves. He reached for something from his toolbox. The man's body blocked Juan's view of his hands, which now were busy installing a tiny video camera and listening device. The lens of the wireless camera had a 360-degree fisheye view of the room. The microphone was powerful enough to pick up every conversation, and the small camera could zoom in to see what Juan was typing on his laptop.

Detective Michael Kazimir and the Kew Gardens Russians now had eyes and ears on Juan. They had been tracking Juan's every movement for the past few days, using both technologies to ping his cellphone and old-fashioned shoe leather on the street. The Russians had followed Juan to the hotel. What they didn't know yet and were eager to discover was the identity of his City Hall source.

The Russians—stationed in a room on the same floor as Juan—now had eyes on his door and the entire 16th floor hallway, and now, they could monitor him inside his room.

The Russian maintenance guy gathered up his toolbox and headed toward the door.

"Shouldn't give you a problem now, sir," he said.

He left quickly and Juan got back to work, unaware that his every keystroke and every utterance now was being recorded by Kazimir and his men.

Kazimir's number-two man, Mikhail, monitored all the video feeds, including a tiny remote they had planted in the hotel lobby. He was reliable, a former KGB operative who fled Russia when the Soviet Union fell apart in the early '90s. Kazimir had used him as an undercover when he was still on the job with the NYPD and investigating the Russian mob bosses who took over gambling, sex, and drug rackets in the Brighton Beach section of Brooklyn, then spread their operation out to other parts of the city. Mikhail never got made. His cohorts on this job had no idea he had helped Kazimir when he was a cop.

Mikhail noticed a well-dressed woman boarding the elevator in the lobby and getting off on Juan's floor.

"We might have something," Mikhail said to Kazimir, who was on site, monitoring the entire surveillance operation. "Check her out."

Kazimir stared at the woman.

"She looks familiar," he said. "Run her through facial recognition."

The software the Russians were using contained tens of thousands of images from public and proprietary sources, including government employees and news photos that had been published or were online.

The room the Russians occupied looked like a mini National Security Agency field operation. Laptops and PCs were everywhere with double-screened monitors.

"We got a hit," Mikhail said. "She works at City Hall."

Mary popped up almost instantly on the facial recognition software as she had been photographed many times in the background of news photographs featuring Mayor Giuliani. They didn't even have to tap into any secret government databases to find her. All the publicly available news sites had her in their archives. The most recent entries identified Mary as a top and trusted aide to Rudy and as the widow of a hero FDNY rescue team member who had perished on 9/11.

"Shit!" Kazimir said to no one in particular. "An aide to Giuliani. Great. This just got more complicated."

Mary tapped lightly on Juan's hotel room door.

"Juan, it's me."

This time, Juan didn't hesitate.

He looked quickly through the peephole to confirm she was alone and then opened the door.

Juan paused from his writing to greet her. They hugged as she closed the door behind her.

As they emerged from the friendly embrace, he looked her straight in the eye. "Are you sure you are ready for this?" he asked again.

"I've left City Hall for the last time," she replied. "I don't know what my new life will bring, but it's no longer back there. I'm going wherever the truth takes us."

She smiled at Juan as she uttered the words. A feeling of great relief came over her once again, even in the midst of this very tense situation that she found herself in. She felt Bill was looking down on her and that he would approve.

She carried a paper photocopy of the Maldanado resignation letter and report, just as a backup. She had highlighted the sections she thought were significant and handed them to Juan. He had highlighted essentially the same sections, but it was good to have another set of experienced eyes looking at the material. They were all business now.

"Are you almost done writing?" Mary asked.

"I'm about halfway through. Should be done in about an hour. I've got the top of the story pretty much written, and the rest should follow pretty quickly. Here's the lead. See what you think."

Mary read the opening sentences of Juan's story as she sat down on the bed next to the desk where he had set up his laptop. She slipped off her high heels. As she read it, she let out a long, low gasp, thinking of Bill and how he had died. She wondered what communications, if any, he had received on his handy-talkie radio. Had he been given any time to escape? She wondered—as so many other family members who had lost FDNY loved ones—whether the men they knew would have left the Towers even if they had received the order to evacuate. Her Bill was a rescue expert. He was trained to get other people out of very difficult spots. If he had a chance to save even one other person, it's likely he would have stayed until the end, evacuation order or not.

She could live with that. What she longed to know was if Bill and the other men even had the chance to make that call for themselves. Did they even have enough time to escape? She knew these were questions that likely would never be answered.

"Keep typing," Mary whispered to Juan. "This is powerful stuff. The whole city needs to read this. And the nation."

Juan turned back to his laptop and resumed writing. He was used to filing on deadline, usually in the midst of the din of a newsroom. He was on a roll now, and the words were flowing easily. He could block out most anything to focus on the story.

Mary, meanwhile, was faxing a copy of the report to a number that McFeeley had provided, using the portable fax machine Juan had bought at OfficeMax. The fax number connected to the headquarters of the Newspaper Guild, the union that technically still represented the editorial workers at the *News* but that had been effectively crushed when Schwartz bought the paper. McFeeley still had friends there, and he had arranged for the president of the guild, Bill Guida, to stand by at the fax so no one else in the guild office would receive the document. It was a backup plan. Just in case.

Looking on from the adjoining room via the tiny but powerful camera his men had installed, Kazimir now squirmed in his chair as he adjusted the angle of the camera to zoom in on the documents being faxed. They bore the FDNY insignia. There now was little question as to where Juan was getting his information. The leak was right under the mayor's nose.

He pressed his men for confirmation of Mary's identity. He needed to be certain before he took his next step.

"You are sure that is her? Does Giuliani have any other staffers who look like her?"

"No way, boss," Mikhail said. "It's her. One hundred percent."

Kazimir didn't mind going after bad guys on behalf of private clients—employees who were stealing from their employers, corrupt buildings department officials taking kickbacks from contractors—but this job, surveilling a reporter and his source, a 9/11 widow, is where his work got dicey.

He had friends who were killed on 9/11, and he knew what Juan and Mary were trying to do was honorable—although he doubted it would ultimately make any difference. He had been around the NYPD and FDNY too long to believe a newspaper story could change behavior within the departments.

And he had bills to pay, and this was a cash job.

He called his client, Wedley, on the throwaway phone he had issued Wedley at their initial meeting. "We've got a development. The reporter's source is a top aide to Giuliani, a woman who lost her husband firefighter on 9/11. She has access to FDNY files. A top FDNY official has resigned over the radio and communication issue, and he put it all in a letter to the mayor. He spelled everything out: the faulty radios, the effort to replace them, and the inability of the FDNY command to reach everyone with the order to evacuate. The woman has the letter, and she gave it to Juan Gomez. He is getting ready to publish. What do you want us to do?"

Wedley didn't hesitate. "You have to stop him. Do what you have to do, but don't let him send that story."

Kazimir hesitated. He didn't want to be involved in roughing up a reporter. Surveillance was one thing. Direct intervention, quite another. He put up a roadblock, hoping to slow his client down.

"That will be an extra $500,000," Kazimir replied coolly. "Our original deal was to follow him, not to get into any kind of an encounter with him. He is a member of the working press. The NYPD will not be able to ignore his complaint if we go after him. And his source is a top aide to the mayor."

"I'll pay it," Wedley responded, knowing he had little choice. "Just don't get caught."

Kazimir did not reply immediately.

"Are you sure about this?" he responded. "This will bring down a lot of heat."

"Yes. Do it," Wedley replied. He hung up, leaving it to Kazimir to decide how far to go to stop Juan.

Kazimir thought it might go down this way. He had prepared his men in advance for this possibility. They brought what they needed for the job—ski masks, small arms, and a getaway route back to Queens. Kazimir had a plan. Get inside the room, take Juan's laptop, notes, and any valuables. They would make it look like a robbery. The girl they didn't plan on. She made it more difficult. Another potential witness and another person to restrain.

He turned to his men—all Russian, all accustomed to executing this type of operation.

"Plan B is a go," Kazimir said inside the room where they had been surveilling Juan and Mary. "Get in and out of there in eight minutes. Got it?"

Mikhail nodded approval on behalf of himself and his crew.

They had rehearsed it in a warehouse in Queens, even setting up the bed and desk and furniture like it was in Juan's hotel room. They left nothing to chance. Each had their assignment.

The Russians quickly packed up their equipment from the surveillance room. Mikhail sent the equipment with one of the men to a van they had parked in a garage on W. 54th. Kazimir stayed behind with one laptop still hooked up to the video feed from Juan's room. He would leave as soon as he could confirm—with his own eyes—that the job was done.

CHAPTER TWENTY-EIGHT

Mikhail used a small scrambler device to trick the key card entry lock on Juan's hotel room door into thinking it was reading a master key card. The door entry lock turned green and, in an instant, the four Russians were inside, handguns drawn.

"Move away from the laptop now," Mikhail told Juan, pointing his gun at Mary's head while the others aimed at Juan.

Juan froze. He considered hitting the send button but looked at Mary and thought otherwise. No story was worth dying for, and no story was worth getting Mary killed.

Mary's heart was racing. She had never been in this kind of situation, face-to-face with men with guns. It was one thing to quit her job and help Juan, it was quite another to be her now, staring down these men. But she did not panic.

She knew what Juan was thinking. "Do it, Juan. Hit send. They can't stop you," she screamed before one of the Russians pushed her to the ground and put duct tape over her mouth and used it to cuff her hands behind her back.

Juan shook his head to signal to Mary that he wasn't going to provoke these men. Not now. He recognized

Mikhail's voice as that of the "maintenance man" who had entered his hotel room earlier, allegedly to fix the AC unit. He realized now that he must have planted a bug and that everything he and Mary had discussed was now on tape, possibly on its way to City Hall or their surrogates.

"Who hired you guys?" Juan asked, ever the reporter, even with a gun to his head. "You can tell whoever it is this isn't going to work. The story will still get out."

"Just do as we say. No one needs to get hurt," Mikhail said in broken English. "But you should find another story to work on. Some people—some important people—don't need you poking around in their business. This is no game. We know where you live. We know your kids' names and where they go to school. Your Jennifer is a very pretty girl. I'm sure you want to keep her safe. Think about it. Is it really worth it? The next time, we will not be so nice."

Juan did as he was told. He was still processing. They knew his daughter's name? He had been threatened before, but never anything like this.

Mikhail told the other Russians to dump the contents of Juan's briefcase on the bed along with Mary's handbag. They took Juan's reporter notebooks, his tape recorder, the laptop, the fax machine, his cell phone, and the hard copy of the report Mary had delivered. They took Mary's wedding ring and the gold cross she wore around her neck that Bill had given her. They emptied Juan's wallet—it had three credit cards and forty dollars in cash.

Then they bound their hands and mouths with duct tape and tied them to two chairs, back-to-back. They were in and out in less than seven minutes, one minute ahead of schedule.

Kazimir watched it all on his live laptop video feed from the surveillance room. He packed up and left two minutes after Mikhail gave him the thumbs-up sign that they had reached the street. Kazimir didn't want to be seen on the hotel surveillance cameras exiting with the Russians. He took the elevator directly to the parking garage level, walked to his car that he had outfitted with phony plates, and drove back to Queens.

"It's done," he reported to Wedley after he emerged on the Queens side of the Midtown Tunnel. "That story isn't getting into print, at least not tonight."

Wedley told Kazimir that he had transferred the $500K and hung up. Then Wedley made one more call on the throwaway phone, reaching out to his City Hall contact, the person who had helped him win the radio contract and who had as much as him to lose if the story went public.

"I bought us some time but probably not much. You have to come through on your end now."

Lou Amato, the mayor's chief political operative, took Wedley's call and listened carefully but said nothing. He was within earshot of the mayor, but not even the mayor knew of his connection to Wedley. If the mayor ever learned what Amato had done—forging a relationship with FRRC's owner, taking trips with him and then the cash, lots of it, to help steer the FDNY radio contract his way—the mayor would have fired Amato on the spot and turned him over to the US attorney.

Amato's relationship with Wedley had started innocently enough, as these things do. Wedley had reached out, saying he wanted to help the mayor's campaign. Legal contributions were made to the mayor's reelection campaign from Wedley's company. Once he maxed out on the campaign limits, Wedley asked Amato what else he could do to help. At lunch and dinner, Wedley came with envelopes of cash. He didn't ask Amato what he was doing with it. But he did ask for help with the FDNY radio contract, and Amato fed him inside information about how to stay one step ahead in the contracting process.

Now, Amato was in deeper. FRRC had helped to direct an attack on a *News* reporter in an effort to keep the lid on the radio story. And Amato was in bed with FRRC, even if he had no direct, prior knowledge of the attack on the reporter.

Amato stepped outside the mayor's office to call Schwartz on his private line at his corporate real estate office, high up in the Chrysler Building on Lexington Avenue, across town from the *News*'s grimy newsroom.

"Did you know Juan was ready to publish? I thought you said you had this covered?"

"Baldwin has assured me he is on this," Schwartz said.

"Baldwin obviously doesn't know what the fuck his own reporter is up to," replied Amato, his voice nearing a scream. "We had to clean it up on our end. Now you have to double down and do your part. Do what you promised. Make sure nothing gets into the paper on this. It would hurt the city's efforts at recovery. It would hurt the mayor. You know that. You want him to be president as much as I do. Think of what he could do for you if he reached the White House. We have to clean up the mess downtown and start to rebuild as soon as we can. Everything else is a distraction," Amato told the publisher.

"I understand," Schwartz replied. "Don't worry."

Back in the hotel room, Juan and Mary struggled to free themselves.

Juan used his free fingers to rip at the duct tape binding Mary's wrists. And Mary did the same until both of them were able to free an arm. It was a tedious process, giving the Russians plenty of time to get away before Juan was able to reach the phone in the room and hit "O" for the operator and call for hotel security.

The Sheraton security guys—all retired or off-duty NYPD—arrived quickly. They removed the remaining duct tape from Juan and Mary's mouths, legs, and torsos. It had been many years since the security guys had seen an in-the-room robbery like this one. They didn't know what to make of it. They knew not to disturb the scene, and they had already called it in to the NYPD's robbery unit at the Midtown North precinct. Detectives were on the way.

"What happened?" asked Tom Lisante, the head of the Sheraton security office, a retired NYPD captain with thirty years on the job. "Are you two okay?"

Juan identified himself as a reporter for the *News*, and Mary said she worked at City Hall.

Lisante took notes as Juan described the break-in and the threats to his family. Once he realized Juan was a member of the City Hall press corps, Lisante called his old bosses at One Police Plaza to give them a heads up. He didn't want them to be caught off-guard. He knew the potentially sensitive nature of this break-in.

Within ten minutes, NYPD brass would be on the scene, including Kevin Burns, the police commissioner's top communications guy who held the title of deputy commissioner for public information.

Juan did not tell Lisante anything about the story he was working on or what he was doing in the hotel room with Mary. He didn't want any of those details to be in a police report.

Just before the NYPD brass arrived, Mary had slipped into the bathroom and emerged holding a small flash drive in her hand. Before she left City Hall, she had made a backup of everything and put it on the flash drive. She had stored it in her bra for safekeeping. She wanted her own copy, just in case Juan failed to get the story published. Now, she gave it to Juan without a word.

"What's this?" he asked quietly, careful to not let the security guys in the room hear their conversation.

"You didn't think I would leave City Hall without backing up my files, including the email from Maldanado to the mayor? I was going to show it to you later. It was my insurance policy. It also has a draft of the story you sent me earlier today to my personal email."

"Mary, you are an angel," Juan said.

They kept their conversation out of earshot of the arriving NYPD detectives.

"We need to get to a computer so we can send what we have to McFeeley."

"There's a public computer in the business office on the first floor," Mary said, ever the efficient assistant who made it her business to know where the backup systems were located in any situation.

"Let's go," Juan said.

Burns held up a hand to block them from the door.

"Where are you going? We're not finished here yet."

"Kevin, I'm on deadline," Juan replied. "I don't have time to explain, but I need to get to a computer. I can fill you in later, but, right now, I have to file.

"And, Kevin, I need a favor. The guys who broke in threatened my family. They know where I live, and they know Jennifer's name. Can you get a detail over to my kids' schools and to my house, just until this is over?"

Burns and Juan had known each other for more than a decade. Burns immediately read how serious this was. He knew not to try and get in Juan's way. The detectives could finish questioning him later.

"Okay. Done. Text me the address of your kids' schools. As long as you promise to come to the precinct later and finish answering the detectives' questions. This doesn't make a lot of sense right now. These guys weren't after a laptop and the forty bucks in your wallet," Burns said, stepping aside.

"No, they were not, Kevin. You are right about that," Juan said. "They were trying to stop me from filing this story, which is why I need to get to a computer. I promise to fill you in later and come down to the precinct—after I file."

They hustled to the Sheraton business office and scanned the room, settling in at the one open terminal.

Juan slid the flash drive into the port on the side of the desktop. The files popped up quickly and, within a few seconds, Juan was typing away again, picking up almost where he had left off.

Juan asked Mary to call McFeeley to alert him to what had happened.

McFeeley picked up the phone on the first ring.

"Is this Mr. McFeeley?" Mary asked, careful to get confirmation before she continued.

"Yes, this is McFeeley. Who is this?"

No one in the newsroom called him Mr. McFeeley. And he didn't have time for a crank call.

"This is Mary Sullivan. I am a friend of Juan's. I work at City Hall. He asked me to call you. He's right here, but he's typing."

"Good, tell him to hurry up."

"There's been a little glitch, and he wanted me to fill you in. Four men, four Russian men, broke into the hotel room where Juan was working on the story, tied us up with duct tape, threatened Juan's family, and took his notes and laptop. They didn't hurt us. We managed to call security. The NYPD is up in the room right now. We are in the hotel's business office. Juan is filing from a public computer. I had the report on a backup flash drive, so we didn't lose too much time, but there has been a delay. And it is likely that whoever broke in is working with City Hall and with your boss at the paper. Juan wanted me to warn you that the bosses probably are aware of what we are up to or will be very soon."

McFeeley didn't know quite how to respond.

"Are you two okay?"

"Yes, we are fine, just a little shaken up."

"Tell Juan I will handle the bosses here and not to worry. Just get that story over to me as fast as he can, okay?"

"Understood. I will tell him."

Juan didn't look up from the screen.

"Let me guess, he said to send the story in as fast as possible?"

"You got it. And he said not to worry about the bosses at the paper. He said he would deal with them," Mary said. "He seems like a good guy. I'd like to meet him sometime."

"McFeeley is a good egg. He's a little rough around the edges, but you would like him. If he says he will handle something, you can count on it. I don't know how McFeeley is going to get this story past Baldwin and into the newspaper, but I will leave that to him. I'm almost done. Let's get ready to move."

CHAPTER TWENTY-NINE

McFeeley settled into his regular booth in the back of TJs, a small, dark, workingman's Irish pub on Ninth Avenue and 35th where the bottled beers were still three dollars, and there were only two kinds of brew on tap—Bud and Bud Light. TJs was trapped in 1960s décor with cheap, wood paneling on the walls, a string of half-broken Christmas lights above the bar, and only two banners hung on either side of the one, wall-mounted TV—one for the New York Yankees and one for the New York Giants. Mets and Jets fans were out of luck at this establishment, which served as a second home to the pressmen, drivers, typographers, and other union crafts whose physical labor each night made the printing and distribution of the *News* possible.

The union guys would stop in before their afternoon and overnight shifts began—before the presses began to roll—dressed in their blue-and-grey uniforms for a couple of quick beers to help them get through the night. The writers and photographers at the *News* also had adopted the place as their after-work hangout, mainly for its close proximity to the newsroom and its cheap drinks. It was the one place where the blue-collar *News* workers and the white-collar reporters and editors occupied the same space, although they didn't usually talk to one another.

The uneasy standoff inside TJs between the union guys and the growing number of hipsters of the *News*'s newsroom staff represented a wider conflict unfolding across the city. The West Side near the paper was slowly being transformed, like so many other NYC neighborhoods. A few hip restaurants already had moved in, and, slowly, the strip joints and peep show/video businesses that had already been pushed from Times Square also were being squeezed out of Ninth and Tenth Avenues as rents slowly escalated. The city's real estate barons had big plans for this piece of the West Side of Manhattan. The LIRR rail yard, west of Penn Station, was one of the last large tracks of open-air space available. The cash-strapped MTA, which ran the city's subway, rail, and bus systems, was trying to sell the development rights to the highest bidder. There were rumors of a new football stadium going in or maybe high-rise apartments. TJs' owners were hanging in, hoping for a big score down the road. But, for now, the place remained a shot and beer domain of the working man.

McFeeley nodded to his regular waitress who did not bother to ask him what he wanted. She brought over a cold Bud from the tap and a shot of Jameson's.

McFeeley sipped the beer and watched the door.

The first union leader, Tommy McBride, arrived a few minutes later and sat down across from McFeeley. The *News*'s two other union bosses, Michael Flynn and Anthony Impellitari, joined them in short order, and the waitress brought over more beers and shots. These three men—the sons of Irish and Italian immigrants—had extraordinary power within the News's printing and distribution plant. They got guys hired, fought periodic management attempts to lay them off, and, essentially, could dictate how, when, and if the newspaper got printed and delivered on time.

When Schwartz bought the paper, he gutted the newsroom union and installed Baldwin as his top editor, but he knew he had to strike a deal with these men or risk chaos on a nightly basis in the production and delivery areas.

Flynn was the most powerful of the three. He called the shots within the pressroom. He was a six-foot, red-headed, self-educated union leader with a silver tongue. He also headed up the council of unions—eleven unions in all—that had the keys to virtually every other aspect of the News's operation. He and his men had no love for publishers and their kind. Schwartz had been squeezing pennies out of the operation ever since he took it over, cutting overtime, reducing manning on the presses, and constantly pressing for union givebacks.

McFeeley had skillfully forged a close bond with Flynn over the years. And he also knew Impellitari, the leader of the Teamsters Local 5 that represented the News's 300 truck drivers. Without the drivers, the paper simply would not make it onto the streets of New York. Local 5's members could make the paper arrive on time each day—by about 4:00 a.m. throughout the key distribution points in the five boroughs of the city—or make sure the bundles hit the street a half hour after rush hour was over, effectively killing that day's street sales. And McBride, the shop steward for the typographer's union, controlled the composing room, where the paper's front page and other inside pages were laid out each night. McBride admired McFeeley's headline writing skills, which he had seen him execute on deadline almost every night.

The union leaders all knew someone who had died on 9/11. The 343 men from the FDNY who perished were working-class guys like them who had come from the same neighborhoods as their members—Bayside, Flushing, Flatbush, Co-op City, Bayridge, Bayshore, Rockville Centre, Smithtown. The union leaders showed up this afternoon at TJs because McFeeley had asked them to and because he told them it was related to 9/11.

It was rare for the top three leaders to be in the same place at the same time. They each had tremendous egos and were usually leery of each other's motives. They jockeyed constantly for power within the council of unions.

McFeeley went straight at it, appealing to their sense of patriotism, which was running high.

"Baldwin is trying to kill a story about the firefighters. It's an important story, one that reveals how most of them were killed because they never got the word to evacuate. Their radios weren't working. City Hall doesn't want the story out. It goes against their 'everybody died a hero' line, which is simply untrue. The families of the 343 firefighters who were killed deserve to know the truth. The city needs to know the truth. And I need your help getting this story in the paper tonight and on the streets. Without you, I can't pull this off. I am essentially running a mutiny, doing an end run around Baldwin.

"A lot of those firefighters didn't have to die, and this story, if it gets published, will hold City Hall accountable."

The three union leaders looked at each other quizzically, then looked at McFeeley like he had two heads. They knew McFeeley to be a level-headed editor, but this was a big ask, one that crossed a line in the sand.

"Bill, you know this stuff isn't our bread and butter," McBride said. "Why should we risk a big fight over this? And, if it's such a good story, why wouldn't Baldwin want it in the paper?"

McFeeley looked at each of them straight in the eye.

"I don't know for certain why. I can only speculate on that, but I have a pretty good idea. You have to remember, Schwartz first and foremost is a real estate guy. He's not a newspaperman. The *News* is just a toy for him, a way to get him on the Sunday morning talk shows and win invitations to the White House and Gracie Mansion every now and then. He's got major property holdings in Manhattan, including downtown. The real estate guys are all really nervous that businesses will flee downtown and that the place could become a ghost town. We're talking about hundreds of millions in real estate values going up in smoke. Baldwin knows this, and he knows how to curry favor with his boss without being told what to do. He doesn't want the *News* going after the mayor over the radios or anything else. Not now. He wants the focus on the cleanup and recovery effort. The developers want to rebuild as soon as possible. Anything else is just a distraction as far as the real estate community is concerned. They want this all behind them.

"And, it is possible the city didn't update the radios because of payoffs between the contractor and some bigwigs for the city. That part is only a theory, but it's one we are working on. Either way, bottom line, the radios didn't work when the guys needed them most, and most of the guys did not hear the order to evacuate. The guys in the North Tower didn't even know the South Tower had collapsed."

McFeeley went in for the close. "Tommy, didn't your cousin work at the firehouse right across from the Trade Center? Ten House, right? Anthony, Mike—didn't you have friends down there that day? This isn't just another story. This one is personal."

"Let me get this straight," Flynn asked McFeeley. "You're saying City Hall knew the radios didn't work, and they sent those guys in anyway? And then had no real way of getting them out? You're saying City Hall is trying to keep this all under wraps?"

"Mike, that's pretty much exactly what we have found and what this story will say," McFeeley responded, "which is why it's so important to get out. I wouldn't be asking you otherwise."

Flynn and the others paused for a moment to let McFeeley's words sink in.

Flynn spoke first.

"This is war you are asking us to start. You know that? If we do this, Schwartz will hold us all accountable."

"I know what I am asking," McFeeley said. "There are times in this business when you have to stand up. This is one of those times. If we let him, Schwartz is going to run this paper into the ground. He's letting City Hall dictate coverage of one of the most important events of our day. We can't let that happen. If we do, the paper eventually won't be worth a dime. And when Baldwin or Schwartz start asking questions, you can put it all on me. Just say this is a story we were given by McFeeley, and he is in charge of the newsroom."

McBride spoke next.

"You're asking an awful lot. This will be a hard sell to my members. They care about their paychecks, not about whether the boss is in bed with City Hall. In fact, we assume he's in bed with whomever he needs to be in bed with to keep this place afloat."

The leader of the drivers' union—Anthony Impellitari—who had been quiet until now, stood up.

"I've heard enough. The guys who died down there were our guys, our brothers, our fathers, our cousins, and our neighbors. The firefighter's union is as much a trade union as we are. McFeeley here is saying they need our help to get this story out. McFeeley's always been straight with us, and I have no reason to doubt him now. It's our job to deliver the papers once they are printed. You get this through the composing room and the pressroom, and we'll get those papers on the streets no matter what Schwartz or Baldwin says. You can count on that."

Flynn and McBride looked up at Anthony for a moment, not quite knowing what to make of him. He had just dared them to chicken out.

"Okay, we're in too," Flynn said.

"Us too," said McBride. "We can't let Anthony take all the credit here."

The four men shook hands and downed their shots and beer. It was a deal. Ironclad now as they were all witnesses. Personal honor was at stake.

On McFeeley's order, they would go in a few hours with the front page he sent them, circumventing the normal channels that Baldwin would be able to monitor from his computer. By the time Baldwin discovered what was happening, it would be too late, the story would be on the *News*'s presses, loaded on the *News*'s trucks, and dropped on every corner bodega and newsstand in town.

They all knew they were risking their jobs. McFeeley would take the direct hit—he was ready for that, eager for it. It would be his legacy in the business. The union leaders would have to stand together; Schwartz and Baldwin knew they couldn't put out the paper without them. As long as they were all in it together, there was little Schwartz and Baldwin could do to stop them, at least not tonight.

Tomorrow, there would likely be hell to pay. But the story would be on the street by then.

CHAPTER THIRTY

Juan had written the story in his head so many times that his fingers flew over the keyboard now, and the words came pouring out. Mary looked over his shoulder and kept an eye on the door, scanning for anyone—another set of Russians, the police, Baldwin himself—who might storm in and try to stop them.

Juan read through the top of the story quickly. He had sent the first few paragraphs to McFeeley so he could start working on the headline. Juan reread the lead:

> The 343 FDNY firefighters who perished while responding to the 9/11 attack were doomed by poor radio communications, little or no coordination with the NYPD, and a critical breakdown in the fire department chain of command at Ground Zero, according to internal City Hall documents.
>
> A secret city report confirms many firefighters inside the towers likely never heard the order to evacuate the buildings. The radios and communication system the firefighters depended upon on 9/11 did not function as intended.

The *News* obtained a copy of the bombshell report as well as internal emails documenting the findings and frantic efforts by some city officials seeking to keep the report from being released.

The report was kept under wraps even as family members of FDNY members who died on 9/11 repeatedly called for a full investigation.

Federal prosecutors and the FBI are now investigating the links between the firm that provided the radios and city officials. The report documents repeated attempts to replace the radios with newer technology, efforts that were repeatedly stymied by inept management at the least and possibly by a corrupt bidding and procurement process.

Meanwhile, a top-ranking FDNY official who was charged with investigating the deaths of the 343 FDNY members on 9/11 has resigned, citing conflicts with City Hall over his investigation and the long delays in trying to improve FDNY radio communications and technology so that firefighters could better communicate in a situation like they faced on 9/11.

Juan's flip phone suddenly buzzed to life. It was McFeeley. "The lead you sent looks good. This is dynamite stuff. You are going to rock the town with this story. Keep it coming. Send it to me in takes, one page at a time, so I can run it down to the composing room. We have no time to waste."

"I'm sending it as fast as I can," Juan said, irritated at McFeeley's nudge. "Don't post anything on the web until after the first copies roll off the presses and are loaded onto the trucks."

"I know what to do," McFeeley responded. "You just keep typing."

Both McFeeley and Juan wanted the story in the print edition first. They recognized the reach of the internet, but both were old school, with ink in their blood. They wanted the story on the front page first. They wanted The Wood.

McFeeley had many years under his belt of writing catchy, classic, *News of New York* front-page headlines. He was considered among the best at it in the business. He was only now beginning to test out the headline for Juan's story, scribbling various versions on a dummy sheet that he would hand to the composing room foreman at just the right moment. He was leaning toward:

FAULTY FDNY RADIOS DOOMED BRAVEST ON 9/11

--City Hall Cover-Up Charged

In a city still reeling from the losses of 9/11 attack, that headline was sure to wake up the town—and sell some newspapers.

McFeeley did not ever ask for the input of his reporters when writing headlines. They were usually too close to the story. This time he decided to make an exception, given that

Juan and his source had put it all on the line for this one. He faxed over a proof to Juan.

"This works," Juan told McFeeley. "You got it."

Juan paused for a second and pondered the look on Baldwin's face when the cover of the *News* would hit the streets of New York in a few hours.

But Juan was getting ahead of himself. First, he and McFeeley had to run the gauntlet to get the story past Baldwin and into print.

McFeeley had a backup plan in place in case Baldwin got wind of what he was doing. He had alerted a friend at the rival *New York Post*, David Dunleavy, a top columnist he could trust, to check his email for a story in the morning that he might want to follow. It was a tease, and a dangerous one. Normally, *News* editors would be loath to give the competition any kind of a heads-up about an exclusive breaking story, especially one as big as Juan's piece. But McFeeley explained the situation in a guarded, completely off-the-record fashion, just as a double fail-safe against Baldwin's possible last-minute intervention. If all else failed, McFeeley would email the story to his pal at the *New York Post* and let them break it as "*THE STORY THE NEWS OF NEW YORK REFUSED TO PRINT.*" It would be a double embarrassment for the *News*, but it would at least guarantee that Juan's story was published. Dunleavy tried to pump McFeeley for the details, but McFeeley refused and swore his friend to secrecy, except to say it was a big one. Dunleavy reluctantly agreed to the terms McFeeley laid out.

For the third time in the last hour, Baldwin stuck his head into McFeeley's office.

"Where the hell is your star reporter? What is he up to?" Baldwin barked.

"He hasn't checked in in a while," McFeeley responded, without looking up from his computer screen or stopping from taking a drag on his cigarette.

"I need to know the minute you hear from him, okay?" Baldwin ordered. "And nothing he files is to make it into the paper without my seeing it. Are we clear on that?"

"Roger that, boss," McFeeley said, again without looking up.

Baldwin also made his wishes known to all of the sub-editors on the city desk, just in case McFeeley was up to something. He had promised City Hall that he would keep a close eye on Juan, and that is exactly what he intended to do.

Baldwin had no way of knowing that McFeeley—always a careful maneuverer in the newsroom hierarchy—had made a decision months ago to retire at the end of the year. After forty years in the news business, it was time. He had squirreled away enough money to survive, and, in a year, he could collect social security. That, along with a small monthly pension from the *News* (which he became vested in before they froze and eliminated the plan), would allow him to spend some time in Florida where he liked to fish.

What better way to go out the door at the *News* than to defy Baldwin's order on a story like this?

It would take all of McFeeley's skill to get the story on the front page and on the *News*'s website in direct defiance of Baldwin's order. It was the equivalent of a newsroom mutiny that he was about to lead. He knew he would be fired on the spot once Baldwin figured out what he had done. And there would be no severance this time around. Just a security escort out the door.

At the 4:00 p.m. news meeting, where all the top editors, including Baldwin, gathered to review stories that would make up the next day's paper, McFeeley had left Juan's story off the story list and made up a dummy front page with a story about how the discovery of more human remains at Ground Zero had once again slowed up the cleanup process downtown.

None of the other editors knew what McFeeley was planning.

He didn't want them to be fired after the fact, and he wouldn't be able to protect them, so it was best that they weren't involved and could honestly deny any knowledge of the plot.

Baldwin reviewed the dummy front page at the end of the news meeting.

"Every time they find another human fragment, they have to stop the entire cleanup operation. This is getting ridiculous. Good story. Let's go with it."

He knew City Hall would approve.

He put his initials next to the headline, meaning he had signed off.

McFeeley waited until 6:00 p.m., when Baldwin had checked out for the night.

"Did you ever hear back from Juan?" Baldwin asked before heading for the elevator.

"Nothing yet, boss. He must be tied up with a source. I'll let you know when I hear from him."

"You do that. I want a call."

"You got it."

The real front page carried the classic, screaming head-line McFeeley had settled upon:

FAULTY RADIOS DOOMED 343 OF
FDNY'S BRAVEST ON 9/11

The smaller sub-headlines drove the scandal to City Hall's doorstep.

City Hall Tried to Deep-six Damning Report
Feds Investigating Radio Malfunctions

There was a buzz now in the composing room as the union shop stewards and veteran typesetters slowly began to realize what McFeeley was up to. They had laid out the dummy front page earlier in the day, so they knew now that the previous version was being scrapped in favor of this new front-page story.

And they were savvy enough to know the new story was dynamite, a direct hit at City Hall on the most sensitive subject of the day.

Every paragraph Juan was sending now was being set into type in almost real time, as it arrived.

McFeeley cleared the way with each shop steward at every step of the process.

"We've got a new front page," he told Jimmy, who was in charge of the typesetters on the night shift. "Rip up the old one. This one is going to blow the town wide open."

"Roger that, boss," Jimmy responded. He had gotten word a little earlier from McBride, his union president, that

McFeeley was up to something that could get dicey but that it had the backing of the union leadership. Everyone was to clear a path for McFeeley tonight.

Quickly, the composing room men made up the new front page and began setting up the story, photos, and side-bars on the first six pages of the paper. There was no other story of import.

Next, McFeeley called over to the shop steward in charge of the presses, six floors below the composing room, in the basement and first floor of the building.

"Put it on the press," he ordered Tommy, who oversaw the pressmen.

"You got it."

Slowly, the presses were beginning to fire up to speed, sending a rumble through the entire building. It was a com-forting sound to those on the upper floors. They knew it meant the newspaper would make deadline and hit the streets on time in the early morning hours.

The front pages were always put on the press last, to give reporters and editors the maximum amount of time to make last minute updates and changes.

In the early morning hours, the bundles of papers would be sorted and loaded onto waiting trucks that would drop them at newsstands throughout the five boroughs in time for the a.m. rush hour. If McFeeley's plan went as intended, Baldwin and Schwartz wouldn't find out about the mutiny until the paper reached their doorsteps.

McFeeley called Juan at the hotel.

Mary answered his cell phone so Juan could keep typing. An NYPD officer had now joined them, standing guard outside the small business office where Juan was typing.

"I'm holding the press run. He's got to send the rest of the story now!" McFeeley shouted over the din of the composing room, where the typesetters were awaiting the last few takes of the front-page story.

Mary didn't need to relay the message. Juan had heard McFeeley screaming through the phone.

Juan hated the pestering calls from editors on deadline. Did they really think that their queries would make him write any faster?

In this case, though, he heeded the call.

"I'm done. Tell him I just sent over the last page. He's got it now. We are heading back over to the newsroom. The rest is up to him and the guys in the plant."

CHAPTER THIRTY-ONE

DECEMBER 17

Baldwin was not someone to be underestimated. McFeeley knew this. But he didn't anticipate Baldwin's next move. A little before 8:00 p.m., Baldwin unexpectedly reappeared in the newsroom. A few minutes later, Schwartz huddled with him in his office.

The NYPD had tipped off City Hall to what had happened at the hotel. And City Hall came down hard on Schwartz. They knew Juan was up to something.

City Hall had their own spies inside the newsroom, friendly reporters willing to rat out what other reporters were up to in order to curry favor with the Giuliani administration. While only McFeeley, Juan, and the tight circle of union leaders knew the full details of the plan, it had started to leak out internally that Juan was on to something big.

"Are we going with a new front page?" Dean Wang, the city editor, asked McFeeley. "The composing room guys say you ordered up a new headline."

McFeeley liked Dean, who was a loyal lieutenant. He didn't want to see him get fired. But he didn't want to directly lie to him either.

"I got this one," McFeeley replied. "Take a long dinner break. It's better if you stay out of it."

Dean looked perplexed, but he yielded to his boss.

The two watched from the city desk as Schwartz and Baldwin engaged in what looked like a heated exchange.

"I just got a call from City Hall," Schwartz told Baldwin. "They are worried about questions Juan has been asking. They say Juan is way off base on some story about radios not working on 9/11. Why is Juan spending time on this? It's history. It's not going to bring those guys back. What's important is the cleanup and the rebuilding effort."

Baldwin walked over to the large wall of glass in his office that fronted the newsroom. He turned and closed the blinds. This was not a conversation he wanted the reporters and editors to see. They would be trying to read lips and body language, sending out instant messages among themselves trying to interpret what was being said.

"I've got it under control," Baldwin assured his publisher. "I'm letting him run around on it for a while, but nothing is going to get in the paper. I've locked the place down. He won't have enough confirmation for us to run the story. He'll make a big stink about it when I kill the story, but he'll get over it."

"That's not what I am hearing," Schwartz protested. "I am hearing he's got enough to go with now and he's ready to publish. Do you even know what your own reporters are up to?

"I don't need City Hall calling me. You realize what we have on the line downtown? You know what we face here, as a city. That whole area could become a ghost town. We don't need any distractions. The mayor is doing his best to keep the feds at bay so he can run the cleanup out of City Hall and get it done as fast as possible. If the feds take over, it will take years to clean it up. We have to support the city. This is no time to be taking potshots at City Hall. How the fuck were they supposed to know Al Qaeda was going to use our own civilian aircraft against us and bring those buildings down? No one anticipated that type of attack. Whether the radios worked or didn't work, it doesn't matter. It's not fair to try and hold the City Hall accountable for that. We have to hold the terrorists accountable, and that's Bush's job. You need to control your troops here in the newsroom. Get them focused on the cleanup. Get them focused on the future of this city, on the future of downtown. Put some pressure on these fucking insurance companies that are already dicking around and don't want to pay out claims to rebuild. That's the story."

The more he talked, the more agitated he got.

"I didn't buy this newspaper and subsidize it all these years so that you and your left-wing staff could turn it against the business community at a time like this. You understand?"

Baldwin tried his best to calm Schwartz down. He didn't want him storming out of his office in a huff for the rest of the staff to see.

"I'm on your side," Baldwin said, groveling now, giving up any pretense of being an editor with any real independence from the business interests of his publisher and boss. "I will take care of this. Don't worry. We have to let this play itself out. It will be worse if it looks like you and I are trying to kill a story that would be damaging to City Hall. The *Post* could get a hold of this and blow it up into something. You don't want that. Let me handle it. Just tell the folks at City Hall to keep their cool."

"They have enough to worry about," Schwartz shot back. He opened the blinds of Baldwin's office, just wide enough for him to peer out at the newsroom, now filling up with reporters on deadline. "They don't need your staff hounding them, trying to second guess what went on at Ground Zero in the moments after the attack."

Baldwin was quick to remind Schwartz that those pesky reporters were his troops. "They are your staff, too," Baldwin said, softly, hoping not to incur Schwartz's wrath again.

Schwartz looked back at Baldwin. "I pay you to keep them under control. Do your job."

Baldwin did not need any further interpretation. Schwartz's directive was clear, as was the implied threat to Baldwin's own survival if he failed to control Juan and keep the radio story out of the paper.

"I got it. Don't worry," Baldwin said, one more time.

Schwartz left Baldwin's office and the reporters working at cubicles nearby were careful to pretend not to be paying too much attention. They picked up phones, typed on their keyboards, looked busily at documents on their desks, all the while trading instant messages among themselves on the newsroom's computer network, asking each other what they thought Schwartz was up to and agreeing that he did not look happy and neither did Baldwin. This usually meant something bad would be happening soon.

Back in Queens, after the hotel raid on Juan and Mary, Kazimir packed up a few things and decided it was time to get out of town for a while. He checked his account. The cash was there. It would last quite a while.

Before he left, he reviewed a set of tapes he had not told his client about. Kazimir trusted no one, including his clients. He had ordered his Russian pals to tap Wedley's phone, as well as Juan's, and had captured all of Wedley's conversations with Amato. the mayor's trusted aide at City Hall.

The tapes laid bare the inner workings of the backroom dealings between City Hall and FRRC. Amato's language and intent were crystal clear on the tapes. Kazimir thought for a moment of making a second score. He could try to blackmail Amato and maybe pick up another $500K. Instead, his old NYPD detective instincts kicked in. Part of him was still a cop. He packaged up the tapes carefully—no fingerprints—and sent them to the special agent in charge (SAC) at the FBI's New York office—26 Federal Plaza, New York, NY. The SAC would know what to do with them. And Kazimir would sleep a little easier.

CHAPTER THIRTY-TWO

DECEMBER 17

After taking it on the chin from Schwartz, Baldwin now was out for blood. He stormed over to the city desk, where McFeeley was still reviewing the fake front page with Dean.

"Get me Juan right now. We need to talk to him together," Baldwin said, hovering directly over McFeeley. "Call him on his cell phone. Do what you need to do to find him."

This time, McFeeley looked up from his screen. "I will try, but I told you, he hasn't checked in in a while, and I think he is with a source. What's the urgency?"

Baldwin leaned in. "The urgency is the publisher just made it very clear that he thinks Juan is wasting his time chasing this radio story. And I agree. We need to shut this story down. Now."

McFeeley knew better than to argue at this point.

"Okay, Bill," McFeeley replied. "I'll track him down."

"Come find me the minute you hear back from him."

Baldwin went back to his office, closed the door and the blinds, and fidgeted with his office thermostat.

McFeeley called Juan on his cell. This time Juan picked up.

"Baldwin is really on the warpath. I can't stall him much longer. Stay out of the newsroom for a while until I figure something out and we have more time to get the story on the presses.

"Who is Mary, by the way?" McFeeley asked.

"Mary works for the mayor. I will explain later. She's my source inside City Hall. She's left the administration but backed up all her emails. They'll come after her, but she's got it all on a flash drive. She's bulletproof. And now she's willing to go on the record if need be."

"Call back in five minutes. Baldwin can't exactly kill a story you haven't filed yet and that he hasn't seen. If I put you on the phone with him, don't argue. Just yes him to death, okay? Can you do that?"

"Yes, boss. As long as you get the story on the presses and on the street."

McFeeley glanced at the newsroom clock, a four-sided, wood-encased relic that hung from the ceiling, right over the city desk where the top editors coordinated the day's news coverage. The clock stood as a reminder of the newspaper's past, values, and traditions.

The hands on the big wooden clock on this day in the *News*'s newsroom indicated it was just a few minutes before 8:00 p.m.—crunch time as the final deadline for tomorrow's front page loomed.

Baldwin could still put a halt to the paper if he found out what was going on.

McFeeley called Tommy McBride, Michael Flynn, and Anthony Impellitari. He sent each of them a copy of the story. He wanted them to see for themselves what was at stake and make sure he had their support. They each gave it a read and agreed again to go forward with their plan. No one backed out.

By 8:30, Tommy's guys had made up the front page and set the story into columns on pages three, four, and five with photos of the 9/11 destruction of the World Trade Center, an FDNY handy-talkie radio, and a head shot of FDNY probie Peter Murphy in his helmet and fire gear along with excerpts blown up from the confidential report. They included a shot of Peter Wedley, III, owner of FRRC. It was a powerful-looking package. Juan's byline appeared above the story on page three. McFeeley ordered up a sidebar story on the attack on Juan and Mary in the hotel room. He wanted it to be part of the record. He had the paper's police bureau chief handle the story, based on accounts from official NYPD sources. The headline for the sidebar read: "*News Reporter & Source Attacked by Thugs Trying to Stop Story.*" A headshot of Juan ran with it along with a photo of the trashed hotel room.

McBride, Flynn, and Impellitari personally appeared in the *News*'s pressroom to make sure all went smoothly and to send a signal to their men to make sure this edition of the paper hit the streets on time.

Baldwin came back over to the city desk and again asked about Juan's whereabouts.

"Did you hear from him?"

"He should be calling in any minute."

Just then, the phone on the city desk rang, the line used by reporters calling in from the street.

McFeeley punched the flashing button to answer.

"It's Juan. What's so urgent? I was with a source."

"Baldwin needs to speak with you. You're on speaker."

"Juan, this is Baldwin. I want to know what you have on this radio story. You're rattling some cages at City Hall. I want to know if it's worth it."

Juan thought carefully about how to respond.

"It is a dynamite story. I can't talk now because I am on the street. Let me brief you in person. I'm on the way in."

Juan was trying to buy some time. Another thirty minutes and the story would be in print.

"Well, I have serious concerns about whether this is even a story at all based on what I've heard from my City Hall sources," Baldwin barked, loud enough for half the newsroom to hear him. "You are going to have to make one hell of a case."

"I'm on my way."

Juan hung up abruptly without giving Baldwin time to ask another question he didn't want to answer.

Baldwin looked scornfully at McFeeley, as if this was all his fault. He said no more. Baldwin retreated to his office. Both men knew this was going to be a long night.

By 9:30, the early edition of the newspaper was spinning and thundering its way off the presses and onto conveyor belts to be bundled by zone and loaded by hand onto the fleet of Teamster-driven trucks. The copy boys brought up the first copies for the night editors to proof one last time before the full run got underway.

There was no way now for McFeeley to conceal the real front page any longer. The game was up. He watched carefully as one of the copy boys delivered an edition to Baldwin.

Baldwin glanced at the headline and at the first few pages and ran out of his office, waving the front page in the air. He didn't wait to reach the city desk before he started screaming.

"What the hell is this? I did not authorize this front page! McFeeley, is this some kind of joke?"

"No joke, boss. It's a solid story, and it's going on the street."

"Over my dead body. McFeeley, you're fired. Get out."

Baldwin then called down to the pressroom on a special line that went right to the pressroom foreman.

"Ed, stop the presses! The story on the front page is wrong."

"No, it's not, Billy. McFeeley signed off on it a few hours ago."

"I know, but he should not have. It's wrong. You have to pull it. I'm coming downstairs."

McFeeley followed Baldwin down to the pressroom. Baldwin took the elevator. McFeeley took the back stairs, leaping down two at a time, and beat him there.

"Ed, whatever you do, don't stop the presses, you hear me?"

The union leaders gathered around the foreman and nodded their support of McFeeley.

Baldwin strode off the elevator and onto the pressroom floor.

"I said to stop the presses. Why are they still running? That story has to be pulled."

The foreman and three union leaders stood directly behind McFeeley.

"The story is staying on the front page. No one is going to stop the presses. Not tonight," McFeeley said defiantly. "Juan has done a terrific piece of reporting that the city deserves to read."

"You're fired. You have no authority here anymore. Get out of the way."

Baldwin reached for the red emergency STOP button that could cut power to the presses.

Flynn, McBride, and Impellitari stepped in front of McFeeley and blocked Baldwin's path. The three were each over six feet, towering above Baldwin. The pressmen on the catwalks along the sides of the giant presses stopped in their tracks to watch.

"You are all fired, too," Baldwin screamed. "I'm the managing editor. You can't do this."

The union leaders stood firm. And their men took their signal from them. The presses kept rolling.

Flynn stepped forward and went nose to nose with Baldwin.

"Why don't you go back upstairs now, Billy, and tell Mr. Schwartz that you did your best to stop us. We're running the show tonight. And McFeeley is our editor on this one. We're not going to leave him or our FDNY brothers hanging. Not this time. They paid for this edition with their lives. In a few more minutes, the trucks will start to roll, and there is nothing you can do about it."

Baldwin couldn't believe what was unfolding. A mutiny. Right in his own newsroom and pressroom floor. He would get Schwartz to fire every last one of them.

He stormed back into the elevator to call Schwartz.

Within a half an hour, the first early editions would hit the streets as the trucks rolled across the city, dropping off their fresh bundles at key newsstands in Manhattan, Queens, the Bronx, and Brooklyn.

McFeeley stayed in the pressroom to head off any other attempts to stop the presses. He called Juan and told him to avoid the newsroom and come directly downstairs to the pressroom floor.

Juan parked his car next to one of the *News*'s iconic delivery trucks. He ran into the pressroom area via the truckers' entrance to avoid notice. Mary joined him.

The union leaders and McFeeley greeted Juan and Mary as the presses roared overhead and a web of newsprint produced hundreds of copies of Juan's front-page story each minute.

"You know we are going to get fired," Juan shouted in McFeeley's ear, above the din of the press's powerful motors.

"Baldwin already fired me. Feels great. It will be a great way to go out," McFeeley responded.

Impellitari walked over to Juan to shake his hand as the other union leaders looked on. "You did good, kid," Impellitari said as the first of the *News*'s trucks began moving behind him, starting their early morning runs to every corner of NYC and beyond. "I'm just a truck driver, but even I get how important this story is. Schwartz and Baldwin can go kiss my ass on this one. We're not backing down."

By the time dawn broke, every newsstand in the city and in the tristate region had its bundles of *News* copies, the front-page headline screaming at every commuter who walked past in the morning on their way to work, catching the subway, Metro-North, the LIRR, and NJ Transit.

The story was out.

CHAPTER THIRTY-THREE

DECEMBER 18

Tim O'Brien, the news director at the city's leading all-news radio station, 1010 WINS, woke as usual at 4:00 a.m. to get ready to shape the station's all-important drive-time broadcast. More listeners were tuned in to 1010 WINS between 6:00 a.m. and 9:00 a.m. than at any other single point in the day. And more commuters listened to 1010 WINS than any other all-news radio station in the city. On most days, 1010 WINS lived up to its tag line: "You Give Us Ten Minutes, and We'll Give You the World." Once a news story made it to the thirty-minute "wheel" of a station like 1010 WINS and was repeated every half hour, it became news that would not be ignored.

By special arrangement, O'Brien had the early editions of all the newspapers hand delivered to his apartment on E. 57th Street each morning as soon as they became available. He scanned the headlines of the city's tabloids over his first cup of coffee, looking for key stories he would have to chase. Before he even hit the 1010 WINS newsroom at 4:45 a.m., he already was assigning stories to reporters from home via email and making calls to subeditors who were nearing the end of their overnight shifts. Together, they would help set the agenda for what tens of thousands of 1010 listeners would hear across the metro area as they readied themselves for work, got in their cars, or put in their ear buds as they headed out the door toward the subway.

This morning—three months after 9/11—one story stood out. The *News*'s front page indicated a major break in 9/11 coverage and a turning point in the ongoing effort to fully understand the attack and the city's response to it.

O'Brien, a hyper news junkie who had scrapped his way up the ladder from a street radio reporter by spending hours chasing police and fire department scanner bulletins, called immediately into his city desk—the heartbeat of 1010 WINS's twenty-four-hour news operation. He reached his counterpart, Richie D'Esposito.

"Did you see the *News* story yet?" O'Brien barked into the phone.

"Not yet, boss, I just got through the *Post*. Nothing much there."

"Well, pick up the *News* and fast," O'Brien ordered. "Their front page is dynamite. They are saying the firefighters' radios malfunctioned on the morning of the attack and that the FDNY crews that were in the Towers on 9/11 had no way of communicating. The firefighters likely didn't hear the order to evacuate or even know that the South Tower had collapsed. And the story references a possible City Hall contracting scandal. The city should have ordered better radios but didn't and then covered it up. This is going to be big. We have to jump on it. Assign everyone we have coming in on the a.m. shift. We'll need reaction from the FDNY families and official comments from FDNY brass and City Hall. And try and see if we can get Juan Gomez, the *News*'s reporter who broke the story. I want him on the air live this morning. This will be the story of the day, and it's got legs."

"Got it, boss," D'Esposito answered while scanning the *News* story for possible angles he could assign his troops to pursue. "We'll get someone over to FDNY headquarters and see if we can get someone to talk. And I'll make sure we are at the mayor's morning briefing so we can ask about the story and get a reaction."

And so, it went across the media landscape this a.m. at virtually every radio and TV outlet in town. News directors and editors scrambled to figure out how best to follow the *News*'s front-page story.

Meanwhile, the US attorney for the Southern District of New York, the most powerful prosecutor's office in town, a post once held by Rudy Giuliani, also reacted quickly to the story and to the information Kazimir had mailed to the FBI.

Within a few hours, FBI agents had fanned out across the city, serving subpoenas and executing search warrants at the midtown offices of the FRRC, at City Hall, and at the Stillwell law firm. FBI agents, wearing their signature blue windbreaker jackets with yellow "FBI" emboldened on the back, seized truckloads of boxes from each location, giving the TV news outlets a great visual as they carried the documents out from each location. News4, the flagship NBC affiliate in New York City, broke into its daytime programming at midmorning to carry the images live, showing the FBI agents at work. Other TV crews staked out the mayor at City Hall, hoping to confront him leaving or entering the building, while other reporters hounded the FDNY deputy commissioner for public information to see if the fire commissioner would answer questions on air.

The press corps was in a full frenzy.

At the *News*, Baldwin was summoned to the publisher's 10th floor office.

Schwartz was there with the head of HR and the paper's general counsel. The moment he walked into the room, Baldwin knew his fate had been sealed.

Schwartz got right to the point. "They outsmarted you, Billy. They got a story in the paper—my paper—without you even knowing it was going to press. Clean out your stuff. You're done."

Baldwin thought it fruitless to argue at this point. But he got in one last shot at Juan and McFeeley. "Boss, I'm the editor, and I take responsibility. But this was a mutiny that involved more than just Juan and McFeeley. The unions were all in on this. I tried to stop them last night, but they refused. They were backing McFeeley. You should clean house, starting with Juan and McFeeley. They have betrayed this paper."

"Billy, it's no longer your concern," Schwartz shot back. "You let the rabble in the newsroom run the show. HR will walk you out. We'll have someone pack up your office. I don't want you back in the newsroom. The lawyers will be in touch on severance."

Schwartz was smart enough to know when he had been outplayed. He was, after all, a sharp businessman. He didn't dwell on lost battles. He cut his losses and moved on. Baldwin was now damaged goods, disgraced, outmaneuvered, and undermined in his own newsroom. There was no question he had to go and go quickly. How to handle the rest of the mess remained an open question.

As he was being escorted out, Baldwin passed McFeeley in the lobby. Both men stopped cold, face-to-face for the first time since the story hit the street.

"You Irish prick. I made you city editor, and you stabbed me in the back. You went around me, and you betrayed me and this paper and the publisher," Baldwin said, his face inches from McFeeley's.

McFeeley took a step closer to Baldwin, leaning in. He had confronted many a bully on the Brooklyn streets of his youth. Baldwin was no different.

"Billy, you betrayed yourself a long time ago when you got into bed with City Hall. Juan was just following the story. The firefighters downtown are the ones who got screwed on 9/11. That's where the facts led us, and that's the story that deserves to be told. You can go kiss the mayor's ass if you want to, but that's not what this paper stands for, at least not what it used to stand for before you came along. We're here to tell their story, not the fantasy spin the mayor's people have been feeding you."

By this time, the faceoff had drawn a small crowd, including a couple of reporters, editors, and security guards who were stationed nearby to screen all those trying to gain entry up to the newsroom.

Without warning, Baldwin lunged at McFeeley and tried to sucker punch him. He missed. It was an awkward, wild swing. McFeeley swung back, hitting Baldwin directly in the nose with a short, hard jab. Baldwin's nose was broken, and he started bleeding profusely.

The guards stepped in immediately, separating them, but not before the commotion drew an even larger crowd and additional reporters on their way into work had gathered to watch the brawl. The reporting staff let out a cheer when McFeeley's punch landed on Baldwin's nose. They slapped McFeeley on the back as he made his way back up into the newsroom.

Baldwin brushed off the guards, headed out onto W. 33rd Street, and into a waiting yellow cab. He didn't look back. The mess in the newsroom was no longer his problem.

A few minutes later, Schwartz appeared in the newsroom. The TVs in the newsroom were all carrying reports on Juan's scoop concerning the faulty radios.

Ever the opportunist, Schwartz saw now that the *News* had a tiger by the tail, its biggest scoop in years. He decided simply to ignore the mutiny that had occurred—not even acknowledging it except for the firing of Baldwin—and ride the wave instead. He knew he would have to field some unfriendly calls from the mayor's people, but he had little choice but to push ahead, now that the story was out.

He called McFeeley into the publisher's conference room.

"I just fired Baldwin. I should fire you, too, except this is the biggest story we've had in years. Baldwin was inept. You and Juan outsmarted him. You are now the editor-in-chief. Congratulations. Keep milking this story as long as we can."

McFeeley was momentarily taken aback. He wasn't expecting this development from Schwartz. He had to admit, it was a smart play. But he didn't want to get trapped into an untenable position, serving as the publisher's next tool in the newsroom, doing the bidding of City Hall. With Baldwin out and the radio story hitting it big, he figured he had some room to negotiate.

"I will take on the editorship on one condition. We will take this story wherever it goes, including into City Hall. I won't pull any punches," McFeeley said, eager to set his own ground rules. "And you stay out of the newsroom."

If Schwartz balked, McFeeley would walk. He had planned to retire by the end of the year anyway.

"I understand," Schwartz replied. "The newsroom is yours. I won't interfere in the coverage on this."

Juan and Mary had stayed at the paper until 2:00 a.m. Rather than drive all the way to Queens, Mary had agreed to take the shorter ride back to Brooklyn with Juan, where she slept in his guest room.

When morning broke, Juan made eggs with onions and peppers for the kids and Mary. He sliced fresh pieces of avocado and tomato to dress up the eggs. There was bacon and fresh bagels too. It was a celebratory breakfast.

Jennifer woke before the others and saw the front page of the *News* on the kitchen table, where it always was every morning. Except this time, it had an even bigger, bolder headline than usual—and Juan's byline was above the front-page story.

"Your story made the paper," she said, glancing at the lead and the sidebars. "This is what you were working on this whole time?"

Juan nodded and kept stirring the eggs in a large skillet. Jennifer turned on the TV and flipped through the morning news channels. Juan's story led every broadcast.

"This is going to shake up things at City Hall. You should have told me this was what you were doing. I'm sorry if I was a pain. I get what you do at the *News* is important."

"Jen, honey, you and your brothers are the center of everything I hold dear. The story is important, but nothing is more important to me than you and your brothers. Always know that, even if I am not around sometimes."

Mary emerged from the guest room and introduced herself. Jennifer recognized her from her photo in the *News* as the City Hall aide to the mayor who had helped her father break the radio story.

"Nice to meet you, Jennifer. Your dad never stops talking about you. You should be very proud of him today."

"I am. But I don't want his head to get too big. He's already all over the TV."

Mary and Juan laughed.

"I think he's going to ride this wave for a few days, at least, so you better get used to it."

"Yeah, until I get fired," Juan said, only half-joking.

"Why would you get fired, Dad?" Jen said. "This is such a big story."

"Some folks at City Hall did not want this story to come out. But don't worry. We'll be fine. I can always get another job in this town."

The boys all joined them around the breakfast table as Juan dished out the eggs and bagels.

Just then, the house phone rang.

It was McFeeley.

"Believe it or not, you still have a job. Schwartz fired Baldwin, but he's keeping us. He just offered me the editorship. Go figure. He sees which way the wind is blowing on this one, and he's decided to let us run with it."

Juan put McFeeley on speaker and had him repeat the good news for all to hear.

"So, there is a God? I didn't plan on that one," Juan said. "Baldwin is really out?"

"He's gone. They walked him out," McFeeley assured him.

Juan looked over at Mary. "Maybe there is justice in the world after all," he said.

Their eyes locked for a moment, and Juan felt a connection, one he had been keeping at bay. Perhaps they were just giddy at their victory. But Mary sensed it too.

"Alright, we're heading in. See you soon."

"We've got a lot of work to do now," McFeeley reminded him. "The story is hitting all over town. Everyone is picking it up. What do you have for a follow? This is our story, and we need to stay ahead of it."

No rest for the weary, Juan thought to himself.

"We'll get you something. We need to stake out the mayor. Can you send someone over there? I'm going to work the feds to see if their raid of FRRC turned up any new evidence."

He hung up with McFeeley and looked over again at Mary.

"What are you going to do now? You can't go back to City Hall."

"I know," Mary said. "I'm done there."

"Why don't you come to work at the *News*? McFeeley is the new editor. He can make it happen. And we need a researcher to help with this story."

"That might work, at least for a few months until the baby comes," Mary said, genuinely touched by his offer to help her restart her career.

"A baby? You're pregnant?" Jennifer asked, suddenly suspicious.

"Yes, my husband was killed on 9/11, but he left me the most precious gift of all."

"Oh, congratulations!" Jennifer said, relieved. She gave Mary a hug.

"You will make a great mom," Juan said. "And someday you will tell Bill's kid what you did here to honor him and his FDNY brothers."

Mary fought back tears. The job. 9/11. The loss of Bill. Being pregnant. The prospect of being a single mom. Breaking from City Hall and the life she knew. It was all catching up to her.

"I know how lucky I am. It's such a blessing. I'm going to do my best to make Bill proud."

"You shouldn't worry," Juan said, trying to reassure her. "Being a parent is the most fantastic journey of your life.

And you will have plenty of help—if you want it—from the FDNY family. You know they take care of their own."

"I hope that's still true after they read your story and once they figure out that I helped you," Mary said.

"They are going to have your back now more than ever," Juan replied. "You helped shed some light on what happened on 9/11. The rank and file will realize the importance of what you have done, even if the brass doesn't."

CHAPTER THIRTY-FOUR

MAY 19, 2004

A steady spring rain fell outside on W. 12th Street. Inside the auditorium of the New School, former Mayor Giuliani settled in for two hours of testimony as a star witness before the 9/11 Commission.

This would be the eleventh of a dozen public hearings the Commission would hold in Washington, DC and in the New York area before issuing its final and definitive report on the terrorist attacks on the United States. The ten-member panel was chaired by Thomas H. Kean, the former Republican governor of New Jersey, a Princeton-educated academic who came from a long line of US senators, governors, and high-level GOP presidential appointees.

Kean was well-respected by both political parties for his evenhandedness and fair demeanor. It was no surprise when President George W. Bush turned to him for the politically sensitive task of leading the 9/11 Commission.

The Commission was nearing the end of its work. It had examined virtually all aspects of the attack on the WTC and the Pentagon, from the rise of Bin Laden and Al Qaeda to how the 9/11 attackers infiltrated and organized themselves, to the missed signals and failures of the CIA and FBI in preventing the attack. The subject of today's hearing was to examine the emergency response in New York City after the planes hit the WTC.

Drawing on his years of experience as a federal prosecutor, Giuliani made his best case to defend the city's response on the morning of 9/11. He said no city could have been totally prepared for an attack the scale of which the nation had never experienced. He praised the response of the FDNY and the NYPD, giving them credit for saving tens of thousands of civilians who were safely evacuated from the North and South Towers before they collapsed.

Whatever shortcomings in the response, he reminded the panel and the public that the real villains were the terrorists, not city officials who did their best under the most trying of circumstances to save lives.

"We have to channel our anger," the former mayor said during the second day of hearings on the city's response. "Our enemy is not each other, but the terrorists who attacked us.

"Blame should be directed at one source and one source alone: the terrorists who killed our loved ones."

It was a masterful performance by the man dubbed "America's Mayor" after the 9/11 attack, the man who had been selected as Time magazine's person of the year in 2001.

Everyone in the room, the panel members and press included, knew that the mayor himself narrowly escaped death on the morning of the attack, fleeing downtown after the South Tower fell, leading a cadre of city officials and reporters north, covered in the white ash that enveloped everyone who was there that day.

Giuliani had been able to bask in the patriotic glow of 9/11 ever since. Indeed, few disputed that his actions in the immediate hours after the attack, when he was the highest ranking and most visible elected official speaking to the nation, had helped hold the city and the country together.

But Sarah and the 9/11 families at the hearing were not buying it, not today. They had had enough of the glowing reports of the mayor's actions and resented what they viewed as "kid-glove" treatment he received by 9/11 Commission members, who barely asked the mayor a hard question about the communication breakdown among the FDNY and NYPD on the morning of the attack.

Sarah, sitting only a few rows behind the mayor, steadied herself, calling on all her inner strength and courage to be ready for this moment. She was just a mom from the Bronx, she thought, unaccustomed to the big stage she unexpectedly found herself thrust upon. She didn't really want to be here. The bright TV lights and fifteen cameras in the room were directed at the mayor, not her. Until she quietly stood up, holding a homemade sign.

"Fiction"—it read.

Sarah held it up high above her head as the mayor spoke.

The TV news cameramen instinctively focused their lenses on Sarah and her sign as the mayor continued to testify, unaware at the moment that he was being challenged.

This was the moment the reporters had been waiting for—the Mom v. the Mayor.

Other 9/11 family members saw what Sarah was doing and rallied, coming to her aide.

"Lies," yelled one widow.

"Ask him about the radios," another shouted. "Why didn't the fire department radios work?"

The 9/11 Commission chair, Tom Kean, banged his gavel, calling for order and urging the audience to "stop wasting time."

Sarah held fast as security moved toward her. She silently held the sign high the entire time. Her heart was racing.

Then, her husband Tom, wearing a well-worn NYPD cap, stood up too, right next to her. This time, he was the one holding the framed photo of their son in his FDNY helmet. Sarah saw him and smiled. Their eyes met, and Tom nodded his admiration for her, a fleeting gesture that in a moment said he now knew what she had been fighting for all these months. The cameras whirled again, this time in his direction. The 9/11 Commission security—all NYPD—recognized their former colleague and stopped their advance.

The Commission chairman again banged his gavel, calling for order.

"You're the ones wasting time," Sarah shouted at the Commission members. "Why aren't you asking any real questions about what happened? My son was murdered because of the city's incompetence."

The Commission hearing adjourned, and the press descended on Sarah and her group of 9/11 family members.

The mayor held his own post-testimony briefing, just yards apart from Sarah and the 9/11 families. The mayor knew not to attack the 9/11 widows. He was too smart to fall into that trap. That was a no-win proposition. Instead, he said he understood how emotional these hearings can be for families who have lost loved ones. And that sometimes people can get carried away.

Standing in the rain outside the hearing room, Sarah unleashed her most direct attack to date on City Hall.

"The ugly truth is many firefighters were sent to their slaughter that day. There was no leadership. There was no coordination. There was no communication. The city let them down.

"We want to know, we demand to know, what happened. Why didn't the radios work? Why was my son and hundreds of other members of the FDNY put at risk and then not told to get out in time? What is City Hall hiding?"

EPILOGUE

SEPTEMBER 11, 2005

Mary arrived for lunch at Ellen's Cafe near City Hall pushing an umbrella stroller with Billy Jr. in it. He was four now, pushing five fast. She could take him to a restaurant at this age without making a scene. He liked tuna fish sandwiches, and he knew he would get an ice cream later if he was good at lunch. The kid had his mother's crystal-clear blue eyes and blonde hair, and he already weighed forty pounds. He was going to be a bruiser, just like his dad.

The heavy and sticky summer air had given way to early fall temperatures. The leaves on the trees in City Hall Park had started to turn colors. Families lucky enough to be able to escape the city during the summer had returned, and the streets were bustling again. Kids were back in school.

Mary had just attended the annual September 11th reading of the names of the nearly 3,000 victims of the attack, including the first responders. Mary attended every year. This was the first time she brought her son.

Rudy was there, along with all his former mayoral aides. They did not talk or even exchange greetings. They still considered Mary an outcast. But all of Bill's surviving FDNY colleagues were there, and they invited Mary to sit with them during the reading of the names. The reading took hours. No politicians were allowed to speak. Just family members of those lost who rotated turns reading the names. It was a dignified and solemn event, covered live by all the major local news outlets.

Afterward, Mary strolled up Broadway pushing Billy in the stroller to meet Juan for lunch. This had become an annual ritual now, although Mary and Juan also stayed in touch throughout the year.

"You're looking great," Juan said, greeting Mary. "And who is this guy?"

"I'm Billy Jr.," Billy said without missing a beat. "And I am four! And I am going to kindergarten."

"Really? Four years old? That's pretty old!"

They settled into a booth by the window so they could see the others returning from the reading of the names, many in uniform, passing by as the afternoon evolved.

"How was the ceremony?"

"Very nicely done. They are still working on the pit, so they had it across the street in the park. I always like to go. I feel close to Bill whenever I am there. I'm looking forward to when they build the permanent memorial."

"How's it going at the paper?" Mary asked as they ordered, and she took out some crayons for Billy Jr. to scribble on the placemat.

Mary had worked for Juan a few days a week as a researcher for a year after the story was published. But then she had decided to stay home full-time to raise her son, at least until he started school. Juan still called upon her from time to time to do freelance research assignments. It kept her busy, and she enjoyed the work and being connected to journalism. She thought about starting a freelance writing career once Billy Jr. got a little older.

"The paper is struggling. It's one wave of layoffs after another. All the ad dollars are going to the internet, it seems. The writing is on the wall. I'm not sure how much longer I can hang in, to tell you the truth."

"They are always going to need good reporters who know how to really investigate a story. Don't give up."

"I guess I could always go into PR," Juan said, half joking. "Maybe I'll become the flack for the fire department! I hear it pays well!"

"Stop it. You are a reporter. Stick to what you know. Even if the *News* goes down, there will be other news outlets that will need you and your skills."

"You are too kind. I hope you are right. Jennifer is in a pre-med program at NYU, so I need to squeeze out a few more years to pay for the tuition and her student loans. I could have bought a house in the Hamptons with the amount I am sending NYU every month. It's crushing. And then I have to put the two boys through school. I am never going to get out of debt."

"It's the best money you will ever spend, and you know it," Mary said. "Jennifer has turned out to be a fine young woman. You should be proud. And you must be making some money off the book."

Juan had turned the 9/11 radio story into a bestselling nonfiction book. It had done well. Twenty weeks on the *New York Times* nonfiction bestseller list. His agent was negotiating now with the Hollywood folks to see if they could sell the option to make it into a movie. The royalties would definitely help with the tuition bills.

"I am very proud of Jennifer and the boys. And the book has done well. Life is good. And what about you? This guy is getting big. Are you keeping busy? And any dating prospects? You are allowed to have a life, you know."

"Oh, stop," Mary blushed. "I think Bill was my one and only. I am focused now on raising this guy. He keeps me plenty busy. But I am in touch with a lot of the other 9/11 widows and the guys from Bill's firehouse. Some of the guys who worked on The Pile are starting to get sick. Weird types of cancer. They say it is related to all the crap they breathed in down at Ground Zero. There is a research team up at Mount Sinai Hospital that is tracking it all. The guys are starting to organize to make sure they get health benefits. I am going to help them. Seems like a worthy cause."

"Really? Cancers. From Ground Zero? Sounds like a story," Juan said.

They exchanged a knowing smile.

"Keep me in the loop on that."

"I will."

AFTERWORD

In the aftermath of the 9/11 attack, the city's firefighters were lauded as heroes. The public showered FDNY firehouses with gestures of goodwill, from flowers, food, and memorials to trips to Disneyland. Elected officials also rushed to praise the efforts of the FDNY. Having suffered the greatest loss of life of any of the first responders, the FDNY became the focus of an outpouring of adulation, sympathy, and hero worship.

Much of the praise was warranted. Firefighters rescued and helped guide many civilians to safety. However, the city's overall response and that of the FDNY in particular was badly managed. The lack of coordination among responding agencies, the poor or nonexistent radio communications, and the general sense that the operation was a colossal screwup that resulted in unnecessary loss of life was a given among many ranking and rank and file firefighters. Those sentiments were confirmed by the 9/11 Commission Report issued in July of 2004 following a series of public hearings the Commission held in New York and in Washington, DC.

Chapter nine of the 9/11 Commission Report documents in great detail the failings that occurred among the responding agencies during the WTC attack, including the malfunctioning of radio communications among firefighters during the initial response and even after evacuation orders had been given, orders many firefighters likely never heard.

The 9/11 Commission Report identified four problems that hampered radio communications among firefighters, including difficulties of radio communications in high-rise buildings, too many firefighters trying to communicate all at the same time on the same radio channel (Tactical Channel 1), firefighters being on the wrong radio channel, and some off-duty FDNY firefighters who responded to the WTC without any radios.

"Significant shortcomings within the FDNY's command and control capabilities were painfully exposed on September 11th," the Commission concluded in its final report.

Former FDNY Fire Commissioner Thomas Von Essen, who responded to the WTC after the attack, acknowledged many of the communication issues that plagued the response when he tried to sum up the extraordinary situation his men faced during his testimony before the 9/11 Commission on May 18th of 2004. His words are worth repeating here:

"We had hundreds of firefighters who, without hesitation, put themselves in danger to save lives. It is important to remember that every firefighter who responded did so out of an unwavering commitment to the job, to the people of this city. No one could ask for a more dedicated fire department. We have heard civilians in the buildings say over and over how much it meant to them, how much hope and security it gave them, to see firefighters going up the stairwells as they were coming down.

"Let me speak for a moment about the communication issues on 9/11. There were problems with communications. Nothing worked all the time. Everything worked some of the time. Cell phones, the point-to-point department radios, all alternately worked and did not work. The unprecedented circumstances had an understandable impact on the communications plans and systems. One of the biggest problems was the amount of traffic on the radios that day. Firefighters normally use their radios to talk to each other point-to-point. They do not go through a central dispatch. And that is very important in an operation—firefighters need to be able to talk to each other about the conditions they are facing at the scene of a fire. The downside is that due to the limited number of channels available, only one transmission can be made at a time, and it limits the use of that channel by another firefighter. With a few hundred firefighters at one operation, the radios were overwhelmed with competing transmissions. In the communications industry, this is called 'stepping on each other.' We had never had an emergency operation of this size, and so we had not experienced this difficulty to this extent.

"We also know there was difficulty with the repeater system in the towers. Like everything else, it worked and didn't work. Some chiefs used it for some of the time, and some did not because they had tested it, and it didn't appear to be working correctly at that point. What matters most is whether the radio and repeater difficulties had a significant impact on the operation or on the evacuation of the buildings. It is, of course, impossible to know the definitive answer to that question—and anyone purporting to have the definitive answer is being less than honest. We do know that evacuation orders were given, both before and after the South Tower collapsed. What we will never fully know is how many received the evacuation orders and how many did not—how many continued the operation despite the orders, or how many were on their way out but just didn't make it in time.

"We've heard the evacuation and 'Mayday' orders on tapes and on videos, and both civilians and firefighters have stated that they heard the evacuation orders. We know that firefighters and other emergency rescue personnel passed on these orders to each other. We know that some evacuated and some did not, even after receiving the orders. We've been told of situations where NYPD emergency service unit officers, who were evacuating, passed the evacuation orders on to firefighters who were climbing up, firefighters who acknowledged receipt of the orders, and then continued to climb.

"To understand all this, it is important to understand what it means to be a firefighter. Firefighters do not run away. They do not leave if they think they can stay. They will not leave their brothers. This, of course, is not to say that the firefighters who were able to evacuate were in any way less courageous or dedicated. It means simply that, as it has always been with firefighters in the New York City Fire Department, when faced with critical decisions, firefighters do what they believe the immediate situation requires of them. For many firefighters, an evacuation order means 'get the civilians out, get all my guys out, and then I go.' One team on their way out may have stopped to help some injured civilians, another team may have just cleared a floor and escorted the civilians down. We will never know what decisions many of our firefighters made that day. But I do know that firefighters do not abandon civilians in distress to save themselves. Without question I wish so many more had evacuated. The emptiness from the losses that day has never left me, not for a moment."

ACKNOWLEDGMENTS

Any factual error of time or place in this work is the sole responsibility of the author. The author, however, wishes to gratefully acknowledge the works upon which he relied during research for this book, including: *102 Minutes: The Untold Story of the Fight to Survive Inside the Twin Towers* by Jim Dwyer and Kevin Flynn; *Grand Illusion: The Untold Story of Rudy Giuliani and 9/11* by Wayne Barrett & Dan Collins; *The 9/11 Commission Report: Final Report of the National Commission on Terrorist Attacks Upon the United States.*

Ranking members of the FDNY, including former First Deputy Commissioner Michael Regan, contributed to the author's knowledge of some of the complex issues they faced during the worst day in the history of the fire department of the city of New York. Regan provided a valuable read of the manuscript, along with key encouragement and endless insight into the inner workings of the department.

My editor, John Paine, deserves enormous credit for his unique and expert editing skills and for helping to draw out the full story and help organize it in a way that would be best for the reader. I am deeply indebted to him for guiding a former newspaperman and first-time novelist toward whatever success this book finds. My agent, Ed Breslin, provided a thoughtful round of reads, key edits, and, most importantly, encouragement and enthusiasm for the work as he labored to find it a home. My former *Daily News* colleague, the beloved Tom Robbins, deserves a special thanks for introducing me to Mr. Breslin. Without them, this book may never have seen the light of day. The editing team at Post Hill Press, led by Managing Editor Aleigha Kely, provided valuable advice and treated the manuscript with expert care as they labored to make it better. A special thanks to Post Hill Publisher Anthony Ziccardi for taking a chance on a first-time novelist.

Joseph M. Finnerty of Finnerty Osterreicher & Abdulla, a dedicated First Amendment lawyer, provided valuable advice and critical reads of the manuscript, along with encouragement. I am fortunate to have the benefit of his legal counsel.

Long time NYC publicist, former newspaperman and City Hall guru, Morty Matz, helped in ways big and small, offering encouragement and advice while in pandemic lockdown on the Upper East Side.

To the extent I am able to write with any authority about New York, I owe much to my *New York Newsday* and *Daily News* colleagues who, over many years of their own expert reporting, conversation, debate, and analysis, helped school me in the ways of the city, including the late Jim Dwyer, a great friend and voice for New York; Kevin Flynn, Tom Robbins, Paul Moses, Mike Arena, Tom Curran, Rich Galant, Jerry Capeci, Russ Buettner, the late

Jerry Schmetterer (who generously provided key advice on book publishing), Tom Zambito, Willie Rashbaum, Ellis Henican, Richie Esposito, Sal Arena, Wendell Jamieson, Tom Maier, the late Bob Greene, the late Don Forst, Arthur Browne, Rich Rosen, Michael Moss, Jennifer Preston, the late Barbara Strauch, the late Wayne Barrett, the late Bill Boyle, and the late Mike McAlary. My City Hall and Room 9 colleagues also helped inspire, educate, and inform, including Bill Murphy, Bruce Lambert, the late Mickey Carroll, Carolyn Daly, George Arzt, Bob Liff, Juliet Papa, Tony Guida, Marcia Kramer, Joyce Purnick, Dave Seifman, Joel Siegel, and Kevin Davitt. Many friends, some of whom I had the honor to serve with during my time in state and local government, also have contributed greatly to my understanding of power and politics, including Tom McMahon, Frank McLaughlin, Robert Tierney, the late Bob Keating, Michelle Adams, Prof. Mitchell Moss, Mike Clendenin, Frank Gribbon, John Banks, Jerry Skurnik, John Sabini, Tom Suozzi, Anthony Cancellieri, Retired 1st Grade NYPD Detective Mike Sapraicone, Tim Lisante, John Donnelly, Tim Driscoll, Shelly Cohen, Tom Stokes, Peter Gerbasi, Helena Williams, Mary Curtis, and Arda Nazarian.

My colleagues at New York University also have provided unwavering support over the years and a second journalistic home, especially Prof. Mary Quigley and Prof. Yvonne Latty.

My FDNY and NYPD brothers-in-law, Mike, Ralph, and Charlie Piscopo, along with the late Uncle John Scalzo and Joe Portoghese, provided forty years of education in the ways of civil service along with hours of FDNY stories and insights into the workings of the city of New York. They also entertained with endless "Battle of the Badges" banter. Retired FDNY Lt. Charlie Piscopo gave key advice about firefighting operations. They are not responsible, however, for any of the content in this book.

My children, Chris, Craig, and Ana, were in high school and grammar school at the time of the 9/11 attack. On more than one occasion, including the day of the 9/11 attack, I had to leave them to cover a story while working as a newspaper reporter. On 9/11, I was among the fortunate ones who were able to return home to their families. I hope I never took that for granted. My children have been a source of constant inspiration, pride, and joy. I thank them for bringing so much meaning and purpose into my life. My youngest, Ana, a writer and editor at *People* magazine, has been a special source of inspiration as she battles breast cancer. I so wish she never had to bear this cross, but her courage and determination in the face of often difficult treatment options has been a teaching moment about the power of optimism and perseverance for all of us.

I also thank the newer members of our family, my daughters-in-law Erica and Danica and our two wondrous grandchildren—Stella and Cooper—for their love. They bring it all to the next level and have started our next generation. My children and grandchildren have taught me so much over the years about family, fun, and unconditional love.

I am forever indebted to Madeline, my wife of more than forty years and my lifelong partner, who has helped in everything I have accomplished as a journalist, teacher, media advisor, PR guy, boat captain, and father, and who provided a critical early read of the many drafts of the manuscript. She has always been the lighthouse in my journey, guiding me back to safe harbor—no matter the adventure—and giving me reason to return home. She indulged me by giving me the time on nights and weekends to craft this story and urged me not to give up in trying to find the voice to tell it and get it published.

Finally, I wrote this book in part to try and shed some light on the efforts and challenges faced by the firefighters who responded on 9/11 and especially to the 343 members of the FDNY who did not make it home. I am inspired by their bravery, even when the department and the city let them down, and I hope their sacrifices are never forgotten.

ABOUT THE AUTHOR

Photo by Ana J. Calderone

J oe Calderone served as investigations editor of the *New York Daily News* at the time of the World Trade Center attack and helped cover the FDNY in the aftermath of 9/11, including documenting the problems firefighters had communicating via radio that day. Calderone worked as a newspaper editor and reporter for more than twenty-five years, including covering City Hall for *New York Newsday*. While with *Newsday*, he was a member of a team of reporters that won a Pulitzer Prize for local reporting. He is a long-time adjunct instructor at New York University's Arthur L. Carter Journalism Institute, where he teaches investigative reporting. He considers himself fortunate to have attended Holy Cross High School in Flushing, Queens, and he holds a Bachelor of Arts degree in United States history from the University of Maryland at College Park.